CARTEL HUNTER

A THRILLER

ROBERT GOLUBA

EVERTOUCH PUBLISHING

ISBN: 978-1-7330513-6-1 (Paperback)

ISBN: 978-1-7330513-7-8 (eBook)

Edited by Karen Sanders

Cover Design by Miblart

Sign up for my email newsletter at **RobertGoluba.com/newsletter**

This book is dedicated to the courageous men and women who serve in the armed forces and the US Air Force Pararescuemen who answer the call to save lives and aid the injured anytime and anywhere.

CONTENTS

Chapter 1

Jason Mulder soared over the hostile Afghan landscape prepared to save more soldiers and civilians, unaware that he'd soon be forced to take lives instead.

The US Air Force Pararescueman, or PJ, caught an initial glimpse of the carnage on the ground as the pilot maneuvered the HH-60G Pave Hawk helicopter into the canyon and banked. Through the open helicopter door, Staff Sergeant Mulder observed three groups of US Army medics working to stabilize wounded soldiers.

"I've got eyes on three," Mulder radioed of the three severely wounded men to the pilot and crew from his wireless headset.

"Roger," the lead pilot responded. He circled the helicopter landing zone or HLZ for a second time within the narrow canyon in northeastern Afghanistan.

The HLZ was outside a small outpost of a dozen civilian structures built at the base of terraced farm steppes descending from the foothills of the towering, beige mountains.

First Lieutenant Campbell, the combat rescue officer or CRO leading the team of six US Air Force pararescuemen across two helicopters, radioed the tactical operations center thirty miles west at Bagram Air Base. "Final status report?"

"Three US military. Two with gunshot wounds. One amputee below the knee from an IED. Four deceased civilians. Two are minor children. Over."

This was a challenging mission, even for a deployment in Afghanistan. Wounded brothers were bad enough, but dead children tested the limits of how much war a person can stomach.

Lieutenant Campbell turned toward Jason and the other PJs on board. "Y'all going to be cool on this one?"

Jason replied with a thumbs up as he tightened his Kevlar vest for the hundredth time since they scrambled twenty minutes earlier.

"Intel said it was going to be hot. Lead team, maintain air support. We'll load all the wounded and transport them to Bagram," Lieutenant Campbell commanded.

"HLZ has been swept for IEDs but is hot with small arms fire," came from the pilot.

Jason felt his heart pounding while he kept his eyes on the bombed-out buildings through the red dot reflex sight of his M-4 rifle. His body tensed at the orange tracers zipping between their helicopter and the ground two hundred feet below, followed by a Kalashnikov rifle report. Before Jason could turn his body and return fire, the right gunner sent bursts from his .50 caliber machine gun into the source of enemy fire. No more shots came from that area.

"Get us down now," Campbell barked into the headset. The pilot started his countdown twenty seconds later.

"Five, four, three, two, one, wheels down."

Once the dust settled under the slowing rotors of the helicopter, Jason unhooked his safety harness and jumped from the aircraft. Twenty yards out, he took a knee and scanned the structures and hills while Campbell met the medic from the army unit. Once he had the medical reports, Campbell waved four soldiers carrying a stretcher to load the wounded warrior. The army ranger infantryman suffered from a pair of 7.62-millimeter rounds that tore through his triceps and forearm, shattering his ulna bone. After they secured the soldier in the patient bay of the helicopter, a second stretcher with a combat engineer from the 75th Ranger Regiment arrived. His tan desert-camouflaged pants were soaked with blood, and the medic reported he was still bleeding from the slug in his left calf.

Four soldiers shuffled the last wounded man, a fire support specialist who'd been on the receiving end of an IED explosion, toward the waiting helicopter. Jason joined the men loading the specialist and saw the tourniquet and bandages above what remained of the soldier's left leg. They loaded their fellow ranger onto the helicopter, and Jason climbed inside. Turning to shut the helicopter door, he saw the dead civilians huddled together near a wall. Jason surmised by the position of the mangled bodies that the father and mother tried to shelter their children from the incoming rounds and shrapnel. He stared at the bodies and noticed movement in one of the buildings. Jason pulled the M-4 rifle slung across his back to eye level. He looked through his sight and observed an elderly Afghan woman clinging to a young girl, maybe eight years old, inside the bullet-ridden walls of the windowless stone structure. Although they were seventy-five yards away, Jason could see blood spatter on their white garments.

"Three cat alphas aboard and secure," Jason heard on his headset. That was the signal all three severely injured soldiers were ready for transport and he should shut the helicopter door. Jason grabbed the door handle and looked at the woman and child. He thought the woman looked in his direction with eyes that could penetrate the thickest armor.

Is she pleading for help?

As Jason assessed the situation, he saw movement in the foothills a hundred yards from the structures in the tiny village. Jason recognized the uniforms of two Taliban soldiers descending from positions higher in the foothills toward the row of homes. This was terrible news for the rangers, the civilians, and everyone on the helicopters. Jason knew he had to get the injured soldiers to the hospital within the golden hour of sixty minutes after the initial call. He saw another PJ, Senior Airman Garza, and Lieutenant Campbell preparing IV bags, and before Jason could debate himself for another second, his boots were back on the dusty earth outside the helicopter.

He darted left toward a low wall about three feet high and dove behind it to obscure his movement toward the civilians.

"Mulder, where are you going? The LZ is hot. Return to exfil ASAP!" Campbell radioed.

"Give me two mikes. I have eyes on the enemy moving into position to fire at our bird."

Campbell responded, but Jason didn't hear his team leader. He was in a zone. Jason hunched over and scurried along the wall to get into position for a shot at the approaching Taliban fighter. Once he was outside the building with the woman and girl inside, Jason raised his head above the wall and saw both fighters had dropped to within fifty yards of the civilian enclave. Jason had to act now or they'd have the tactical advantage once inside. He raised up, positioned his elbows on the waist-high wall to steady his M-4, and lined up the red dot sight on the chest of one of the Taliban soldiers. Jason steadied his breath and squeezed the trigger. The man dropped and tumbled down the hillside until he skidded to a stop under a cloud of dust. Jason moved his rifle five degrees to the right to find the second soldier. That's when debris from the wall smacked his exposed cheeks as the second Taliban soldier fired at

Jason. He ducked and moved his position behind the wall ten feet to his right. When Jason peered over the wall again, the Taliban soldier reached the bottom of the foothill and was yards from the civilian structures. Jason watched him disappear into a building three or four down from his current position.

"Shit! Now he can move anywhere inside those buildings," Jason said to himself.

He leaped over the wall and lowered himself quietly into one of the single-room homes. Jason inched toward the opposite side of the room to get a better angle at the last location of the enemy when he heard a noise. It sounded like a whimper from a puppy. Jason spun around until he was face to face with the older woman and the young girl. The woman had her hand over the girl's mouth, and Jason saw the tear-filled brown eyes of the young girl pleading for him not to hurt them.

Jason slid toward the girl and put his index finger to his puckered lips. "Shhh. I won't hurt you, but be very quiet," Jason whispered. He could tell by her eyes that she didn't speak English, but understood him.

As Jason turned around, he witnessed a rifle barrel advancing through the open window. He assumed the Taliban fighter found him first and expected to see a muzzle flash and then black. Instead, a wide grin formed on Jason's face. It was Senior Airman Garza.

He looked down at Jason and then at the woman and girl. Jason stood to warn Garza that the enemy was still in the area when he saw the Taliban soldier drop into position for a shot over Garza's shoulder. Jason raised his M-4 and shot past Garza's head without aiming. A nanosecond later, he heard the report from the Taliban fighter's Kalashnikov and a slug whiz by his head.

Jason's round must have hit his arm and changed the slug's trajectory. Jason whipped his head back to his right to see if the slug struck Garza, but Garza was standing in the same spot. Instead of dropping for cover, Garza raised his weapon and unloaded a half dozen rounds into the injured Taliban fighter.

Jason fist-bumped Garza and said, "Let's get back to the bird now." On his way out, Jason leaned over and put his hand on the woman's shoulder.

"I'm sorry for all this, but you're safer now."

Mulder and Garza darted back to the HLZ while watching for additional enemy combatants. Garza jumped into the helicopter bay first, and then Jason followed, shutting the door behind him.

Seconds after their wheels left the ground, the .50 caliber machine guns roared to life again on both sides as more enemy fire targeted the pair of helicopters. The PJs didn't flinch as each one straddled a patient lying on a stretcher. Forty minutes after scrambling, both helicopters departed the valley for Bagram Airfield to transport all three victims to the hospital for surgery.

Jason took the ranger with the gunshot to his calf. He did a blood sweep by feeling around the soldier's body to ensure it was his only injury. As soon as he confirmed the calf was the only wound, he felt a tug on his shirt sleeve that almost pulled him off his patient. It was Lieutenant Campbell.

He pushed down his headset and yelled into Jason's ear so only he'd hear. "What the hell happened back there?"

Jason leaned toward Campbell's ear. "I saw two Taliban getting in position to fire on our birds."

Campbell glared at Jason, the anger evident in his red face and fiery eyes. Jason had never seen him so furious in the two months he'd known his CRO.

"Take care of your man. We'll deal with this in the after-action review."

Campbell let go of Jason's shirt and returned his attention to his semi-conscious patient. Jason did the same. He found a vein and inserted a needle into the ranger's arm inside a helicopter that felt like it was bouncing back to base.

"Got it!"

The ranger's blood pressure improved, so Jason turned to see if Garza or Campbell needed assistance. He saw Campbell struggling to insert the IV needle into the amputee's arm.

"He's lost too much blood. IO," Jason suggested over the radio.

Campbell shot Mulder a look that said, "no shit" and found the intraosseous infusion device in his kit. A few beats later, the amputee screamed as the device penetrated his femur above the knee and deep into the bone marrow. Nobody took a breath until the blood drained from the clear bag into the IED victim.

"Vitals are improving," Campbell reported as he kept his eye on the monitors.

The helicopter landed outside the NATO hospital fifty-seven minutes after initially scrambling to the call. Campbell, Mulder, and Garza transported the three rangers to the hospital staff and joined them in the ER to update the doctors on their status. It was only a sentence or two, but that was all the hand-off needed before the hospital staff whisked the wounded to surgery.

The ride to the tactical operations center for the after-action report was quiet. Jason sensed Lieutenant Campbell planned to hang him out to dry in the meeting.

CHAPTER 2

Blood and sweat were smudged across the faces of the four PJs and the CRO sitting around the table as they waited for Captain Whitney to arrive. Jason tugged at his collar as he prepared for the after-action report—or AAR—of their recent rescue mission. His knee bounced under the table as he considered what Lieutenant Campbell might have included in his report. The compact, windowless room felt like it was getting smaller with each passing minute.

Once Whitney arrived and assumed his position at the end of the table, each man took turns sharing what worked and what they had to improve in future missions. Once it was Campbell's turn to speak, Jason's stomach did somersaults as he waited to get smoked by the chief rescue officer. Jason waited and waited, but Campbell made it sound like a textbook mission.

"Good work. Those boys will live because of you," Whitney said. The meeting ended, and everyone rose from their seats.

"Mulder, stick around for a minute," Campbell said.

"Yes, sir."

Campbell waited for everyone to leave and then leaned against the wall.

"Know why I didn't say anything in the AAR?"

Jason shook his head.

"Because you're a good PJ. You know your medicine and all three men made it to the hospital within the golden hour. However, that doesn't mean what you did was right."

Jason tilted his head and pursed his lips. "Sir?"

"I called you back over the radio. You shouldn't have gone into the village."

Jason didn't see anything wrong with his actions. He was trying to protect the civilians and everyone else in the helicopters. It was still the right thing to do in Jason's mind.

"I just wanted to protect those civilians and all of us from the bad guys."

Campbell let out an exaggerated sigh. "I know this is your first deployment here and you want to make a difference in this war. We all want to help save lives, but you're a little too gung-ho when it comes to protecting innocent bystanders. I get it, but we only make contact with the enemy when absolutely necessary. We don't go looking for a fight."

Jason nodded.

"The guys we saved today put their lives on the line every day and depend on us to render medical care as soon as we arrive. Marines, sailors, soldiers, and airmen die if we make a mistake. Injured or dead PJs can't help the men and women down range when they need us most. Don't forget why we do what we do."

"So that others may live," Jason recited the Pararescue motto.

"Exactly! Don't do it again."

Campbell left the room, and Jason fell back into a chair. He raked his fingers through his short, mahogany brown hair and leaned back until he faced the ceiling. Jason wasn't sure he'd change anything he did today, but understood the need to be more careful in the future.

The following day, Jason woke up and opened his journal. He had a new thrilling mission to document when he noticed the date was May 12, a special date that lingered in his mind. It was the date he decided to join the United States Air Force and became a PJ, and like everything in Jason's life, he did it in a dramatic fashion.

Five years earlier, Jason Mulder strutted across the scorching sidewalk on the University of Arizona campus in Tucson, Arizona. It was final exams week, and classrooms were buzzing with students full of anxiety and caffeine. Ten minutes into an exam with two hours allotted, Jason stood and slung his backpack over his shoulder. The other students looked up from their papers and watched Jason stroll to the professor's desk and hold his exam over the gray plastic tray with *Completed Exams* written on it with a black marker.

The professor held up his hand before Jason let it drop.

"You know once an exam is in the completed exam tray, you cannot remove it."

Jason considered the promise to his high school girlfriend and then let the exam fall into the tray. "I know."

The professor yanked Jason's exam from the tray and flipped through all four pages. "It's blank."

"I know."

"You'll fail this class."

"I know."

Two words were all it took for Jason to end his aspirations for a degree in biology and a career in the biomedical field. He departed the University of Arizona campus on the last day of his freshman year and never returned. It was a year longer than he wanted, but Jason didn't want to break his promise to Gaby. He'd promised his high school sweetheart he'd go to college with her, and he'd kept his end of the promise even though she couldn't. Jason stored all of his belongings from his dorm room in three moving boxes and put them in the bed of his truck. He had one stop to make before returning home to Payson, Arizona.

He pulled into an unremarkable strip mall in Tucson that he'd visited several times over the past year. Once inside the United States Air Force recruiting office and the door shut behind him, Jason asked for Staff Sergeant Wilson. A minute later, a stout man in his forties with a bald head walked up the hallway in his dress blues uniform. He smiled when he noticed Jason.

"Great to see you again, Jason. What questions do you have for me today?"

"I'm ready to join."

The smile vanished from Sergeant Wilson's face, and he motioned to a nearby table.

"Let's have a seat."

Jason sat across from the Air Force recruiter as he opened a folder and laid several pamphlets on the table.

"I'm happy to hear that you want to join the United States Air Force, but I've seen you in here several times this year, so I want to be sure you're ready. What occupation did you decide on?"

"I want to be a pararescueman and be part of the Guardian Angels team at the 48th Rescue Squadron with the guys down at Davis-Monthan Air Base," Jason replied confidently.

Wilson leaned forward. "Pararescuemen are Air Force Special Operations Forces personnel attached to other special forces units like the Navy SEALs and the US Army Rangers while deployed. They are the only combat forces in the Department of Defense specifically trained and equipped to conduct combat rescue operations in the world's most remote areas. It requires intelligence and some of the most rigorous physical standards in the military. PJs must be elite swimmers, have great physical endurance, then pass all the medical courses. Over seventy-five percent of the people that start the pararescue pipeline fail. Does that sound like something you can do?"

Jason nodded.

"What's your fitness level and skills in a pool?"

"I've had martial arts training since junior high. Shotokan Karate for four years and Krav Maga the last two. I ran the 800 meters for three years on my high school track team, and I've been a lifeguard since I was fifteen. I've been following a workout a PJ recommended online for the last six months, so I feel pretty good about it."

"Whatever you're doing now, double it," Sergeant Wilson barked.

A look of shock flashed on Jason's face for a second, then he slowly nodded.

Wilson took a drink from his water bottle and stared at Jason.

"Are you sure you're up for it?"

"Yes, sir!"

"It's Sergeant."

"Um, yes, Sergeant," Jason replied.

"Why do you want to become a PJ?"

Jason's smooth forehead wrinkled. "Why?"

"We've talked about other career paths during previous visits. Just last time, we spoke extensively about Special Missions Aviators. They're often with the PJs on combat search and rescue operations but with twenty fewer months of training. You could get started on your Air Force career sooner if you take that path. So why a PJ?"

"I want to serve and defend this great nation," Jason replied with a proud smile.

Wilson tossed his hands in the air and let them drop to the table. "Don't give me that canned bullshit answer, Mulder. I want to know why you want to put yourself through two years of hell to wear a maroon beret?"

"I was going to the U of A for BioMed, so I like the EMT training."

"Why do you want to be a PJ?"

Jason cleared his throat and squirmed in his seat. "I want to be on a team of the most elite special warfare operators."

"Nice try. Why a PJ?

The office was quiet for what felt like five minutes, but twenty seconds later, Jason blurted out the truth that he couldn't contain any longer.

"I want to protect my family, my friends and everyone I care about against anything in the world that tries to harm them!"

Wilson leaned back and rocked in his chair. He never took his eyes off Jason.

"Okay, that's more like it. Don't forget that when you feel like you're going to puke or die in the pool. Remember it when you're a quick air horn burst from making the pain go away. Never forget why you chose to become a PJ and fight like hell for it to be true."

Jason nodded.

"Do you have any questions for me?" Sergeant Wilson asked.

"Yeah. How soon can I leave?"

CHAPTER 3

It is my duty as a Pararescueman to save life and to aid the injured. I will be prepared at all times to perform my assigned duties quickly and efficiently, placing these duties before personal desires and comforts. These things we do, that others may live.

Pararescue Creed

Jason resettled into his two-bedroom apartment on Joint Base Lewis–McChord, or JBLM, southwest of Tacoma, Washington. He'd returned to base after three consecutive deployments in Afghanistan where Jason's crew successfully rescued sixty-three US military members, eighty-nine members of the Afghan National Army, and fifty-seven Afghan civilians. Thrilled to return to the Pacific Northwest, Jason could focus on training and supporting civilian rescues instead of treating amputees caused by mines and IEDs. He had two months left in his current contract with the Air Force and was eager for less excitement for a few weeks before he re-enlisted for another six years.

After Jason unpacked, he booked a flight home to Arizona for Easter weekend. He was eager to see his family for the first time since he'd returned from Afghanistan. A week later, Jason arrived at Sky Harbor International Airport in Phoenix, Arizona, and his family gave him a hero's welcome. His little brother, Josh, was the first to reach him after he passed through the secure doors. Jason hugged Josh first, then his mom, Celeste, and his dad, Phillip. His other brothers, Kevin and Noah, waited at home to greet him. During the ninety-minute drive to Payson, a central Arizona town of 16,000 residents nestled a mile high in the Tonto National Forest, Jason filled them in on his latest deployment.

"Have you decided yet if you'll re-enlist?" his dad asked.

"I'm planning on it. I just need to meet with my career adviser to sign the new contract."

Phillip parked his SUV, and Jason unfolded his six-foot-two frame from the backseat onto the gravel driveway in front of the ranch-style home. It was a modest home with chocolate brown siding and dark green shingles, making it look like an overfed tree set back a hundred feet into the forest. Ponderosa pines soared twenty to thirty feet above the roof line, making the house appear smaller than a five-bedroom, three-bathroom home. A detached two-car garage sat back from the house with a vast wood patio separating the two structures. Over the decades, the well-worn deck hosted hundreds of meals, parties, and late-night discussions. The adjacent fire pit directly behind the patio came in a close second for family gatherings and memories.

Jason stretched and did a full three-hundred-and-sixty-degree turn to take in the property he'd lived on his entire life until he left for the Air Force. He took a deep breath, and the pungent aroma from the pine resin and dry Arizona air tickled his throat.

"I like the Northwest, but I sure miss this."

"I'm so glad you're back," Josh chirped. He hadn't stopped smiling since Jason walked through the security doors at the airport.

The family moved inside. Jason dropped his bags and met with the rest of the family, which had grown since his last visit. His older brother, Kevin, and his wife, Carrie, had their first child, so Jason met his niece, Kayla, for the first time. Next, he barged into his younger brother Noah's room and punched him several times for not coming to the airport to see him. Jason continued the pseudo-beating until they were both laughing. After the initial greetings, the entire family moved outside to the patio to catch up. Carrie and Kayla went to bed around ten, but everyone else stayed, telling stories until the early morning.

The next morning, Jason went for a run before anyone else was awake. When he got out of the shower, Josh was looking at the bookshelf in his room.

"I didn't expect to see you up so early," Jason said.

Josh didn't respond as his fingers moved across several shelves of books. "Have you read all of these?" His fingers continued to the next shelf until he chose a book and opened it.

"Most of them. Some more than once."

Jason left and returned two minutes later, fully dressed. Josh sat on his bed with one book open and two by his side.

"Whatcha looking at?"

"You have all these weird books I've never heard of. *The Screwtape Letters* by C.S. Lewis, *Bushcraft 101* by Dave Canterbury, and *Meditations* by Marcus Aura—"

"Marcus Aurelius. What's so weird about them?"

"I've never heard of them. What's a screwtape?" Josh asked.

Jason laughed. "What are you reading now?"

"I just finished all the Mitch Rapp books, and they were awesome. Now I'm reading the last Scot Harvath book. Books with action are my favorite."

"I have all of those too. Try the *Gray Man* series next. You'll love them."

Josh flipped through several pages of *Bushcraft 101* and looked up at Jason. "Are we still going to build that off-grid house together?"

"Absolutely! I've saved up enough to buy land this summer. I wouldn't let anything get in the way of you and me building that house together."

Jason had floated the idea of building an off-grid house to his family a couple of years earlier. It became a joint plan with Josh when he'd expressed his desire to help build it. Now Jason had ample savings to buy the property, and soon they'd construct their off-grid house and leave a legacy of their brotherly teamwork for future generations.

"How about grabbing poles and fishing up at Woods Canyon Lake?" Jason asked.

Josh's eyes shot up. "Seriously?"

"Go get dressed."

Josh bolted out of the room and returned a minute later wearing the blue jeans and t-shirt he had worn the day before.

"Are those the same clothes you had on yesterday?"

"Yep. I'm saving the environment. I recycle."

Despite the ten-year age difference, Jason and Josh had a special bond. Jason's older brother Kevin was his senior by three years. The eldest Mulder son loved fast cars and football as far back as Jason could remember. Noah was born two years after Jason and he preferred to play video games, earning him the title of the official electronics expert in the family. Jason played sports and tinkered with gadgets, but was most passionate about reading and everything related to the outdoors like hiking, camping, hunting, and fishing. Josh shared the same passions.

The duo arrived at Woods Canyon Lake and claimed the rocky peninsula that jutted into the clear, cool water before the other anglers arrived. Jason cast his line and sat down on a smooth boulder. He watched his fishing line cut through the reflection of the pine trees shimmering on the lake's glass-like surface. Then, out of the corner of his eye, he caught Josh's hazel eyes fixed on him - an eye color shared by all the Mulder boys thanks to a Spanish mother born and raised on the north coast of Spain and Dutch father from Eindhoven, Netherlands.

"Is something wrong?" Jason asked.

"Why do you need to re-enlist in the Air Force?"

Jason looked back at his line for a few seconds and then at Josh. "It's what I do. I protect people."

Josh seemed to take in the response for a moment and then nodded.

"Will you have to go back to the war?"

"I hope not, but anything is possible. If I do, I promise I'll be safe."

"Good."

Three hours later, they had caught only four fish, but the aim of the fishing trip was a success. Two brothers spending quality time together. The rest of the week flew by with more fishing, hiking, grilling, and trips to the gun range. It was thirteen months since Jason was last home, and the clocks seemed to move at warp speed during his trip.

On the morning of his departure back to JBLM, Jason ate breakfast with his mom and Josh while his dad loaded his bags into the SUV. This was the most challenging part of every trip home, but it was hardest on Josh. Jason and his parents had developed an understanding that it was part of his job, but for a fifteen-year-old sophomore in high school that worshiped his older brother, it was still difficult to say goodbye.

Jason stood up to leave, and his mom held up her hand to stop him.

"Josh has something to ask you before you go."

Jason spun his chair around and sat down in front of Josh.

"Sure. What do you want, buddy?"

"Well—"

Josh started to speak and then stopped.

"Go ahead."

"Well, since you are good at biology, can you help me with my plant science project?"

"I'll help any way I can. What are you doing?"

"We have to find as many native plants as possible and then identify them. It's twenty-five percent of our grade, so I thought we could go deep into the forest and collect some plants nobody else will find like you did in High School."

"That sounds like a blast. I'll be back in seven weeks for Memorial Day. Will that work?"

Josh's shoulders slumped, and his head dropped. "No. It's part of our final grade, so it's due the week before."

"Sorry, Buddy, but Mom is a science teacher, so she'll be a good stand-in for me while I'm away."

"I know, but Mom doesn't know how to go deep in the woods like you. She won't rappel down a cliff to get the best plants, and she'll probably get us lost."

Jason stood up, ruffled Josh's hair, and pulled him in for a bear hug.

"Then I suggest you study some maps so you can help Mom navigate. Don't rely on somebody to find your way. You need to be prepared for anything."

Josh wiggled out of the bear hug. "Okay, but I was mostly hoping to spend some time with you."

They stared at each other, and Jason turned to leave the room. "Give me one minute."

Jason returned with two objects.

"These will help when you go with Mom to look for your plants. This is my first compass, and the pamphlet is my plant identification guide." Jason handed both to Josh.

"Thanks!"

"I have to leave now, but I'll take you fishing, hiking, and shooting when I get back."

"You promise?"

"Absolutely!"

Jason responded with conviction, but it was a promise he couldn't keep.

CHAPTER 4

Celeste Mulder stomped down the hallway and pushed open Josh's bedroom door.

"Turn off the video game and get ready to go."

"Just another few minutes. I've never been on this level," Josh replied. He kept his eyes glued to the character on the monitor.

"That's what you said ten minutes ago. It's going to take over an hour to get there. I need to get back home at a decent time today."

Josh did not respond. His tongue emerged between his lips as his fingers moved back and forth across the controller.

"Joshua Mulder. I'm not going to drive you if we don't leave soon!"

Celeste's tone seemed to snap Josh out of his game induced trance. He straightened and paused the game. "Fine. I want the Helianthus arizonensis. It's hard to find, but Jason found one and he said that's how he got an A in the class."

"The helia what?"

Josh sighed as if everyone on the planet should have full knowledge of Helianthus arizonesis. "The Arizona sunflower, but it may not be blooming yet. Can we go next week instead?" Josh asked as he reached for the controller again.

Celeste put her hands on her hips. "No! Your plant science project is due soon, and you've already put this off for too long. Grab your shoes and meet me in the car in five minutes."

Josh smiled. "Okay, mom. I'll be there in four minutes."

Celeste snagged two water bottles from the refrigerator and found Phillip reading a book and drinking iced tea in the shade on the back patio. His favorite place to lounge around on weekends.

"Josh and I are heading out to collect some plants for his school project."

Phillip looked at his watch. "It's getting a little late to be heading out to the forest."

"I wanted to go earlier but got busy. I'll be home for dinner."

"Okay. Where are you going?"

"We're heading to the forest road off Young Highway near Canyon Creek. I think it may be in Navajo county."

"Why so far?" Phillip asked.

"Josh has researched the plants he wants to find, and they grow wild in that area."

"I believe that's on the Fort Apache Reservation. Be sure to buy the permits before leaving and be careful."

"We will. I'll text you when we get there."

Celeste and Josh left Payson and drove up the Colorado Plateau until they crossed 7,000 feet of elevation. The Colorado Plateau extends hundreds of miles through northern Arizona, with sheer cliffs towering two-thousand feet over the carpet of emerald forest below. Next, they took the Young Highway toward Young, Arizona, and meandered through mountainous terrain covered by pine forest as far as the eye could see.

The unpaved forest road appeared, and they left the highway for a rugged dirt path. They bounced in her mid-size Chevy SUV until they arrived at an overlook near Canyon Creek on the Fort Apache Reservation.

"Okay, Josh. We've come pretty far. Can you find the helia sunflowers around here?"

Josh looked around. "We need to find a south-facing slope. Let's cross the creek and go up the other side. I see a couple of suitable areas over there."

Five minutes later, Celeste parked and locked her car. Josh darted up the rocky embankment while she texted Phillip: *Finally made it. I'll text you when we leave.*

Celeste watched for a confirmation the text went through but received a notification that she had no signal. She walked several steps away from her SUV to see if that provided any bars on her cell phone when Josh called her.

"Come on, Mom. I need your help finding them. If they're blooming, they each have eight golden petals."

Celeste marched up the hill and was out of breath once she reached Josh. "Where should we look?"

"Not here. We need to check over that ridge."

Celeste scanned the area as her lungs refilled with air. "Can't you look harder around here?"

"That's why I wanted Jason to take me. He would have taken me anywhere I wanted."

"That's not fair Josh," Celeste whispered, the hurt evident in her voice. "I know I can't take you the same places as Jason, but I'm here and I'm trying to help you the best I can."

Josh turned his gaze from the hillside to his mother. "I didn't mean it like that. I'm just bummed Jason couldn't come, but I'm glad you're helping me. We just need to check the other side of the ridge."

Celeste's lips briefly turned skyward with a smile. Although Josh was often overeager and annoyingly impatient, he was respectful to his parents like all of his older brothers. Celeste recognized this was Josh's way of apologizing, so she forgave him and refocused on finding the plants Josh wanted. "Okay. Let's go."

Josh raced up the last twenty yards. Once he reached the summit, he dropped his compass and plant guide.

Celeste climbed five more steps and stopped to catch her breath. The elevation made it hard for her to climb any faster. She looked up to her destination and noticed Josh frozen ten yards above her.

"What's wrong?"

Josh didn't answer. Her gut signaled that something was wrong, so she mustered all her energy to reach the top of the ridge next to Josh. Celeste followed his gaze and noticed what stopped Josh in his tracks. A dozen or more men worked inside two camouflage tents underneath a dense canopy of trees. It was practically invisible in the forest, but she observed industrial-sized stainless-steel vats and steam rising from a metal chimney in one tent. Several men milled around outside the tent, and Celeste noticed they had assault rifles slung over their backs. Her heart raced as her eyes panned to two armed men standing guard at the edge of the small camp.

The instinct to flee consumed Celeste. She grabbed Josh's hand and began retreating in one coordinated move. "Let's go!"

Their abrupt departure down the hill caught the attention of a man holding a rifle, and he yelled to three others. Seconds later, the armed men were in pursuit of the intruders. The Mulders had a good head start down the hill while the four men still had to climb the ridge. Celeste slid down most of the embankment and unlocked her car before their feet hit the dirt road. She jumped in, buckled up, and started the car while Josh slammed his door shut in the front passenger seat. Celeste pulled the stick into Drive, did a quick U-turn and spewed rocks into the air as she sped away. She exhaled loudly as the SUV pulled away from the men on foot. A half minute later, Celeste adjusted her rearview mirror and gasped. A beefy black truck kicked up a cloud of dust as it closed fast on her and Josh.

Celeste navigated the descent down and over Canyon Creek. She took the curve on the other side of the creek faster than she should have, and the SUV careened across the rocky dirt road before the front tires regained traction and straightened out. Celeste slammed her foot down on the accelerator to put distance between them and their pursuers, but the black truck continued to gain on the slower SUV.

Josh was on his knees facing the rear of the vehicle. "Faster Mom. They're getting closer!"

Celeste felt the fear in Josh's voice in her bones and pressed harder on the gas. She turned to Josh and shouted. "Sit back down and get your seatbelt on."

Josh ignored her command. His eyes widened as the black truck filled with angry men got within a car length of their SUV. "They're right behind us now."

Celeste and Josh entered the steep incline of the west bank of Canyon Creek when the black truck got within inches from their bumper. No matter how hard Celeste willed the SUV to go faster, the small V-6 engine was no match for gravity and the steep grade they climbed. The men in the super-duty truck had no such problems with the V-8 powerplant under their hood.

The truck moved to their left in the narrow road and Celeste could see the driver and front passenger clearly in her mirrors. The image of the scowl on the driver's face and the determined look on the passenger holding a rifle at the ready seared into her brain.

She heard honking and saw waving arms from the men in the back cab. Celeste assumed they wanted her to pull over, and that was never going to happen. She was halfway up the west side of Canyon Creek and would be back on Young Highway in under ten miles, which had more traffic and a cell phone signal to call for help. Celeste focused on making it up the hill as fast as possible, so she pushed the gas pedal to the floor.

The pursuers may have realized the same thing because that's when the first shot came through the back window.

"Josh, get down." He immediately dropped down into his seat and curled up to make himself a smaller target.

The second shot punctured a hole in the windshield between Celeste and Josh. She ducked down for a second and noticed the hairpin turn at the top of the hill was fast approaching after she popped back up. Celeste wouldn't dare slow down a single mile per hour to enter the switchback curve until the last moment. When the SUV was seconds from either taking the turn or driving off the top of the cliff above Canyon Creek, she braked, but instead of slowing down, the SUV sped up. The truck rammed into their vehicle and accelerated.

"Hang on Josh!"

The SUV blew past the turn and raced down the steep bank of Canyon Creek. The driver of the truck braked and skidded to a stop a foot or two from going over the same cliff.

The SUV rolled several times as it traveled more than two-hundred feet, landing on the roof in a thicket of shrubs near the dry creek bed. Once the vehicle came to a complete stop, Celeste opened her eyes and blinked multiple times as the engine sputtered and died. Dust filled the cabin, and her upside-down orientation added to her confusion. She raised her right hand and felt the crumpled metal pushing against her head. She pushed the deflating airbag out of the way, unbuckled her seatbelt and let her body drop to the roof of the overturned SUV. Pain shot up her spine, and Celeste felt like she might pass out as she tried to move around to find Josh. She looked around and confirmed he wasn't in the vehicle, so she tried to call for him. She opened her mouth to scream several times, but nothing came out. It was like a nightmare, but worse. This was real.

Celeste dragged herself through the broken window and crawled outside. She tried to stand, but her legs wobbled like a baby fawn, and she collapsed. Celeste fought the approaching blackness as she leaned against the SUV. Her baby boy was nowhere to be seen and the pain in her heart was impalpable. Celeste looked left and right as she rested her head against the remains of her SUV. She wanted to yell, crawl, or do anything to find Josh, but blackness closed in until it enveloped her like a tsunami. Seconds later, Celeste Mulder fell unconscious.

At 7:30 p.m., Phillip grew concerned that he hadn't received a text from Celeste, and they still weren't home. He called Noah first to see if he'd heard from his mother, and when he hadn't, Phillip called Kevin at work. He worked for the Colorado Springs fire department, and when Phillip shared his concern about Celeste and Josh, Kevin didn't mince his words.

"Dad, call the police now and report them missing. They are in the middle of nowhere and anything could've happened to them. I doubt they have a cell phone signal to call for help, and it'll be dark soon. Hang up and call the sheriff right now."

Phillip did just that, and twenty minutes later, a Gila County Sheriff's deputy arrived at their house to get a description and the last known whereabouts of Celeste and Josh. The deputy finished taking his notes and said, "I'm going to make some phone calls, and I'll let you know what's going on."

By the time the county dispatcher figured out if it would be a state search and rescue response or a federal team, since it was on the Fort Apache Reservation, it was too late for an aerial search. "Unfortunately, it took several calls to get the right agency sorted out, so a helicopter is not an option right now, but we'll send ground teams out to look for them," the deputy said.

Phillip paced in the family room, wondering why Celeste hadn't texted him or arrived home. He considered calling Jason to tell him, but he didn't want to concern his son if it was just a silly misunderstanding. What if Celeste and Josh stopped for a bite to eat and just forgot to call or text? He decided he'd call Jason once he had answers on their whereabouts.

Just before midnight, the Gila County deputy knocked on the door to tell Phillip they found nothing and called off the search for the night. They'd resume the search in the morning and send up a helicopter at first light.

"Call us if you hear anything from your wife," the deputy said.

"I will."

Phillip paced for hours until he was so exhausted that he passed out in his recliner. He woke again with another knock at the door. This time it was the elected sheriff of Gila County and the department chaplain. Phillip's heart sank at the sight of the two men.

"Tell me you've found them," Phillip said as he opened the door.

The sheriff removed his cowboy hat and held it to his chest. "I'm sorry, Mr. Mulder, but we have bad news. The aerial search and rescue team spotted your wife's vehicle at the bottom of a cliff near Canyon Creek. They airlifted her to Honor Health in Scottsdale in critical condition."

"And my son?" Phillip asked. His lips trembled as he waited for the response.

"I'm sorry. Officers found your son thirty feet from the vehicle. It appears he was thrown from the SUV as it rolled down the side of the cliff. Unfortunately, he was deceased when we arrived."

Phillip took several steps back and fell onto his couch. The sheriff and chaplain left, and now he had to have the most painful conversation of his life with his boys. Phillip was most concerned about Jason.

CHAPTER 5

Jason completed the third mile of his five-mile morning run around Joint Base Lewis–McChord under a light mist. He kept his phone on do-not-disturb to avoid distracting texts until he completed his workout and listened to his eighties and nineties heavy metal music so loud that he didn't hear the Air Force Security Force SUV pull up next to him. Jason stopped running and turned off his music after the airman honked.

"Staff Sergeant Mulder?"

"Yes."

"Please come with me. The commander wants to see you."

Jason knew it had to be bad news if Security Forces picked him up and took him straight to the base commander. He assumed it was deployment or career-related, but it was much worse.

When Phillip couldn't reach Jason on his cell phone, he'd called the base and shared the bad news. The commander told Jason about the accident, and his assistant helped him get a flight to Phoenix a few hours later. Eight hours after receiving the call, Jason arrived at the hospital in Scottsdale, Arizona. He entered his mom's room and found his father and his brothers, Noah and Kevin. They all hugged and gave Jason the chair closest to his sleeping mother. He read the IV bag hanging by her bed and watched the readings on her heart monitor before sitting down.

Jason held his mother's hand in silence. The rhythmic ticks and beeps of the monitors and hum of the fluorescent lights were the only sounds in the room until Jason asked the question torturing him since he received the news.

"What happened?"

Noah, Kevin, and Phillip all looked at each other, and then Jason's father answered.

"The sheriff said she took a hairpin turn too fast and rolled down the side of a cliff near Canyon Creek. She had her seat belt on, so it saved her life, but she suffered a fractured tibia, a broken clavicle, and internal bleeding. They've already removed her spleen and are watching one of her kidneys. Your mom also has a severe concussion, so she's in awful shape."

Jason nodded. He knew better than most visitors the grave condition of his mother.

"Has she been awake or spoken yet?"

"She's opened her eyes a few times but hasn't said anything."

"Josh?"

Phillip broke down in tears and couldn't answer him. Finally, after several failed attempts, Kevin responded.

"He didn't have his seatbelt on. Josh didn't survive the crash."

Nobody said a word for several minutes. Jason felt all the eyes in the room on him, waiting to see how he'd react. They knew the special relationship he had with Josh.

Jason stood and looked at his mom's chart dangling at the end of her bed. "When's the funeral?"

Phillip wiped his nose with his handkerchief. "I haven't finalized anything yet. I've been here all day. I was hoping you three could help."

Jason nodded. "Where is he? I'd like to see him now."

"Are you sure that's a good idea, son?"

Jason's lower lip quivered. "No, but I still want to see him. I want to see him now."

Phillip gave Jason the address of the funeral home in Payson.

Four days later, Jason and Noah helped a home health team set up a hospital bed in the family room for their mother. Celeste insisted she leave the hospital early to give Josh a timely burial. Her doctor finally relented if a nurse could visit their home three times a day to administer medications and monitor Celeste's condition.

The following day, Phillip helped a wheelchair-bound Celeste to the front of the funeral home next to a closed casket. The only evidence of the individual inside was the framed picture on top of the casket of Josh with a beaming smile while holding a two-pound brown trout.

Jason had driven himself to the funeral, so after they laid Josh to rest, he waited in his truck at the cemetery until everyone left. Once the last vehicle departed, Jason stood over the gravestone several shades lighter than its neighbors. He bent over to kiss the smooth granite marker, and his knees gave out. He lowered his head and closed his eyes so he didn't have to read Joshua Phillip Mulder etched in stone another time. Jason hadn't cried in six years but teetered dangerously close to a total breakdown. He took deep breaths to push the tears away, then he felt Josh's hug around his waist like he never wanted to let go when Jason returned home after Afghanistan. He heard Josh's high-pitched giggle when he tried to prank his older brother but always gave it away with his laugh. Knowing he'd never see that smile again destroyed all his remaining defenses. Raw emotion bubbled up and burst into the open like a flash flood through a slot canyon. Jason was no longer in control. He had to let grief run its course. He sobbed like no other time in his life until his stomach ached and his eyes burned, but it ended as fast as it started. Jason stood up, wiped his eyes, and ambled back to his truck.

Two hours later, friends, family, neighbors, and classmates of Josh filtered in and out of their home to offer their condolences. The house grew warm with all the people, but the walls closing in drove Jason outside. He walked across the back patio, leaned his head back, and inhaled the cool twilight air. Not long after, the heat left Jason's body as the back door opened and Noah joined him.

"How are you holding up?" Noah asked. He leaned against the railing next to Jason.

"I'm fine," Jason lied.

"I know it has to be extra tough on you because of how close you were to Josh. Plus, you lost Gaby in a similar way."

"It's tough, but I'll survive." Jason pulled a two-inch splinter from the railing and tossed it into the backyard. "How about you?"

Noah cleared his throat as tears welled up. "You know, I'd be better if I thought it was just an accident."

Jason pinched his eyebrows at the unexpected response. "What do you mean?"

Noah crossed his arms. "I don't think it was an accident. The deputy says Mom had to be going twenty to thirty miles an hour faster than she should have to end up that far down the bank by the creek. Mom never drives that fast. She's a cautious driver. Plus, Josh always wore his seat belt."

Jason nodded. "True. What do you think happened? Do you think someone intentionally ran them off the road?"

"I do."

Jason thought about it for a few seconds. "What are you going to do about it?"

"The White Mountain Apache Tribe police seem to think it was an accident. I was hoping we could go out to the crash site to see if we can find any evidence of foul play before you leave."

Jason let out a loud sigh. "I don't know, man. If the police already went over everything, I don't know what additional evidence we'd find."

"We don't have to do it, but you know your way around the forest and rugged terrain better than most people. I just thought you'd be able to find any clues if there are any."

"I'll think about it."

Noah straightened and moved to the door. "Are you coming back in?"

"I'm going to stay out here a few more minutes."

Jason returned to the edge of the patio. He stared into the woods behind their house while questions swirled in his head like a dust devil.

Did Mom misjudge her speed heading into the curve? Why didn't Josh have his seat belt on? Why would Mom drive so fast?

More questions scrolled through his mind, but only one included an answer.

Jason went inside and found Noah in the family room. He was talking to their Aunt Clara on the couch.

"Can I borrow you for a minute? I need help with something," Jason interrupted.

"Sure."

Noah followed Jason down the hall and into Noah's bedroom. He shut the door once Noah was in the room.

Jason locked eyes with Noah. "I'll go look around the accident site by myself. I can't promise I'll find anything, but I'll take a look."

"Why don't we go out there together?"

"If someone intentionally ran them off the road, they may still be out there, and it could be dangerous. I'll only do it if I go alone."

Noah leaned forward and gave Jason a hug. "Fair enough. I just need to know whether it was an accident." Noah's voice cracked, and his eyes filled with tears.

"Me too."

CHAPTER 6

Jason's mind was still swimming with questions as he stared at the rotating ceiling fan in his bedroom. Instead of sleeping, he laid in bed most of the night considering the hundreds of potential scenarios for the accident.

The first rays of sun beamed through his window, so Jason laced up his running shoes and departed for his morning run. With each step, Jason mentally replayed the possibilities of what could have happened to Josh and his mom. He ran faster and faster until he had to stop and put his hands on his head to catch his breath. Although Jason was only two miles into his five mile run, he couldn't wait any longer for answers regarding Josh's questionable death. Potential evidence was waiting in the canyon deep in the forest, and Jason needed to find it.

Two hours later, Jason parked on the Fort Apache Reservation near the area where White Mountain Apache Tribe police said his mom and Josh drove off the road. Jason found broken branches and disturbed dirt the width of a midsize SUV's rear tires. He walked to the edge, leaned over, and looked down toward the creek. Jason saw red and white pieces of the taillights and the glint of broken glass reflecting in the sun yards from the rocky creek bed. This confirmed the high rate of speed at which his mom and Josh went off the road. He returned to the switchback curve that was almost like making a full U-turn.

"Why would she drive so fast into this curve?" Jason asked aloud.

Jason returned to his truck, drove farther into the forest, and parked near a clearing on the other side of Canyon Creek. *This is where I'd go if I was looking for rare native plants*, Jason thought.

He walked up and down the road but saw no evidence of Josh or his mom.

"Where would Josh go to find those plants?"

Jason looked up from the road and noticed the treeless ridge above the other hills. He let out a small laugh.

"He'd go for the high ground, just like I taught him."

Ninety seconds later, Jason arrived at the top. He scanned the area. A shiny object caught his attention, and when he stood over it, his jaw dropped. It was the compass and plant identification guide Jason gave Josh before he left. Jason's chest tightened as he flipped the guide over to examine the front and back. He pulled his eyes away from the gift and turned in all directions. He moved along the summit looking for signs of anything out of order when he lost his footing. After regaining his balance, he watched the loose granite tumble down to the bottom. That's when Jason noticed streaks of darker brown disturbed earth among a sea of sun-bleached rocks and soil heading down toward the road. They were in an area few people ever visited, so the disturbed earth screamed recent human activity. Jason slid down as fast as possible and looked up to see if his marks matched the others. They were almost an exact match.

"They came down from that ridge in a hurry. What did they see up there?"

Jason walked to the opposite side of the road to get a better view and noticed tire tracks going in a semi-circle pattern. Upon further investigation, Jason noticed two bare spots in the road, like somebody sped away in a rush. Jason explored the area for another five minutes, and when he couldn't find anything else, he drove the forest access road back to Young Highway. He puttered along the forest road and looked for additional clues along the way.

"What did they see back there that caused Mom to drive away so fast?"

On the way back, Jason stopped at the salvage yard, where they towed Celeste's SUV after they pulled it up from the canyon. As he walked to the location in the back of the property the owner gave him for the wreckage, Jason received a text from his father.

Your mom woke up and thought you had already left for JBLM. She's having a bad day so it would help if you could spend some time with her before you go.

Jason's heart sank at the physical and emotional pain his mom must be feeling. His stomach soured when he saw crumbled metal resembling a silver Chevy SUV.

"How did she survive?" Jason whispered to himself.

The accident smashed the roof so far that it was only a foot above the hood. Jason circled the SUV twice, looking for anything out of the ordinary for a fatal accident. Scratches and dents were everywhere after rolling down into the canyon. Jason was about to leave when several deep black scratches on the tailgate and the rear bumper caught his eye. He tried to rub them off with his finger, but something embedded them into the paint.

He opened his phone to text his dad that he was coming home soon when he noticed something odd in the shattered windshield. A perfect dime-size circle just under the rearview mirror that was easy to miss in glass that looked like it was covered by a hundred spider webs. He'd seen that same signature hole a million times in civilian vehicles in Afghanistan. Jason took several photos of the rear bumper and windshield with his phone.

Jason put his key in the ignition but didn't start his truck. He considered everything he'd found and pondered his next steps. Mother Nature doesn't create perfect circles or black metallic paint, so he was confident his fresh evidence pointed to foul play. What now? Could he effectively search for the truth over a thousand miles away while doing a job that required complete focus? Did he really find evidence of foul play or was his desire for it not to be an accident blinding his judgment?

He started his truck and drove home.

Jason crept into the family room to see his mom. The room that used to host lively debates and competitive game nights was a makeshift hospital room. Noah and Phillip saw Jason enter and followed him into the room.

Celeste's red, swollen eyes were open. Jason moved to her side and gave her a gentle hug. He felt warm tears on his cheek and leaned back.

"How are you feeling? Are the nurses taking good care of you?"

"I still can't believe Josh is gone."

Jason nodded. He couldn't believe it either. Although he wanted nothing more than to tear something apart, he remained composed.

Jason gently touched the bandages covering Celeste's forehead and ears. "How's your head?"

"Better, I guess. I still feel dizzy if I sit up too fast."

"You still have to take it easy, even though you're at home."

Celeste nodded, and tears flowed again. Everyone was quiet for another minute until she broke the silence. "Are you heading back to base now?"

"I'm leaving soon, but I want to spend some time with all of you before I go."

Celeste patted his hand. "Thank you."

A minute later, Jason asked Noah to step into the kitchen. Once they were far enough away, Jason shared what he found.

"You may be right, Noah. Something doesn't add up with the accident."

"I thought so. What should we do now?" Noah asked.

"We need to get to the truth about what really happened. I know Mom told the police she doesn't remember much from the accident, so we may need to press her a little to see if she knows anything that can help provide answers. After that, I'll need a few days to come up with a plan."

"Dad's not going to like that. He doesn't want anyone to push her too hard right now."

"I know. She's still in bad shape, so I won't push too hard, but we have to find out if she knows anything else about the accident."

When Noah and Jason returned to the family room, Celeste inched up in bed. "Is everything okay?"

"Yeah, Mom. Everything is fine," Noah responded.

"Are you sure? You two look like you've seen a ghost."

Jason saw the opportunity to ask one question about what she recalled from the accident. "Mom, do you remember everything that happened that day?"

Celeste fell back onto her bed. "It's all still so foggy."

"That's okay. I went out to the scene and found this."

Jason handed Celeste the plant identification pamphlet. She looked at it, and the sobs turned into shrieks, making Jason's arm hair stand at attention.

"Jason Mulder, don't upset your mother. She's still very sick," Phillip barked.

"I know, Dad. I won't ask her anything else. I should probably head out soon."

"You don't have to leave. Just don't upset your mother."

"I know, but—"

"I remember what happened!" Celeste blurted in a strangled voice.

Everyone stopped talking and moved around Celeste.

"We were in the forest looking at plants for Josh's biology project when we came across a camp or something with several men working in and around it. I assumed it was drugs or something illegal, but when I saw they had rifles, I knew we had to run. I tried to outrun them in my car, but their truck was too fast. They even shot at us a couple times, so I tried to go faster, but I couldn't."

Celeste swallowed hard and wiped fresh tears from her cheek.

"I tried to do everything I could to get away from those guys. The last thing I remember was trying to slow down for a sharp curve and then feeling the truck push us over the edge." Her voice cracked. "I'm sorry. I tried to protect Josh, and now he's dead."

Jason caught Noah looking at him out of the corner of his eye. For the first time in six years, his new top priority had nothing to do with his job as a PJ in the Air Force. It was a very personal mission in his home state.

CHAPTER 7

The crisp, cool Tacoma air slapped Jason's face as he exited his apartment for a run. He laid in his bed thinking about the accident until well past midnight and now he had to shake a morning bout of brain fog. Although he'd have another ninety minutes of physical training once he arrived at his garrison, a five-mile run outside always helped Jason refocus his thoughts.

During his run, Jason considered the steps to investigate the suspicious activity surrounding Josh and his mom's accident. As a non-commissioned officer or NCO of the United States Air Force, Jason was a stickler for following the proper chain of command. Without much more thought he texted a recently retired Security Force member he had known while deployed in Turkey as soon as he returned from his run. It was an added benefit that he now worked as a police officer in Farmington, New Mexico.

Hey, Wallace. It's Mulder. I hope all is well with you at FPD. I have a question on jurisdiction. Who should I contact to kick off an investigation for a crime committed on an Indian Reservation?

Ten minutes later, Jason received a text back from Sergeant Wallace.

What did you do, Mulder?

Jason knew Wallace was trying to be funny but found himself annoyed with the response. He chose to shut down further idle chatter and get right to the point.

It wasn't me. It was my mom and brother. They got into a car accident. My mom was seriously injured, and my brother didn't make it. I suspect foul play, but I don't know who to contact.

Sorry, man. I didn't know.

Jason didn't respond to the text. A minute later, Sergeant Wallace replied.

It can be tricky because tribal police cover all crimes of their members but if it's a major crime the feds usually take over. In your case, I'd start with the tribal police.

Got it. Thanks, Wallace, and stay safe.

Jason tossed his phone on the coffee table. He promised Noah he'd call him with the next steps in three days, and four had already passed. It was time to call, but Jason was holding off because Noah often smothered people with his eagerness to help. Knowing Noah, he'd want Jason to fly home today and have them combing millions of acres of forest for clues or hounding the police until it became their number one case.

After brewing a fresh cup of coffee, Jason called Noah.

"How's it going?"

"It's fine. Mom's moving around a little more, so that's good," Noah replied.

"Dad told me the good news yesterday. The nurses do most of the hard work, but I'm glad you're around to help Dad with her on everything else."

"I'll help as much as I can."

Jason cleared his throat. "Look, I want to follow up on our conversation about potential foul play. I've been doing some digging and I think we should call—"

"I've already taken care of it."

"What? You don't even know what I'm going to say."

"Last night, Captain Selah from the White Mountain Apache Tribe Police Department stopped by to see how we're doing. He worked with the Gila County sheriff on the search for Josh and brought a counselor from their victim's services. She's available to any of us if we need grief counseling. I've already signed up for one session, and I think you and Dad should also consider it."

Jason's eyes narrowed. "I don't need a grief counselor. I need someone in law enforcement to investigate the evidence I found to determine if foul play was involved."

"We talked about that too. Captain Selah said they are shorthanded. They don't have a detective on staff right now but he'll send one of his patrol officers to the area to look around for any clues they may have missed. He'll let me know if they find anything in a couple of days."

Jason rubbed the back of his neck while he considered Noah's response. "I'd prefer a detective that knows what they are looking for, but I'll take what we can get. I was calling with a similar recommendation, but you're already on it, so keep me posted on what they find."

"Sounds good. Do you want the number for the counselor to schedule an appointment?"

"Um, no!"

Three days later, Jason received a call after midnight. He assumed it was Noah because he was the only night owl he knew.

"What's up?"

"I have some new information. Yesterday, a couple of patrol officers from WMAT PD came by the house to interview Mom again, and today they went back to the accident site. They don't think it was foul play."

"What? That's what I was afraid of. They didn't find any evidence of another vehicle involved?" Jason asked. He knew the White Mountain Apache Tribe Police Department was short on resources, but hoped the patrol officers would have found evidence of the black truck.

"Yes and no. The investigators found evidence of an illegal campsite nearby. Based on Mom's report that men with guns were honking and waving at her to stop, they think it was poachers trying to convince her not to turn them in. They apologized for the unfortunate accident but didn't find any criminal activity beyond poaching to pursue. The WMAT PD closed the case as an accident."

Jason fell backward on his bed. "I don't believe this."

"Neither do I. Some teenagers from Show Low were in the forest last night and claimed men in a black super-duty pickup truck chased them all the way back into town. They were afraid for their lives, so one of their parents posted it all over social media. I don't think it's a coincidence that they described the same truck as Mom."

Show Low was another Arizona mountain town similar in size and population to Payson on the opposite side of the enormous Fort Apache Reservation.

The line was quiet while Jason mulled over the similarities.

"Are you still there?" Noah asked.

"Yeah. Were those kids on the Fort Apache Reservation?"

"No. They were somewhere just outside the Show Low city limits. What are you thinking? Should we go over there and see if we can find the guys in the truck?"

"I'd love to march into the forest and take care of these guys by ourselves, but we'd end up in jail instead of them. We have to work with law enforcement on this. We just need to push the right people to dig deeper into the case."

"Okay. How do we do that?" Noah asked.

"If it's near Show Low, that means another jurisdiction and another set of eyes and ears. We may get the Navajo County sheriff to investigate the black truck. I have a lot of leave left, so I'm going to see if I can come home for a few days next week. We need to get them on the case if we want to know the truth and bring the people responsible for Josh's death to justice."

Ten days later, Jason arrived home and surprised his mom. Although she required a walker to get around the house while her fractured leg healed, she looked better. Jason visited with his parents for an hour before going out for a late afternoon run. He wanted a clear head when he went with Noah to visit the Navajo County sheriff's office the next day. His livelihood as a PJ relied on being prepared, and he applied the same principles to life. During his run, Jason considered dozens of questions they could ask him, and he felt ready to speak to someone at NCSO. When Jason turned off the pavement and slowed to a walk on the gravel driveway leading to his house, he noticed Noah's car and a strange SUV parked in front of the garage.

Jason opened the back door, expecting to see a home health nurse helping his mother, but found Noah talking to a young lady at the kitchen table.

"Here he is," Noah announced when Jason entered the house.

A stunning woman with straight midnight black hair flowing past her shoulders, stood and strode toward Jason. Although she was a half a foot shorter than Jason, she was self-assured in her movements and shook Jason's hand firmly. His gaze fell to the toned arms behind the surprising handshake that reminded him of an Olympic gymnast. Jason's eyes moved up to her full lips accented with ruby red lipstick that highlighted her ivory teeth when she smiled.

"Hi. I'm Shanna Dosala. I'm a certified trauma, abuse, and grief counselor with Indian Health Services and a liaison to the White Mountain Apache Tribe Police Department. I've heard so much about you."

The words to respond were lost in Jason's throat, and he stammered until his voice caught. "Hel—Hey—Hi. Nice to meet you."

He didn't know what to expect when he walked in the door, but a stunning woman sitting in his kitchen was not the hand he expected to be dealt.

Noah chuckled. "I told you she was beautiful."

Jason shot Noah a look with such ferocity that Noah immediately quit laughing and genuinely looked afraid for his physical well-being.

Noah walked over to Shanna and stood next to her. "Shanna is helping me sort through all my anger and grief productively over everything that happened. She really knows her stuff."

"I'm sure she does, but right now, I have to prepare for our meeting with NCSO tomorrow."

Shanna moved closer to Jason. "You've suffered a devastating loss, and navigating through everything yourself is difficult. How are you doing?"

Her brown eyes were soft and her voice steady and inviting. Her concern felt genuine, and it disarmed Jason.

"It's tough, but I'm getting by."

"I don't want you to just get by. I want you to heal. Can we talk sometime?"

Jason considered the offer. Shanna made him feel vulnerable yet safe, but Jason preferred to keep his deepest feelings to himself.

"I appreciate the offer, but I really need to go. It was a pleasure meeting you."

Shanna nodded. "Me too."

Noah moved next to Jason as they watched Shanna back out of the driveway.

"You should meet with her."

"That's okay. I wish I could talk away all my problems like some people, but it's not easy for me."

Noah opened his mouth to speak but then closed it. He took two steps away from Jason. "Gaby would understand."

"What does Gaby have to do with any of this?" Jason snapped.

"It's been seven years. It's okay to move on with your life."

"I have moved on."

"A hundred first dates doesn't mean you've moved on. It's just camouflage for your pain. It may fool others, but it doesn't fool me. You haven't had a relationship with anyone since Gaby."

Jason glared at Noah. He wanted to knock the smirk off his face, but couldn't. Noah was right, and Jason hated when his punk-ass little brother was right.

"Be ready to leave by nine tomorrow."

The following morning, Noah and Jason drove ninety miles east to Show Low, Arizona. They pulled off Deuce of Clubs Avenue and parked a block away in the Show Low substation of the Navajo County Sheriff's Department.

They sat in Jason's truck and watched deputies and citizens walk in and out of the front entrance.

"We may have to push them a little to get them interested in this case," Jason said.

Noah nodded.

"They may not be very interested in investigating teenagers chased out of the forest, but we have to make them interested. It's the only way we'll get to the truth."

"I'm ready," Noah said.

Jason and Noah entered the building and the door slammed shut behind them. They were committed now to finding the truth.

CHAPTER 8

Noah walked shoulder to shoulder with Jason to a counter separating the public waiting area from the business area of the police station. A middle-aged man in a uniform with a Navajo County sheriff patch on his shoulder greeted Jason and Noah. He verified their appointment and invited them to sit in a bank of worn chairs. Ten minutes later, a man in plain clothes with a badge and a holster with a Glock 22 service pistol on his belt stood before them.

"Hello. I'm Detective Caldwell," he said as he extended his hand to Jason and Noah. They shook hands and followed Detective Caldwell back to his office. The Mulder brothers sat opposite the detective with a metal desk with a computer on top separating the two parties. Jason looked around the room and noticed only one picture of what looked to be his family on his desk. He assumed Detective Caldwell was a minimalist, all business, or both.

"I understand you have some information to share on a recent incident involving some local teens outside Apache-Sitegraves National Forest."

Noah looked at Jason, which was his cue to respond. "Yes, sir. Did you read the police report on Celeste and Josh Mulder that the WMAT PD provided?"

"Yes, I did. I'm sorry for your loss, and I wish a speedy recovery for your mother."

Definitely all business, Jason thought.

"Thank you. We contacted you because my mom reported seeing a dozen armed men before she was chased by a black super-duty truck that ran her off the road. The vehicle described by the high school boys sounds like the one my mom described. If you find the vehicle, it may have silver paint on the quarter panel or bumper to positively ID it as the same vehicle."

Detective Caldwell took notes while Jason shared his information.

"Did she get a vehicle make?"

"No, sir. Just that it had a crew cab, black paint, and was larger than my Ford F-150."

"Did she see what the armed men were doing?"

"Not exactly. She grabbed my brother and ran as soon as she saw them, but her gut told her some type of illegal activity."

Detective Caldwell nodded and then tapped a few keys on his keyboard. "I see here that the White Mountain Apache Police believe it was a camp of poachers and that they ruled it an accident. So why do you believe we should look for this black truck?"

"The men in the truck shot at my mom. Even if they are poachers, which I don't believe, wouldn't that make them guilty of more serious crimes that deserve investigating?"

Detective Caldwell leaned closer to his monitor and scrolled through several pages. The rhythmic clicking of his mouse was like fingers on a chalkboard to Jason as he waited.

"I don't see any mention of gunshots in the report. On what grounds are you basing that claim?"

"I saw a bullet hole in the windshield of her SUV in the junkyard." Jason reached into his pocket to retrieve his phone with the pictures, when he noticed Caldwell lean back in his chair.

Jason looked up and the detective flashed a sheepish grin. It was the kind of grin a know-it-all has when they are about to educate you on how things work in the real world.

"Well, Mr. Mulder, gunshots in real life are a lot different than on TV or video games. Trained investigators know how to spot them and that didn't happen here. I appreciate your theory, but why on earth do you think you found evidence of gunshots the police missed?"

"Thousands of real-world examples when deployed with my special warfare team in Afghanistan last year," Jason snapped.

Jason was used to being underestimated. He didn't look like former army MP and fictional giant Jack Reacher or the prototypical military badasses in all the movies. He was six feet two inches tall with single-digit body fat and a six-pack under his shirt. Jason was clean-shaven, and a simple T-shirt hid his tattoos of jolly green feet and the PJ motto from view. He let the top grow out an extra inch in his high and tight haircut to part it on the side, and Jason rarely wore clothes that revealed his muscular arms, legs, and chest. If pressed, Jason would admit he relished being underestimated, especially by bullies and foes. He'd dealt with it his entire life. When he was in junior high school, he hated it and busted his ass with martial arts to become an equal to his peers. Now he used it to his advantage. Detective Caldwell probably thought Jason was some yuppie assistant to the assistant manager at a local bank, and now he was backpedaling from his previous attitude.

Detective Caldwell leaned forward and turned his full attention to Jason. "Thank you for your service."

Jason stared coolly at the detective and did not respond. Finally, Noah broke the tension in the room.

"We wanted to share this information because the men my mom saw are dangerous, and if those teenage boys ran into them, they might have moved their operation here. So, we're hoping NCSO could check it out to ensure the safety of the local citizens."

Good job, Senator Mulder, Jason thought with Noah's quick pivot.

Detective Caldwell stood up. "We appreciate the information, and we'll send someone out to the area to check it out."

Jason and Noah also stood up.

"Will you let us know what you've found?" Noah asked.

"We'll be in touch in a few days."

Jason exited the Navajo County sheriff substation with negative vibes from Detective Caldwell. He couldn't place exactly what bothered him, but he didn't think they were going to get much cooperation or effort from Caldwell.

Two hours later, Noah and Jason ate lunch with their mom and dad under the shade of a large umbrella on the back patio.

"I have to get back to work now," Noah said.

He stood and picked up his empty plate. Noah was a software engineer two years out of college, working remotely for a company that manufactured commercial-grade unmanned aerial vehicles or drones.

"Got any cool new products coming out?" Phillip asked.

"Yeah. Our latest drone has longer flight time and range, but the really cool tech is the new Forward Looking InfraRed or FLIR infrared camera we added. It can see through smoke, identify people in the dark, and even detect the heat signatures of people for search and rescue teams."

Noah turned to Jason. "When your enlistment is up with the Air Force, you should start your own search and rescue business. I could get you a deal on our best drones, and you can contract your services out with all the agencies that don't want to buy a full line of SAR drones. They all love the technology, but most don't have the money to buy twenty-thousand-dollar UAVs outright."

Jason thought about it and then responded, "I'm planning to re-enlist for another six years."

Jason didn't want to admit that Noah's idea was pretty good. His younger brother was getting a big head lately with some of his ideas, and as the older brother, it was Jason's job to keep Noah's ego in check.

The next day, Jason packed his bags for his return trip to JBLM. He heard Noah's phone ring.

"Hi, Detective Caldwell," Noah said. Jason walked over and Noah put the detective on speakerphone.

"Do you have an update?"

"We have a couple of deputies in the area where the teenage boys encountered the mysterious black truck, so they're going to check it out," Caldwell shared.

"Okay. Let us know what you find," Noah replied.

Noah hung up and turned to his older brother.

"I hope they find something."

"I hope they actually look."

Noah's face turned from one of hope to confusion, so Jason felt he should elaborate.

"After our meeting, I didn't feel he believed an armed group was running around in the woods. I hope they investigate and not just drive by to pacify us."

"I think they'll do a thorough investigation," Noah replied with hope in his eyes.

Jason kept busy until it was time to leave for Phoenix Sky Harbor Airport to catch his flight back to Tacoma. He wanted to stick around as long as possible to get the scoop from Noah firsthand when Caldwell called back.

Just as Jason was about to leave, Noah's phone rang.

It wasn't Detective Caldwell but someone else from NCSO. The friendly female voice on the other end shared she was calling on his behalf.

"Detective Caldwell is busy right now, and he asked me to let you know that after an exhaustive investigation of the area, they found no evidence of illegal activity or armed men that match your description. We'll keep you posted if anything changes."

"Exhaustive investigation? Did he say that?" Jason asked.

"Yes, sir. Those were his exact words."

Jason figured that Caldwell's eyes must have turned from blue to brown with all the bullshit he was spewing through his messenger.

"Thank you for the call," Noah said. He hung up and tossed his phone onto the kitchen table. "They didn't find anything. Zip. Zilch. Nada. What should we do now?"

Jason looked down at the packed bags at his feet. He knew Southwest Airlines had a later flight that was rarely full.

"I'm going over there to check myself."

"Okay, but we'll have to wait until after five because I have a conference call."

"I'm going alone."

"Why can't I go?" Noah asked.

"It could be dangerous."

"I'm not afraid of danger."

"You should be. The armed men that shot at Mom and murdered Josh won't hesitate to kill again."

Noah stood in silence. Jason could tell it hurt him, so he gave him the real reason he had to go solo.

"Look, man. I have to go alone. I don't want to lose another brother."

CHAPTER 9

Pine trees towered fifty feet over Jason's truck as he bounced along the same dirt path as the teenagers from Show Low that narrowly escaped the black truck earlier that week. His frustration with the Navajo County Sheriff's Office evaporated during the drive like a puddle on a hot Arizona summer day. He understood their reluctance to admit that a group of armed men were lurking in Apache-Sitegraves National Forest, threatening dozens of small mountain communities bordering the forest.

The sheer enormity of the forest was daunting. The combined Sitegraves National Forest and Apache National Forest covered 5.5 million acres or 8,500 square miles. It ran roughly one-hundred and fifty miles from the northwest corner near the Blue Ridge Reservoir east to the corner of the national forest at the New Mexico border. It was fifty miles from the northern to the southern border, creating a national forest nearly large enough to cover the entire state of New Jersey. That didn't count the adjacent national forests to the west and south. Coconino National Forest on the western border added another 2,800 square miles, Tonto National Forest on the southwestern border 4,500, and the Fort Apache Reservation on the southeastern border added more than 2,600 square miles. Combined, the area of contiguous pine forest in

Northern Arizona could cover the entire states of Massachusetts, Connecticut, and Rhode Island if it was picked up and moved two-thousand miles northeast. The prime hunting and fishing paradise for anglers and hunters was a nightmare for a search party. Finding anyone, even a large group of men, in such an enormous area would take equal parts skill and luck.

Several miles into the forest, Jason slowed to ensure he didn't miss any signs of a group of men or vehicles in the area. The forest road led to a T intersection. One direction led into the Fort Apache Reservation, and the other led to an abandoned Navajo County fire observation tower. Jason noticed more tire tracks in the direction of the tower, so he turned and drove until he could see the eight-story tower jutting above the trees. Jason parked in a clearing a hundred yards from the defunct wood structure.

The old truck made ticking noises as the engine cooled after a long drive on a warm day. Jason grabbed his binoculars and scanned the tower. He examined as much as he could see inside the tower and followed the ninety-seven steps down to the concrete platform. Satisfied the tower appeared unoccupied, Jason moved away from his truck and listened for man-made sounds. He did a complete 360-degree turn, inhaling through his nose with each turn to smell anything related to human activity. He learned in Survival, Evasion, Resistance & Escape training, or SERE school, during his PJ pipeline to use all of his senses to gather intel and not rely solely on sight. Jason turned to the hill a half click to the south and noted that it was the next highest point after the tower. He set a destination point on his Casio GPS watch and pushed slowly through the undergrowth. Once he reached the summit, he found a clearing on the south-facing slope. This vantage point allowed Jason to see one-hundred eighty degrees from the southeast to the southwest.

Jason raised his binoculars and panned from right to left and then left to right but didn't see any signs of the men. He sat down on the ground between two juniper shrubs to conceal himself while he let the setting sun drop further from the sky. Occasionally, a different angle of the sun could reveal something new. After fifteen minutes, Jason returned to the clearing and repeated his scan. As he slowly scanned from left to right, a glint of light in the sun's nearly horizontal rays caught Jason's attention in the brush three hundred feet below. The reflected light lasted a few minutes, and then it disappeared as the sun dipped below the horizon. Jason knew the only things to cause a similar reflection in nature were water or ice. It was too hot for ice, and he didn't see water nearby, so he crept down the hill to investigate. One hundred feet down, he reached the edge of a cliff. It was too steep to descend without his rappelling gear. Jason lowered himself into a prone position and peered through the binoculars to get a better look.

In the twilight, he made out a pickup truck under camouflage netting. He focused his binoculars and confirmed it was a black super-duty truck.

Jason's heart raced like it did every time before he put himself in harm's way. He reached into his pocket and pulled out his phone to call NCSO, but it didn't have a signal.

"Damn. I'm going to have to drive out to call the sheriff's office."

As the forest grew darker, Jason turned to hurry back up the hill when he stepped on a small boulder that dislodged and tumbled into the valley below. The snapping limbs and thud at the bottom sounded like someone tossed a bowling ball into the forest. Jason dropped to the rocky forest floor and slowed his breathing to listen for evidence that the men in the black truck heard the commotion. He waited for two minutes. Then, when he thought he must have gotten lucky, an engine started. Jason raised his head above the shrubs and saw the black truck backing out from under the camouflage cover. Its headlights were off, but the white reverse lights lit up the dark shadows in the forest.

Whoosh.

Jason's gut told him to move before his brain registered what had happened. Whenever he experienced a surge of the fight or flight hormone epinephrine, it made a sound in his head like the deep bass you hear when gasoline is tossed onto a fire. It wasn't an audible sound but one felt deep in the bones. Nobody else could hear the involuntary signal from Jason's brain to his body to be on high alert, but he knew it was never wrong.

He had to get to a spot with a signal to call NCSO as soon as possible. So, he broke protocol and pushed through the forest without concern about detection. His objective was speed versus stealth. Jason had to get to his vehicle before the black truck reached him. Ten minutes later, he arrived at his vehicle in the waning minutes of twilight. Jason checked his phone again for a signal. Still nothing.

He climbed into his truck, and a white beam of light illuminated his cabin.

"How did they get up here that fast?" Jason shouted into the empty truck. He turned toward the light source and noticed it wasn't the black truck. It was a spotlight beaming down on him from the fire tower that Jason thought was empty.

He turned the key to start his truck, and the engine turned but sounded like it was underwater. He didn't get the roar from the engine he hoped to hear, so he tried a second and a third time, but it still didn't start. The cabin of his truck fell dark again. Jason looked at the tower and saw the white light lowering in a zig-zag pattern. The person in the tower was coming down. Someone was approaching from the tower in the north while the truck was climbing the hill from the south. He'd be trapped if he didn't move soon.

Jason tried to start his truck again, and when it failed, he slammed his fist on his dash.

"Come on, you old son of a bitch. Start!"

The light from the tower reached the ground just as the truck headlights leveled off into the clearing. The length of a football field separated Jason from people coming toward him from two directions. Based on what happened to his mom, Josh, and the teenagers from Show Low, Jason assumed they weren't interested in talking. They were a threat and were seconds away from his truck.

He turned the key again, and this time it started. It sounded like a cannon blast in the quiet forest. Jason flipped on his headlights and slammed the accelerator. He saw the light from the tower and the truck meet and stop in his rearview mirror as he sped away. Jason slunk lower in his seat to make himself a smaller target in case a slug came in his direction, but none did.

Once Jason was a half mile away, he exhaled and wiped the sweat off his forehead as he hauled ass through the forest. He picked up his phone to check for a signal but tossed it onto the passenger seat when he noticed a new truck parked at an angle on the narrow forest road. The driver opened the door as Jason slid to a stop twenty feet from the truck. Jason's eyes widened as the mountain of a man poured himself into the beam of his headlights. He was at least three inches taller and fifty pounds heavier than Jason. Mountain Man wore an olive drab boonie hat that looked too small for his head and a button up shirt with the sleeves torn off. He crossed his thick arms covered in full sleeves of tattoos and took a wide stance in the space between his truck and the tree line.

Jason exited his vehicle and understood the posture of a man that had no plans of moving peacefully. Jason couldn't go around the truck. He had to go through Mountain Man.

"I don't have any beef with you. Just let me go through and nobody has to get hurt," Jason said.

The man simply stared back at Jason. His dark eyes absorbed the light like two mini black holes. Jason turned around to make sure the people in the truck or tower weren't behind him. He'd be in grave danger if he let himself get pinned between them and the Mountain Man. Jason's concern melted into anger.

Jason waved emphatically at Mountain Man. "I said get out of the way."

Mountain Man responded with a string of profanity and threats in Spanish. He took several steps toward Jason. His walk evolved into a trot. Jason assumed the fighting stance he learned the first month in Krav Maga. He'd trained for situations like this in the Israeli martial art developed for the Israeli Defense Force. Krav Maga was derived from a combination of techniques used in aikido, judo, karate, boxing, and wrestling. It was known for its focus on real-world situations and now Jason was about to test his skills on a real attacker.

As Mountain Man got within a few steps, he wound up like a baseball pitcher and swung his fist to land a moving knockout punch along Jason's jaw. Jason ducked and sidestepped the blow while responding with a palm strike to his chin as he thundered past. The quick, yet effective move sent Mountain Man staggering several yards past him.

Mountain Man regained his balance, grunted and charged again. Jason deployed right and left-hand blocks to each punch intended for his jaw. On the second block, Jason moved inside and delivered an up knee to the man's stomach and retreated to his fighting position. A deep, guttural groan confirming the delivery of sharp pain to his abdomen tickled Jason's ears.

Jason stood outside the beam of headlights and watched Mountain Man gather himself. For a moment, Jason thought Mountain Man may have had enough, but that wasn't the case. He straightened and advanced with the fury of a charging bull. Once again, Jason blocked his roundhouse punch and this time he slid his blocking hand to Mountain Man's shoulder and pummeled him with several right elbows to the face. Fortunately for Mountain Man, his height didn't allow Jason to get a square shot at his nose and he ended up striking more lips and cheek. It was effective though, as Mountain Man's eyes quickly filled with tears and blood flowed over his chin. Jason shuffled back several steps. Although he currently had the upper hand, Jason knew that could change in an instant.

Mountain Man reached up and touched the blood trickling down his lips and across his chin. His eyes squinted at the unexpected crimson on his fingers illuminated by the headlights, and then he licked his index and middle finger to remove the blood. Jason assumed the primal act was intended to accentuate his erratic mental state and warn Mulder of his impending doom. It didn't have the desired effect. Jason was trained to sustain personal defense for up to ten minutes, but also knew how to end a conflict in seconds. It was time to end the fight.

This time Mountain Man came at Jason under control and the two danced around each other for thirty seconds until Jason unleashed a powerful straight punch square in the solar plexus. It was one of Jason's favorite targets because men gasping for air and hoping to avert death by asphyxiation rarely continue to fight. This case was no different. A muffled groan was followed by silent gasping. He opened and closed his mouth like a fish yanked from the water. Seconds later, Mountain Man's chest heaved as oxygen returned, and he gasped to refill his lungs. Mountain Man gathered his feet under him, placed both hands on his chest and leaned forward.

It was the move Jason hoped to see. The seven-year student of Krav Maga lunged forward, sent an up knee into his eye socket and then pushed his head down until it was near Jason's waist. He finished the fight with a hammer fist blow to the base of Mountain Man's head, instantly knocking him unconscious.

Jason checked his six again and took a minute to catch his breath. Once his breathing slowed, he dragged the unconscious man into the forest. He returned to his idling vehicle and passed through the narrow opening between the trees and the truck. Ten long minutes later, Jason arrived on a paved road. He knew he'd have a signal now.

"911, what's your emergency?" the dispatcher asked.

Jason gave the coordinates of both trucks and explained the reason for his call. The 911 operator said she'd pass it along to the NCSO. Jason called Noah.

"I found them. You have Detective Caldwell's cell phone number, don't you?"

"Yeah."

"Call him right now and tell him the 911 dispatcher has the coordinates of the black truck. They need to get someone out there ASAP. I'll be home in ninety minutes," Jason barked and hung up.

Jason turned on the main highway back to Payson and his thoughts turned to the men that tried to capture him in the forest. "Who were those guys?" He wondered if a gang moved up from Phoenix or Tucson into the woods outside sleepy Payson and Show Low. The Mountain Man certainly looked like he'd spent time in a prison or a gang. He'd never heard of such a thing and grew more confused with each mile.

When Jason walked into the house, he saw Noah sitting at the table with his hands on his face.

"What's wrong? Did they find the black truck?"

Noah looked up. "Oh, yeah. They found it."

"So, what's the problem?"

"When the NCSO deputies arrived, they found a truck fully engulfed in flames. It started a small forest fire, and the truck was reduced to a heap of metal and ash by the time they got it out. They'll investigate tomorrow morning when it's light out, but they won't find a shred of evidence in the truck. We're back to square one."

Chapter 10

Jason leapt from his chair in his apartment in Tacoma after his phone dinged on the coffee table. He'd fallen asleep watching TV after a long day of EMT training. Jason never took naps, but he was more exhausted than usual. He had recurring nightmares about Josh nearly every day and restful sleep became more elusive. Every nightmare was the same. Jason arrived at the dry creek bank to find Josh's mangled body lying on a patch of rocks and rust-red dirt. He noted the awkward angles of his limbs and torso. As he approached his dying brother, Josh's eyes locked onto Jason's with a piercing intensity. Jason couldn't look away. Josh never spoke, but the look on his face was enough to convey everything he needed to say. He expected his big brother to save him, but in every nightmare, Josh died right after Jason reached his side.

As a PJ deployed during wartime, Jason witnessed death on his watch. He'd even held soldiers, airmen, and Afghan citizens in his arms when nothing more could be done and they took their last breath. He knew death was part of the job, and he compartmentalized pain accordingly, but Josh's piercing gaze in his nightmares haunted him like no other. Every nightmare reminded Jason that he failed to protect his brother, just like Gaby.

Jason opened the text message on his phone.

It's hard to train a squad when one guy is always missing. I hope you resolve everything at home so we can get back to a full squad soon.

It was from Jason's chief rescue officer and squad leader. Jason reread the text as he ran his fingers through his hair. His CRO was a good guy, and he must be frustrated with Jason's latest request for time off to send the text. Jason would be in Arizona again to pay his respects over the Memorial Day weekend. He was looking forward to going home to see his family and talking to Noah about any new information on Josh's case, but now the heavy weight of guilt landed in his lap. Jason hated letting his team down and he'd done that over the last month. It was too late to cancel his trip now, but he had to think long and hard in the future before taking more leave to go home.

Two days later, a Southwest Airlines 737 touched down just after noon in sunny Phoenix with temperatures already climbing over one-hundred degrees, a stark contrast to Tacoma. It was a shock to the system to go from such extremes after spending two and a half hours in a pressurized tube, but Jason loved the dichotomy of his two homes. His dad picked him up at the curb, and ninety minutes later, Jason walked through the back door in Payson.

"Where's Mom?"

"I think she may still be in bed. She had physical therapy this morning and is usually exhausted afterward. I'll wake her and let her know you're home."

"That's okay. Let her sleep. PT can be grueling, and she needs to recharge. Is Noah home?"

"Yes. I believe he's meeting with Miss Dosala right now. He's been meeting with her at two o'clock on Fridays the past month."

Jason nodded. "I'll go put my stuff away."

When he returned from his bedroom, his mom was waiting for him in the hallway. She hobbled over and gave her son a tight hug.

"How are you feeling?" Jason asked.

"Better. I ditched the walker earlier this week, but it's still hard to get around very fast."

Jason put his hand on her shoulder. "That's normal. Keep up the PT and you'll continue to improve."

Jason went to the kitchen to make a late lunch when he heard Noah plodding down the hall. He was prepared to give Noah a hard time for not saying, "hello," and that's when he noticed Shanna with him.

"Hi, Jason. Sorry I don't have more time to hang out, but I'm late for a conference call. Could you see if Shanna needs anything and then see her out?"

Before Jason could respond, Noah darted back down the hall, leaving him standing awkwardly next to Shanna. He walked over to the refrigerator and opened it.

"Looks like we have soda, beer, and bottled water for the ride. Which one would you like?"

"I'm fine," Shanna replied with a smile.

Five seconds of silence passed until Shanna moved toward the door. "I probably should head back now."

Jason jogged to the door and opened it for her. Celeste Mulder pounded in the thick skulls of her four boys that real men show respect for women.

"Sorry Noah ran off like that. Have a safe drive back."

Shanna took a step toward the door and stopped. "How are you doing?"

"I'm great," Jason said. He twisted and tugged at his watch.

Shanna took another step toward Jason, and they locked eyes. "How are you really doing?" she asked, almost in a whisper.

Jason looked up at the ceiling and then down at the tile floor before he answered.

"I'm having nightmares about Josh."

Shanna nodded. "If you're open to it, I may be able to help you with the pain and confusion you're experiencing. I believe Noah is in a better spot now after just a few sessions. Would you like to set up a time to talk while you're in town?"

"Nah, I'm good."

Shanna crossed her arms and tilted her head. "Can I ask why?"

"Don't really see the benefit, I guess. I'm used to dealing with bad shit in my life and always seem to figure it out on my own."

"That may not be the best long-term solution."

"It works for me."

"Have you had a lot of bad things happen in your life, other than Josh and your mom?"

"Yeah. I was in Afghanistan for a year and several people I knew died. Some were good friends. In high school, I also lost Ga—" Jason stopped. "You know what? I'll think about that talk, but for another time I'm back in town."

"Please do."

Shanna flashed a reassuring smile, turned, and descended the patio stairs to reach her SUV. Jason watched her reverse out of the driveway. As Shanna reached the end of the driveway, his older brother Kevin arrived with his family.

The Mulder family cooked out on the barbecue grill for dinner every evening during the long weekend. Then, once the kids were in bed, the adults enjoyed cocktails and engaging conversation around the fire pit in the backyard.

On Memorial Day, the Mulders attended a parade and visited Josh's grave as a family. Jason stood behind his parents as they held hands and cried over Josh's tombstone. He stood motionless and watched the miniature red, white, and blue flags placed throughout the cemetery flap in the wind. He'd hoped the sting of Josh's death would be a little more bearable now, but the weight of his absence still felt as heavy as the day he heard the news.

Later that night, everyone gathered around the fire pit. Celeste, Phillip, and Carrie had corralled Jason's eighteen-month-old niece all day, so they turned in early. Noah, Kevin, and Jason remained outside. They watched the flames flash bright colors like a peacock and listened to the orchestra of crickets in the nearby forest.

"We should follow up with Detective Caldwell at NCSO while Kevin is in town. Maybe they'll be more cooperative with the three of us, especially since he's a firefighter," Noah stated.

Kevin leaned forward. "I'm game, but it has to be no later than Wednesday. I have to be back for my next shift on Friday morning."

"Same for me," Jason chipped in.

"I'll call tomorrow and get us a quick meeting before you two head out."

It took several calls and some convincing by Noah, but they arrived in Show Low on Wednesday afternoon for another meeting with NCSO.

Once seated in a conference room, the three Mulder boys sat in birth order and by height. Kevin, the firstborn and tallest at six feet three inches tall, sat on the far right, while Jason sat in the middle, and Noah, the second youngest, claimed to be six feet, but Jason teased that he was only five eleven and a half. Combined, they were a formidable force. Caldwell arrived and countered with Deputy Jarvis to better even the playing field.

Deputy Jarvis entered first and sat down across from the Mulder trio. He looked the same age as Kevin, and his uniform hung loose on his wiry frame. As soon as Caldwell shut the door, he launched into his account of the black truck barbecue. His explanations were brief and his tone was terse. His demeanor changed from cool yet cooperative during the first meeting to sheer disdain for the case that his facial expressions couldn't hide.

Kevin seemed to recognize his attitude and intervened.

"Hi, I'm Kevin Mulder. I'm a lieutenant with the Colorado Springs Fire Department. We didn't come here to point any fingers. We're just looking for answers to some unusual activity surrounding our brother's death."

Caldwell exhaled and relaxed his shoulders. "Nice to meet you, Lieutenant. We already have more cases on our plate than we can handle, and the stress level is high in this office. Is there a specific question I can answer?"

"Did you find the owner of the burnt truck?" Kevin asked.

Caldwell pointed to Jarvis. "Go ahead and share what you found."

Jarvis opened his notepad and flipped back several pages. "We traced the VIN to a resident of Whitewater on the White Mountain Apache reservation. It was reported stolen six weeks ago. He hasn't seen it since."

The room was quiet for a few seconds when Jason spoke. "Someone hit me with a spotlight from the fire tower as I was leaving. Did anyone investigate the tower?"

"We didn't go up the tower but searched the surrounding area and confirmed the tower gate had a working lock. We found nothing suspicious during our search," Jarvis responded.

The door swung open, and a grand figure in a police uniform with a white cowboy hat appeared. Jason instantly recognized the man as Sheriff Kellerman from all the political billboards and posters around town for the upcoming election in the fall.

"These the boys you told me about?" Sheriff Kellerman asked while pointing to the three Mulder men.

"Yes, Sheriff. We're just reviewing the latest information from their 911 call," Caldwell responded.

Kellerman reached across the table and shook each of their hands. He was about the same height as Jason, with a barrel chest, salty white hair, and pale leathery cheeks, probably from years in the Arizona sun. The sheriff was a skilled politician, and Jason assumed he took over any room he entered.

"We're going to catch the bastards that caused so much grief for your family. I don't like the idea of troublemakers of any sort roaming around my county. When we find them, and trust me, we'll find them, I will nail them to the wall."

Jason relaxed for the first time in weeks. He could feel the stress and pressure of finding Josh's killers leaving his body like a deflating balloon. Finally, someone in law enforcement shared the same burning desire to catch the perpetrators. Jason turned to Noah and Kevin and sensed they felt the same relief.

"We appreciate that, Sheriff," Kevin replied.

"I don't want you guys out there doing any more of your vigilante stuff. Leave that up to my men, but if you come across anything else or hear something that may help in the search, give it directly to Detective Caldwell."

Jason thought he saw the detective wince out of the corner of his eye.

"It was a pleasure meeting you boys," Kellerman said. He turned and left the room as fast as he entered.

Once again, the room fell silent, and that was when Kevin stood. "Thank you for your time, Detective and Deputy. We'll let you get back to work."

The ride back to Payson was quiet until Noah spoke.

"What do we do now?"

"I'm heading back home tomorrow. The sheriff seems like he's on top of it now. I'm confident they'll get to the bottom of what happened to Josh," Kevin replied.

Noah's head snapped to Jason.

"What about you? You found the armed men last time. Together, we can search until we find them again."

Jason thought about his text from his squad leader. "I'm with Kevin. I'm hopeful they'll take the case more seriously now that it's on the sheriff's radar. Plus, I live a thousand miles away and can't keep flying home to investigate a crime that law enforcement is working on."

"I don't know. I think we should keep looking just in case he was blowing hot air back there. He is a politician."

Neither Jason nor Kevin responded

"So, both of you are okay that Josh's killers are still roaming the woods around here?"

"Don't go there, Noah!" Kevin roared.

Nobody spoke the rest of the way home. After they parked in the driveway, Kevin exited first, and Noah put his hand up to stop Jason.

"Come on, Jason. We need to keep looking for Josh's killers."

Jason felt like he was in a lose-lose situation.

"The sheriff is on it. I think they'll do more now."

"Okay, the sheriff may care, but do you think Caldwell or Jarvis give a shit? They are the people that will have to go out and investigate."

"Just let them do their job," Jason snapped. The pressure of the impossible situation was building to a point of a full explosion.

"But, they—"

"Noah, no!"

Noah stared back at Jason and his lower lip began to quiver. Jason stomped up the stairs and turned before he entered the house. "I have to go."

Chapter 11

Jason checked the calendar on his phone as the rain pelted the window in his kitchen. It wasn't the light mist typical of Puget Sound. Instead, it was a driving rain that prevented his morning run. The meeting after lunch with Technical Sergeant Elaine Hopkins, his career adviser, drew his eye. She was getting more persistent in her efforts to get Jason to sign a new contract for another six-year term. A new contract was a foregone conclusion for Jason two months ago, but the magnetic pull to move back to Payson to help with family was powerful. He questioned whether he should re-enlist for the first time in his Air Force career.

Jason pondered his decision as he entered the squadron building and slipped into his cage. He finished repacking his combat aid kit when the alarm sounded inside the team room. They scrambled for a civilian support mission to assist Oregon Search and Rescue. Jason soon learned their mission was to locate and rescue a group of campers from the University of Oregon swept away in a flash flood on the South Fork McKenzie River. The State of Oregon requested PJs from JBLM because the raging waters might have swept the campers as far as the twelve-hundred-acre Cougar Reservoir, with depths up to four hundred feet. The Air Force

National Guard in Portland was in Kirtland Air Base in New Mexico for training.

Four hours later, the airborne Oregon Search and Rescue crew scanned the central Cascade Mountains for the students while the PJs were close behind in their Airbus H125 helicopter for rescue support. Twenty minutes after canvassing the forest, a call came in over the radio.

"We spotted three individuals near the mouth of the Cougar Reservoir. They're hanging onto trees in swift water. Two have white shirts, and one has a green shirt."

The helicopter pilot responded, "ETA of five minutes."

As the element leader on this mission, Mulder opened the door as the helicopter circled the three students struggling to maintain their grip against the torrent of water pushing them toward deeper reservoir waters two hundred feet downstream.

Five minutes later, they landed on a bridge and exited the helicopter. Jason and Senior Airman Crespo took the south bank and hustled toward the kids clinging to branches. When Jason reached the bank parallel to the students, he felt the power of thousands of gallons of water rushing past him every second. He saw the students clinging to trees at a slight bend in the river. They looked tired and battered. Jason didn't believe they could hold on much longer. Crespo tied one end of the ropes to a towering pine tree at the river's edge and handed the other end to Jason.

"You think you can throw a tow rope across?" Crespo asked. It was about ninety feet across the swollen river.

Jason thought about it for a second. "That's a little far to throw a rope across. Those kids don't have time for us to miss multiple times, so I'm going to swim it across."

"Swim across? That's some serious water out there."

Jason looked upstream. "I'm going to enter up there and then push as hard as I can to cross. It looks like the current will push me into the bend to tie off to the other side. If I'm wrong, I get to go swimming in the big lake today."

Crespo's eyes widened. "What should we do if you get swept into the reservoir?"

"Save them first, and then come get me."

Jason stopped talking. He jogged a hundred feet upstream, put on flippers and a mask with a snorkel, and waded in with a tow rope to the rigging system. He was up to his waist three steps in, and two more steps put Jason chest deep. That was when he felt his feet leave the river bottom. Jason lowered his head into the brown foamy water and dove into the stream. He kicked hard with his legs and made it halfway across before the mighty current in the center caught him and pushed him downstream ten feet every few seconds. He had to get to the other side in less than a half minute or he'd end up in the vast reservoir of muddy water and tree branches. Jason gave it his all for fifteen seconds. When he surfaced, he saw he was coming up to the bend faster than expected.

He tried to kick harder, but the water was too swift. He was still ten feet away from the shore and would miss his last potential exit point before the reservoir. Just as Jason resigned himself to spending time in the deeper waters, he felt a tug at his back, and then he moved toward the shore. Senior Airman Clay Landry from the 943rd Air Force Reserve unit had tied in and waded out to catch him. Jason made it across. He thanked everyone from the 943rd that landed nearby in their helicopter minutes earlier.

They didn't waste any time. They hooked up the rigging to extract the students, and one at a time, the PJs swam out to the students with life jackets and helmets. They used their swift water training to guide the two females and one male student to safety.

The scared and water-logged students were all transported to local hospitals in stable condition. It was a successful mission. Three students were rescued and returned to campus in time for a late lunch.

During the flight back to JBLM, a stout man passed Jason and sat a few rows behind him. His broad shoulders and thick neck made him appear larger than he really was. His light brown hair was short and neatly trimmed while his baby face wore days-old stubble. He had the same plastic straw in his mouth when he pulled Jason from the water.

Jason moved into his row, sat down in the open seat, and extended his hand.

"I'm Staff Sergeant Jason Mulder. Thanks for coming in for me back there. I thought I was in for a long swim in the deep end of the pool."

"You looked like you were having so much fun, I almost let you pass by."

Both men laughed.

"I'm Senior Airman Clay Landry, by the way." The deep timbre in his voice matched the sturdy warrior delivering it.

"What are you guys doing up here from Davis-Monthan?" Jason asked.

Clay took the straw out of his mouth. "We were on our way to Fairchild Air Base in Eastern Washington for water insertion and extraction training. When the call came in, our CO suggested that we get our training hot. We'll catch a new flight from JBLM."

"Perfect timing."

Jason put both hands on the armrests to push up and leave, but fell back into his seat. "How do you like the Air Reserve?"

"It has its pros and cons like anything else, but overall, I like it," Clay responded.

"Have you always been in the reserves, or were you active?"

"I was active four years before I joined the reserves. Spent time at Cannon in New Mexico and Mildenhall in the UK."

"How many PJs do they have in the 943rd?" Jason asked.

Clay thought about it for a second. "At least eight, maybe more."

"Any open slots?"

"I've heard one may open soon for a guy leaving to join the security team of a congresswoman back in DC. Why? Are you interested?"

"No, just curious," Jason lied.

"Well, if you're ever in Arizona, give me a ring. I'll give you the nickel tour of DM and the 943rd Rescue Squadron," Clay said and put the straw back in his mouth.

"I was with the 48th Rescue Squadron at Davis-Monthan right out of the pipeline, so I'm familiar with the base, but I may take you up on that tour."

Jason returned to his seat. "Hmmm. One open slot," he whispered to himself.

Chapter 12

Jason moved from his couch into the tight galley kitchen in his apartment and opened the refrigerator. He wasn't hungry but wanted something to take his mind off the pain of Josh's absence. He grabbed a bottle of Bohemia beer and returned to the couch. The swift water rescue mission was a success, but it jarred memories of his younger brother. It was the type of place where Jason and Josh would have loved to fish together.

Jason scrolled through his phone. He was hoping to see an update from Noah, but his last message from him was two days ago. Jason's mind went to his last conversation with Noah. He wondered if Noah was right and if he was trusting the sheriff because it helped make his decision to go back to JBLM easier. More questions popped into his head.

Will NCSO really investigate the band of men in the forest? Should I go to Payson to help find them?

He hated to request more leave after the last text from his squad leader, but Jason couldn't sit idle while Josh's killers still ran loose. After five minutes of internal debate, Jason submitted his request for leave. Two days later, he caught the next available flight to Phoenix. He didn't tell Noah he was coming, and his dad was teaching again at school, so Jason took a shuttle.

When Jason arrived in Payson, nobody was home, so he put his bag away and went through a stack of mail. He turned on the TV, but after five minutes he turned it off. Jason left to do what he came home to accomplish. He fired up his truck and drove back to the forest where Jason last saw the stolen black truck. Once he was back in the area, Jason approached with caution. He parked near a wide swath of burnt grass and trees a quarter mile from the fire tower. He noticed the rudimentary path for off-road vehicles south of the clearing that he had missed during his first visit. It must have been how the men in the black truck arrived so fast from their concealed location deep in the valley.

Jason walked the perimeter. After a full sweep of the area, he removed his hat to wipe the sweat off his brow, and turned toward the fire tower jutting above the trees. A six-foot chain-link fence with rusted white US Forest Service signs warning people to keep out surrounded the tower. Jason cleared the fence in less than five seconds and assumed local teenagers regularly did the same. He climbed the winding stairs of the wood structure until he reached the observation deck eight stories above the forest floor. It had a roof and four walls with large open-air windows cut out of all sides to provide a 360-degree view of the Apache-Sitegraves Forest. It was apparent that Jason wasn't the first to jump the fence and climb the structure. Empty bottles of hard liquor, beer cans, and cigarette butts littered the ten-by-eight-foot deck. Jason kicked cans out of the way to get closer to the open windows and peer out in each direction.

First, he looked west toward Young and saw the highway and a few homes dotting the landscape. Then, Jason moved from the west opening, and a light brown and cream-colored object intertwined with fast food wrappers caught his eye. When he got closer, he noted it was a foreign currency. It looked like the Euros or British Pounds Jason used during his past stops in Europe. He picked it up and saw Bank of Canada written on the one-hundred-dollar note. He turned the bill over several times.

Why would teenagers drinking beer have Canadian money? Why would Canadian tourists, common visitors to Arizona during the winter, ever wander into such a remote location and climb this tower?

After considering a range of unlikely scenarios, Jason put the Canadian bill in his pocket.

He moved to the side of the tower looking south into the Fort Apache Reservation. He figured that whoever torched the truck probably fled into White Mountain Apache Tribe's sovereign land to avoid capture by the NCSO deputies. That was what he'd do.

A dark, shadowy area eight or nine miles away in the sea of pine piqued his interest. Like the last place Jason found the men, it was a dense cluster of trees nestled in a valley. He strained to see a reflection or any sign of people, but he didn't bring binoculars and couldn't see that far.

"Why didn't I bring binoculars?" Jason asked aloud.

Pissed at himself, Jason kicked aluminum cans across the room. A Pepsi caught his eye after it hit the wall and rolled back. It wasn't because it was the only non-alcoholic beverage in the piles of trash, but it looked different from the Pepsi cans Jason recalled in local stores. He bent over and picked up the crumpled can.

Everything was in Spanish, and it appeared to be bottled in Guatemala.

Jason ran his fingers across the stubble on his cheek as he considered his new find. The armed men used the tower for a lookout, and the trash might provide clues about who was there and where they might go next. Jason pulled black nitrile gloves from his backpack and dove into the trash. First, he picked up an unlabeled eye dropper and several stamps that looked homemade. They looked out of place but didn't offer any clues. Jason tossed them aside and continued to push mounds of trash out of the way. Beneath a pile of crushed Coors Light cans, he found an empty red and white cigarette package. Pall Mall brand cigarettes with Spanish writing: Producto autorizado para la venta en El Salvador.

"Product authorized for sale in El Salvador?" Jason asked aloud.

It wasn't unusual for Central Americans to migrate north to the United States to look for work in Arizona, but this felt different than migrants looking for employment. Jason paced back and forth as he considered the latest piece of suspicious trash. He stopped and rushed back to the location of the discarded homemade stamps. Debris flew everywhere until Jason found another stamp that looked like a black sun painted with watercolors. He recalled seeing something similar in a TV news story about the opioid epidemic ravaging small communities in Arizona. It wasn't a postage stamp but a piece of blotter paper users put in their mouths to extract the synthetic opioid.

Jason let out a sigh of relief that he was wearing gloves. He placed the blotter paper in another pair of unused gloves and considered his unusual lot of clues. Drug paraphernalia was not uncommon in a hiding place like this, but the combination of soda cans and cigarettes from Central America added a unique twist to his findings.

"It's not the local kids," Jason said aloud. "So, that must mean—"

Jason bolted down the stairs two at a time until he reached his truck. The engine turned over, and Jason followed the gravel road until the T intersection and stopped. Instead of turning back to Show Low, he continued straight into the reservation.

He dipped into a valley and then climbed through a thick patch of forest. Twenty minutes later, the gravel road ended and turned into a dirt path that Jason doubted his old truck could tackle. Jason estimated he was near the dark part of the forest he saw from the tower. He pulled to the side of the road and walked a hundred yards into the forest to conceal himself if someone drove down the dirt path. For the next thirty minutes, Jason crept through the woods for one minute and then knelt for thirty seconds to observe the area. He continued parallel to the road until he saw a clearing for overhead electric wires. After gazing across the clearing for several minutes, he saw nothing. He turned back toward his truck, but the breeze picked up and Jason hit the forest floor.

Smoke!

The smell of smoke in a dry Arizona forest was enough to get anybody's attention, but this was even more alarming. It was cigarette smoke. Jason rose just high enough to scan the potential source of the odor. When the wind slowed and the sounds from the forest died down, he heard two people talking. Jason focused his attention in that direction, and that's when he saw movement.

Jason was downwind of the stiff breeze typical on warm days in June. The sounds and smells of the men carried to Jason while the hum of rustling pine needles blunted his movements. He low crawled toward the movement and saw two men in camouflage military-style uniforms. Both were at least a half foot shorter than Jason with black, unkempt hair. One had a thin mustache, and the other a full beard covering his tanned face. Each carried an AK-74 assault rifle, just like his mom described.

Adrenaline exploded and surged throughout his body. His gut told him the two men were dangerous before his brain caught up a second later. He eyed them carefully from his position in the brush.

After observing the men for a minute, Jason doubted they were military because even the worst-trained soldiers wouldn't smoke or talk in a normal voice while pulling security. He watched each man walk a few yards, look around, and then come back for more conversation in Spanish. Jason could make out bits and pieces of their conversation thanks to four years of Spanish in high school and a mother raised on the northern coast of Spain near Santander, but his Spanish had gotten a little rusty in the Air Force. He understood their discussions about shipments, cigarettes, and fast food. They also bitched about recently moving camp to a new location. Jason knew what their discussion likely meant but didn't want to believe his ears.

The shadows cast by the trees grew longer, and Jason didn't want to get caught in the forest after dark, so he retreated quietly to his truck and drove back to Payson without stopping.

Noah waited for Jason on the back patio as he pulled into the driveway.

"Where were you?" Noah asked as Jason exited his vehicle.

"I went back to the tower."

"Did you find anything?"

Jason walked onto the patio, leaned against the railing, and sighed. "I have some good news and some bad news."

"Give me the good news. I don't know if I can take anymore bad news."

"I think I found Josh's killers."

Noah tilted his head as wrinkles spread across his forehead. "Okay. What's the bad news?"

"His killers might be a Central American drug cartel."

Noah stood frozen on the patio. Jason saw his face processing the bombshell, so he turned to enter the house.

Noah grabbed his arm. "A cartel? Are you freaking serious?"

Jason looked inside and saw his dad in the kitchen. He motioned for Noah to follow him to the far end of the patio.

"I found evidence that Josh's killers are probably from Central America. They moved onto the Fort Apache Reservation, and I came across two spotters. They're amateurs and didn't see me, so I got close enough to hear them talking about shipments. It has to be drugs, and they seem to move across jurisdictions to avoid detection. So far, they've been active in Gila County, Navajo County, and the Fort Apache Reservation."

"This is worse than I thought," Noah whispered.

Chapter 13

Victor Romero needed the Arizona operation to be successful for him to maintain his teniente, or lieutenant, role as second in command to the capo in the La Palma Cartel. The micro cartel based in El Salvador was named for its home territory in the country's northeast corner. For years, local authorities had witnessed La Palma's tactics for shrewd narcotics trafficking and ruthless dealings with competitors and dissidents. The organization made up for its small numbers compared to other Latin American drug cartels with its "kill first and ask questions later" mantra. Their capo, Orlando Vasquez, survived civil wars, gang wars, and attempts on his life with that mentality. His time on the streets earned him the nickname El Jaguar, the apex predator in the local jungles, from both his friends and foes. Victor had instincts like his boss that allowed him to reach his twenties, a feat that many other men the same age as Victor did not achieve.

Armed with the equivalent of a seventh-grade education, Victor killed his first person in front of his home days after turning fourteen. Part of Victor's initiation by a local gang required him to steal drugs from a rival gang in San Salvador. When a rival gang member showed up at his tin shanty looking to exact revenge for the stolen goods, Victor took the knife his mother used to dice vegetables for dinner that evening and stabbed the sixteen-year-old gang member eleven times. His rival never landed a single punch. He ran away from home to avoid arrest and lived on the streets for three years before killing again. This time the heat from the police grew too hot to stay in San Salvador, so Victor hitchhiked to La Palma to hide out in his aunt's goat shed, and that was when he met El Jaguar. The capo had a home, a family, and a thriving business of trafficking meth and fentanyl north to the United States. The La Palma boss gave Victor a chance as long as he proved to be an asset to the organization. If not, El Jaguar would kill Victor himself.

Victor started out on the bottom rung of the ladder as a falcon, or lookout, and notified the capos of all police, military, and gang activity in the area. He proved himself in that position and moved up to the rank of sicario, or hitman, where Victor demonstrated a natural ability to kill. He was La Palma's top producer of kidnapping ransom and held a perfect record of assassinations of target rivals. His record was especially impressive because he preferred to kill his targets with a knife. It was quiet and more personal. For Victor, everything was personal.

The rising cartel star married in his early twenties and started a family. His youngest boy recently learned to walk, and his oldest son looked like a future soccer star, which made Victor's head swell with pride. He preferred to have five or six more kids, but his wife insisted they stop at two. She liked to shop and travel to the finest resorts in Latin America, and more kids were not conducive to closets full of designer clothes and frequent lavish vacations. Victor didn't fight her too hard about having more kids. His goals of becoming a top lieutenant were more attainable with fewer children. Her passion for material possessions and his thirst for power made Victor and his wife, Alicia, a strong partnership.

Before the birth of his second son, Victor took Alicia and their son to a five-star resort on Tulum Beach, south of Cancun, Mexico. After Alicia took their son back to the room for the night, Victor enjoyed a cigar with his favorite 100% blue agave tequila at the resort bar. He closed his eyes and enjoyed the cooling breeze courtesy of the Caribbean Sea until three men arrived. They were drunk, loud, and Victor learned later they were from Canada. One man noticed Victor and asked him what brand of cigar he was smoking. Victor was used to being approached by strangers. Despite the vast amount of blood he'd spilled over the last decade, he looked less like a menacing cartel sicario and more like an affable captain on a harbor dinner cruise.

Victor sat up straight and looked at his cigar. He wasn't sure of the brand since he told the bartender to bring him the finest cigar. Victor handed it to the Canadian and he laughed after his examination of the cigar.

"You seem like a man who appreciates the finer things. Try this instead."

The man tossed Victor a Cohiba Behike 54.

Victor immediately knew what he possessed. He smelled his beautiful bundle of Cuban tobacco and smiled. "I like your taste."

One of his friends, the drunkest of the three, staggered over and whispered, "We have more. We smuggle cigars and rum into the United States."

One of the Canadian men shoved his friend. "Shut up!"

"You won't say anything, will you?" the intoxicated man asked.

"Your secret is safe with me. Let me return the favor," Victor replied.

He purchased the trio five rounds of tequila shots over the next hour. Before the two Canadians carried their friend back to their room for the night, Victor found out they moved illegal goods in and out of the United States through Arizona and New Mexico, with stops in Phoenix, Salt Lake, and Denver. They stayed away from California, Texas, and Florida ports and dealt exclusively in Canadian dollars. It was the easiest currency in the Americas to launder since it retained its value and the DEA was hyper focused on US Dollars. The Canadian operation impressed Victor, and he quickly formed ideas of his own operation before he hit the pillow early the next morning.

During a rare meeting with the La Palma boss, Victor pitched his idea to bypass the dangerous distribution routes through Mexico and set up a small fentanyl operation in the United States.

"Not possible," the boss replied coolly.

In a rare show of defiance, Victor disagreed. "I believe it is. Let me take a few men with me to the United States to scout the best place for a mobile operation."

Orlando stared down his nose at Victor. He felt sweat forming under his arms and on his forehead. His choice to disagree felt like the wrong decision with each passing second.

"You have two months."

Victor departed El Salvador with three men and crossed into the United States near El Paso, Texas. They scouted sites all over Arizona, Colorado, New Mexico, and Utah. The four cartel members drove through the most remote areas they could find with access to water. He couldn't believe the vast wilderness in the Southwest United States and had several options for his mobile lab, but one place rose to the top of Victor's list.

Apache Sitegraves National Forest in the mountains of Eastern Arizona was the ideal location for its sparse population, the potential for concealment in the densely wooded valleys, and the contacts he made while in the area. It was mostly free of campers, hunters, hikers, and tourists that plagued the other regions, especially during the summer, when urban dwellers flocked to the forest to escape the heat. Victor also studied local law enforcement and learned that the enormous forest covered several jurisdictions. The thought of using America's laws and rules to his advantage made the Arizona site even more appealing.

The mobile lab Victor planned couldn't produce pills as they did in El Salvador, so he turned to liquid fentanyl from India applied to blotter paper. It wasn't as desirable for the target user, but the appetite for opioids in the US was so strong Victor knew he could sell everything they produced.

A year after meeting the Canadians in Tulum, Victor crossed into the United States through the open desert near Hachita, New Mexico, in the dark of night with a crew of thirteen men. The efficient mobile fentanyl lab only required five men for production, so the other eight could focus on security and resupply.

The operation was an immediate success. La Palma's Arizona operation delivered the first shipment to a local dealer in Tucson at the end of April, with demand for more from buyers from Phoenix, Albuquerque, and Texas. Victor's vision to prove himself to El Jaguar and the rest of the cartel was underway. He had three more months to maximize their deliveries before elk hunting season brought people into their remote corner of the forest. Victor vowed not to let anything, or anyone, stand in his way during his time in Arizona.

CHAPTER 14

Jason reclined alone on the patio while he waited for Noah to get off a conference call. He sat in the outdoor lounge chair with wide armrests and a tall, slatted back as he stared into the woods behind his boyhood home.

Noah arrived and plopped down next to Jason. "Sorry that call took so long. Have you thought any more about what we should do next?"

Jason rubbed the stubble on his chin.

"Yeah. Although the Navajo County Sheriff has more resources, the cartel is operating on the Fort Apache Reservation. The WMAT PD may be more receptive now if they know who is operating on their land," Jason replied.

"Should I call and try to set up an appointment?"

"Let's try something different. This time I want to show up and talk to someone face to face."

"Can I go with you?"

Jason considered the request. He wanted to keep his family as safe as possible with every fiber in his body, and the more Noah was involved, the greater danger he was in. However, Jason sensed Noah needed to be part of the effort to bring justice to Josh's killers for him to have closure, so he capitulated.

"Yeah, we'll go together."

The next day, Noah and Jason departed for Whiteriver, Arizona, the capital of the White Mountain Apache Tribe. After passing through the mountain towns of Show Low and Pinetop-Lakeside in Navajo County, they entered the Fort Apache Reservation. Thirty minutes later, they passed the *Entering Whiteriver* sign, and the dense forest opened up to a horseshoe-shaped valley surrounded by steep mountains. It was Jason's first time in Whiteriver, the largest settlement of the White Mountain Apache Tribe. The natural beauty and the sparse population astonished him. Most buildings were only one story high, including the sole community hospital for over 17,000 White Mountain Apache Tribe community members.

The police station was easy to locate off the main highway that divided the small town. Jason parked outside WMAT PD and both Mulder men entered the station. All eyes in the building turned to the foreigners.

A man pushing his mid-fifties with thinning dark hair in a navy-blue uniform rose from a chair to greet them. He wore a badge with a seven-point gold star with White Mountain Apache Police Officer in bold font surrounding their tribal logo.

"How can I help you?"

"We'd like to report a crime," Noah responded.

The officer stared at Noah, then Jason, and picked up an old landline phone.

"I called Lieutenant Luna in to get your statement. It'll be a few minutes, so grab a seat."

Jason and Noah sat on a hard wooden bench next to the front door until a younger officer arrived. He also wore the same navy-blue uniform but was closer to thirty years old. The new officer walked to the counter, and the caller pointed to Jason and Noah.

He took off his duty cap and waved for them to follow him. "Let's grab a room."

They entered an empty office with the nameplate Captain Selah near the door. The White Mountain Apache Tribe patrol officer took the captain's chair and Noah and Jason sat across the desk.

"Hi, I'm Lieutenant Luna. What are your names?"

"This is Jason Mulder, and I'm Noah Mulder."

"Okay. Tell me what happened."

"There's a drug cartel operating on the reservation," Jason said.

Luna looked up from his notepad. "A drug cartel on the reservation?"

"Yes."

Luna put down his pen and folded his hands on the desk. "What makes you think it's a drug cartel?"

Jason leaned forward. "My brother was killed six weeks ago on the western edge of the Fort Apache Reservation. After the accident, I returned to the crash site and found evidence that a black truck had rammed my mom and brother off the road into a ravine near Canyon Creek. I tracked that truck to the forest in Navajo County just outside Show Low, but when the sheriff's deputies showed up, the truck had been torched. NCSO said they can't do anything else, but yesterday I found them near Forest Road 36 on tribal land. I identified a couple of spotters patrolling the area and trash from Central America in the old fire tower they used as a lookout. A soda can from Guatemala and cigarettes from El Salvador."

Luna nodded. "That's interesting and something we may want to check out, but that doesn't mean it's a cartel. They could just be—"

"Poachers?" Jason interrupted.

"Yeah," Luna replied slowly.

"Your department investigated and concluded a band of poachers chased my mom. They're not poachers. They have Russian-made assault rifles. AK-74s. Plus, I found this."

Jason stood up and dug a clear plastic bag out of his front pocket. He opened it slowly and exposed the stamp-like paper to Luna. The WMAT PD officer looked at the one-inch by one-inch paper, back up to Jason, and then opened a desk drawer with a box of latex gloves. He put them on and picked up the paper.

"Don't touch your face and be sure to wash your hands as soon as you leave," Luna stated as he examined the evidence.

He put the blotter paper down, whistled, and leaned back in his chair.

"I think that's fentanyl," Jason said.

"I typically find pills or powder, but I believe you're correct. It looks like blotter paper with fentanyl. Hang on a second."

He returned with a clear bag filled with a spoonful of water. Luna put the blotter paper in the water-filled bag, zipped it, and shook it for several seconds. Then, he opened the bag again, inserted a blue and white test strip for fifteen seconds, and carefully placed the strip on the desk.

"We need to give it a couple minutes," Luna said.

Noah, Jason, and Luna were quiet while they stared at the test strip. Three minutes later, a single pink line formed on the left side of the test area.

"What's that mean?" Noah asked.

"It's definitely fentanyl," Luna reported.

He placed the test strip back in the water-filled bag, zipped it up, and took off his gloves. Luna sighed and leaned back in his chair.

"Fentanyl use, abuse, and accidental overdosing is a horrible epidemic, and the reservation is not immune to those problems. We had training last month on the fentanyl epidemic, and the instructor told us it's involved in more deaths of Americans under fifty than anything else. More than cancer and even accidents. We lose 175 people a day because of fentanyl poisoning. Teenage overdose deaths have tripled over the past few years."

Luna leaned forward and glared at Noah. "Did you know fentanyl is fifty times stronger than heroin and one hundred times more potent than morphine?"

Noah shook his head. "I had no idea."

Luna reached into his service belt and removed a nasal spray. "Most people don't know that as little as two milligrams of fentanyl, roughly the size of a few grains of sand, can cause a lethal overdose. We all carry this NARCAN® nasal spray now and it's already saved a few lives."

"I also found an empty, generic bottle that looked like a saline solution that you spray into your nose," Jason said.

"That's liquid fentanyl. It appears they don't have a lab to make pills, so they use liquid fentanyl in nasal sprays and paper blotters. We don't need any more of that crap in our community, so if a drug cartel moved in here to flood our schools and streets with more drugs, I'm going to put them behind bars ASAP."

Jason's gut was sending positive signals about Lieutenant Luna. He exuded a calm demeanor, but his eyes were intense. Jason suspected a fiery beast inside the affable exterior, and he wanted to help him capture the cartel.

"I was last on Forest Road 36 and then hiked for a while until I came across the armed men on patrol. I can show you where they are," Jason replied.

"No, no, no. That's too dangerous for civilians. I can't have you out there if there's a cartel in the forest."

"Look, I'm not law enforcement, but I'm currently an Air Force pararescueman with a special tactics squadron in Tacoma, Washington. I've been attached to Army Rangers and Navy SEALs on raids, so I can get you close and stay out of the way so you can do your investigation."

Luna stared at Jason for several seconds and then pulled up his sleeve. He pointed to a tattoo with Old Ironsides written underneath a large number one inside a triangle on his forearm.

"I was a tanker in the army. Got out eight years ago, but at the time, I was a gunner in the First Armored Division out of Fort Bliss, Texas. I know you PJs can hold your own, so I'll let you guide us to the location, but you've got to stay back once we get close."

"Can you get more officers and arrive just after sunrise?" Jason asked.

"I'd like to have two or three additional officers, but resources are tight, so we'll be lucky to get one more. I'll talk to the captain to see who else is available, but we'll have to take what I can get and we'll arrive as soon as possible, but it won't be at sunrise."

Jason pursed his lips, looked down at the desk, then back up at Luna.

"Okay. Call me when you're on your way and I'll meet you at the intersection of Forest Road 300 and 36 and take you the rest of the way."

Noah practically skipped back to Jason's truck. Once inside, he continued to beam with excitement.

"I think we may have the support of the White Mountain Apache Tribe Police Department. We may catch those guys now."

Jason nodded. "I hope so."

He was already running scenarios of his mission with WMAT PD in his head. They didn't have enough men but still had to capture the cartel. The small assault team had to succeed before the cartel killed more people.

CHAPTER 15

Jason tapped his fingers next to his coffee cup while he waited for Lieutenant Luna to call. He'd already completed his morning run, dressed in civilian tactical gear and inspected his first aid kit. He looked at his watch for the sixth time in the last half hour and that's when Jason's phone buzzed on the kitchen table. Jason took the call from Luna and two minutes later he was out the door.

Luna stood next to his White Mountain Apache Tribe-marked police cruiser when Jason reached the intersection of Forest Road 300 and 36. A second member of WMAT PD was in a second vehicle, Sergeant Spencer. Jason exited his truck and met the two men standing next to Luna's cruiser.

"This is Jason Mulder. He's going to show us where he last saw the cartel spotters," Luna said.

Jason shook hands with both officers.

"Are you ready?" Jason asked.

They both nodded.

"Follow me and I'll pull over a half-mile or so from where I saw them."

Twenty minutes later, Jason slowed and pulled to the side of the gravel road as it turned into a dirt path. He got out of his truck and walked back to the two officers.

"They were up that way, just past the clearing for the overhead lines and probably about one hundred yards to the left of the dirt road. Remember, they had rifles the last time I saw them," Jason whispered.

Both officers retrieved the department-issued shotguns from their vehicles and returned to the front of Jason's truck.

"Stay here and we'll check it out." Luna said. "Spencer, you take that side of the dirt road and I'll take this side. Turn down your radio and stay in visual contact to communicate by hand signals until we are clear."

The two officers disappeared into the forest. Jason could hear them plodding through the undergrowth for at least a minute. He thought they were going too fast and making far too much noise, but there was nothing he could do. He tossed dry grass into the air and noted the crosswind was not in their favor this time. Confidence in a successful outcome dwindled with each passing minute.

Jason leaned against his truck and slowed his breath to see if he could hear anything from the direction of the two officers. Ten minutes passed, and Jason had to know more about the status of the two WMAT PD officers, so he took a few steps into the forest and listened. It was eerily quiet as noon approached. The vertical midday sun removed most shadows and places to hide in the woods.

Pop. Pop. Boom.

Jason heard two shots from a rifle followed by a shotgun blast. From his time in Afghanistan, he knew the unmistakable sound of a Kalashnikov rifle.

The eruption of adrenaline slammed Jason's gut and without thinking, he was in a full sprint toward the source of the gunshots. He pinpointed that the shots came from the left of the dirt road.

The side Spencer had entered. Jason jumped over logs and pushed through the undergrowth at full speed to reach the area where he thought he heard the shots originate. When he arrived, he hoped to see Spencer standing over cartel members in handcuffs, but he knew that might not be the case.

Luna flashed into view from the right thirty yards in front of Jason and then dropped out of sight. As Jason neared the scene, Luna jumped up with his shotgun and pointed it at Jason. He stopped and raised his hands. Luna saw it was Jason and yelled out, "He's been hit."

Jason arrived seconds later and observed Spencer lying on his back with the upper right side of his uniform soaked in blood.

"Where are the guys that shot him?" Jason yelled as he dropped to a knee next to Spencer.

"They ran deeper into the forest after I shot back."

"How many?"

"I saw two men running away."

Jason scanned the area and didn't see any imminent threats, so he turned his attention to the injured man.

Spencer's chest heaved as he struggled to refill his lungs, and he moaned as he grasped his shoulder. Jason noticed a hole in his shirt over his chest and prayed he was wearing a vest. He ripped open the officer's uniform and exhaled. Spencer wore a level three vest with a deep indentation over his right lung. Jason knew he likely had a massive bruise under the vest and that breathing was painful, but he was alive.

"They hit his vest with one round, but the other slug hit his deltoid just outside the protected area."

Jason ripped off the officer's sleeve to expose his entire arm. He saw the bullet entry point in the front of his deltoid and raised Spencer a few inches to see a clean exit wound in the back. Blood dripped from his shoulder like a leaky faucet until he lowered him back down.

"Looks like a clean in and out. I need to stabilize him, so can you run back to my truck and grab my first aid kit?"

"Yeah. Where is it?" Luna asked.

"It's in the front seat. While you're there, call for a medivac. Once you've called it in, bring the first aid kit back here as fast as possible. I need to slow the bleeding."

Luna looked up into the woods. "What if those guys come back?"

Jason leaned over Spencer and pulled his shotgun within arm's length.

"I'll hold them off if they come back as long as I can, but you have to hurry. Go now!"

After Luna left, Jason pulled off his shirt, folded it, and placed it over the entry and exit wounds. He applied pressure until Spencer yelped in pain.

"Sorry, buddy. We need to stop the bleeding."

Jason continued to work on the wound until he heard a stick snap from the direction the shooters had gone. He snagged the shotgun and moved behind a nearby tree. Jason couldn't believe what he saw in his sights just over a hundred yards away. An unarmed man stood in the open with his shoulders back and chest out. Strands of long black hair fell across his dirt-stained face as he carefully scanned the area. Jason could see his dark eyes and clenched jaw, even from that distance. His eyes stopped in the direction of the injured officer like a predator locked onto the scent of its prey. The man in tan military fatigues didn't move as much as he stalked toward Spencer, so Jason shuffled out from the cover of the tree and raised his shotgun to eye level. The man stopped, but did not flinch. He glared directly at Jason with a defiant air he hadn't seen since the Taliban warlords back in Afghanistan. Although the man was an average height and build, he reeked of authority and confidence. Jason figured he was the leader and might call on the rest of the cartel to ambush him.

"Come on, Luna. Where are you?" Jason growled to himself. His eyes darted from right to left as he looked out for the other two shooters that might try to flank his position.

Jason's heart raced as the stare-down continued. He knew he was being sized up by the enemy and would not have a strong defense against a three on one ambush. Finally, the leader yelled, "Let's go," in Spanish, and two men appeared from behind trees and followed him. The leader was out of range for a shotgun loaded with buckshot and probably knew it, but Jason had never experienced such bravado from a man looking down the barrel of a gun.

After the men vanished into the forest, Jason waited a few beats and turned his attention back to Sergeant Spencer. Jason felt Spencer might lose consciousness and dropped back to his side. He grabbed his chin and looked Spencer in the eye. "Come on. Try to stay awake."

Spencer returned a faint nod.

"Do you have any family? Any kids?"

"Yeah." Spencer swallowed hard. "I have a three-year-old daughter and my wife is pregnant. I'll have my first boy in four mont—"

Spencer drifted off. Jason gently slapped his cheek.

"Come on, buddy. Hang in there. The medivac will be here soon, and you'll have a great story to tell your daughter and son."

Spencer opened his eyes, licked his lips, and nodded.

Jason heard a vehicle from the direction he'd come bushwhacking its way up the dirt path. It was Lieutenant Luna in the SUV. He jumped out, opened the rear door, and ran to Jason.

"I have a sat phone in my car, so the medivac is on the way. I thought getting him to the landing zone in this would be easier."

"Great call. I'll take my kit."

Jason tore into his medical kit and found what he was looking for. He ripped open alcohol wipes and Celox rapid hemostatic gauze pads impregnated with a substance that helps stop life-threatening bleeding in under sixty seconds. He cleaned around the entry and exit wounds and applied the bandage.

"This may hurt a bit," Jason told Spencer. He pressed his finger into the gauze to push it into the hole left by the AK-74 slug.

Spencer released a weak moan. After Jason removed his finger from the entry wound, he took his pulse. It had fallen dramatically since his last measurement five minutes earlier, so they had to get Spencer to the hospital fast. Jason repeated the treatment on the exit wound and waved for Luna to come next to him.

"Grab his legs, and I'll get his midsection to move him into the SUV."

Once Spencer was in the rear cargo bay, Luna put the SUV into drive and crept out of the forest. They arrived at the clearing near Jason's truck and heard a helicopter approaching. Soon the rotor wash bent the grass and kicked up dust until it landed, and three air medics emerged with a mobile gurney. The five men helped secure Sergeant Spencer; minutes later, the medivac team was airborne.

Jason and Luna watched the helicopter head toward Flagstaff Medical Center, the only Level One trauma center north of Phoenix in Arizona.

"You think he'll be okay?" Luna asked.

"I think so," Jason replied. He trusted the doctors and nurses would do all they could to save him, but he'd seen too many men with gunshot wounds die from their injuries to be overly confident.

Luna turned his gaze from the air to Jason. "I think we have a real problem on our hands. The shit is really going to hit the fan around here."

Jason kept his eyes on the sky.

"No doubt. It's going to hit real hard."

CHAPTER 16

Victor Romero stood on the open tailgate of his pickup truck as men reassembled their production facility under a cluster of pine trees. The notion they had to move operations again after the police discovered them made the pounding in his ears even louder. This time, they moved even deeper into the forest to make it harder for anyone to find them. He knew they had to be nimble to avoid capture, and that was why Victor arrived months early and spent the extra money on building the mobile production facility. However, three moves in two months was unacceptable. That's why Victor did the unthinkable. He went to the front line himself to see the tall, fit American with brown hair that had found them a second time. The hazel eyes and square jaw of the man burned into Victor's memory.

A member of the production team approached Victor.

"Why didn't we go after the other men and kill them so we don't have to keep moving?" the man asked in Spanish.

Victor stared down at the man and his dirty, sweaty face for several seconds before responding. "As I've told all of you before, gunfire attracts the police in minutes. Dead men will attract even more police. This isn't like El Salvador, where we shoot and stand our ground to prove that we did it. Here we have to move quickly after we shoot, or they'll send a whole army after us."

"But—"

"There are no buts. Get back to work and finish setting up the lab so we can produce the next shipment."

The man jogged back to help the others.

Victor jumped down from the truck and called everyone together. He leaned against the truck and put his hands in his pants pockets.

"Eduardo and Carlos, come here."

A minute later, two men stood in front of Victor. They stood shoulder to shoulder out of his reach.

"Come closer, so I don't have to shout.

The men looked at each other and took one step closer. Everyone else in the camp stopped what they were doing to watch.

"How did the tall American find us again?"

Eduardo and Carlos both shrugged.

"Were you smoking?"

"No!" they said in unison.

"That's odd because I smelled cigarette smoke when I came up to see the American after the gunshots."

Neither man spoke. Victor paced in front of them several times and turned to Eduardo. "Were you smoking?"

"No, I wasn't smoking. I swear."

"Carlos must have been smoking, then. Is that right? But before you answer, do you know how much I hate liars?"

Eduardo stood motionless with a blank look.

"So, was Carlos the one smoking?"

Eduardo looked down at the ground and nodded. Before he could look up, Victor pulled his RCT-1 Raven Double Action Out The Front Knife out of his pocket and thrust the blade into

Eduardo's chest. Victor twisted the four-inch stainless steel blade back and forth with one hand and grabbed Eduardo by his arm to prevent him from falling with the other hand. He stared into Eduardo's eyes, still wide with shock, as his soul left his body. Eduardo's body went limp, and Victor let him fall to the ground. He moved in front of Carlos.

"Were you smoking?" Victor asked coolly.

Carlos looked down at Eduardo's lifeless body and back at Victor. His eyes were so wide that they looked like tiny brown dots on a white cue ball. He did not answer.

"I'm only going to ask this one more time. Were you smoking?"

"No!"

"So, Eduardo was smoking?"

Carlos didn't respond, so Victor locked his eyes on him for a full minute. He watched Carlos quake like a leaf in the wind as the smell of urine wafted from the new wet spot on his pants.

"Come closer," Victor demanded.

Carlos turned around and looked at all the men watching him. He swallowed hard and took another step. Victor lunged toward Carlos and grabbed the back of his neck. Victor pulled his ear within six inches of his mouth.

"You know what I hate more than a liar?"

"A rat!" Carlos shrieked.

"Exactly!"

Victor looked up at the crowd. "Don't any of you forget that!" He turned to Carlos. "Bury Eduardo, and never let me catch you smoking again. And change your pants."

Victor turned to the men watching Carlos drag Eduardo's lifeless body out of the camp. He never raised his voice, but the reaction was as if he roared like a lion.

"Get back to work."

They assembled the production lab faster than ever before.

The cartel leader sat on the tailgate. He watched his men resume production and smiled. Victor had kept his promise to himself. Nothing would stop him from success in Arizona. Not the police or a member of his own team. The meddling tall American was the last obstacle he had to eliminate.

Chapter 17

Jason finished his final set of pull-ups and collapsed onto the carpet in his bedroom. After doing pushups, sit-ups, burpees, and then pull-ups nearly to the point of muscle failure, he stayed on the floor and stared at the white ceiling. Two minutes later, he sat up and leaned against the wall as he conducted his solo after-action report.

Jason concluded they shouldn't have entered the woods in broad daylight. The lack of shadows, wind, and insect sounds allowed the cartel members to detect a person approaching their perimeter. He also questioned the number of people assigned to search for up to a dozen armed men. Jason wasn't aware of WMAT PD tactics and procedures for a sting involving an armed group and incorrectly assumed Lieutenant Luna knew better because of his army experience. Now, Sergeant Spencer was in serious condition at Flagstaff Medical Center and it could have been even worse. They all could have been shot and killed. In his unquenchable desire to capture Josh's killers, Jason went against his training and all common sense. He couldn't slip up like this again during any future encounters with the cartel. They were too dangerous. If he did, he'd likely suffer the same fate as Sergeant Spencer.... or Josh.

Jason showered and went into the kitchen, where he found his dad making breakfast.

"I thought I'd make us all breakfast before you have to head back to Washington."

Jason snagged a cup and filled it with coffee waiting in the pot. He leaned against the counter and scanned the room. It was the same coffee maker he remembered his dad using while Jason was in grade school. The cabinets, counters, and appliances were the same. The decorations on the wall and mementos in the china cabinet next to the dinner table were decades old. Jason's lips curved upwards as he recalled all the great family memories forged in his childhood home.

Phillip placed a plate on the table for Jason with a feast fit for a king. It contained four over-hard eggs, four pieces of bacon, and two pieces of toast. Jason required a lot of calories as a PJ and his mom and dad always ensured he had plenty to eat. His dad sat down next to him with his breakfast.

"Did you ever have that meeting with your career adviser?"

"Not yet. It's in a few days."

"Doesn't your current enlistment end soon?"

"Yeah. There are some things I have to figure out."

"I thought you loved being a PJ."

Jason shoved a piece of bacon into his mouth and nodded. "I do."

His father put his elbows on the table and leaned in. "You know your mother and I will support you no matter what you do, but remember the three keys to life I told all you boys growing up. Find something you're good at, something you love, and something the world needs and then give one-hundred percent. Only you can answer what you love but know that the world needs people like you. It especially needs people that protect the innocent against the evil on this planet. Not everyone can do it, even if they want to, but you do it very, very well."

Jason didn't know how to respond. He'd heard his father share his three keys to life with him, Kevin, Noah, and Josh so many times that it was just noise, but today it felt like he read Jason's thoughts.

"Thanks, Dad," Jason said.

"Glad to help." His father stood and returned to the stovetop to start another round of eggs for Celeste and Noah.

After breakfast, Jason went to his room to pack for his early afternoon flight. While he zipped up his bag, his cell phone rang.

"Hey, Jason. This is Lieutenant Luna with the White Mountain Apache Tribe Police Department."

"How's Spencer?" Jason asked.

"He's in recovery. They said the surgery was a success, and he's stable now. I'm heading to Flagstaff as soon as I'm off. Thanks again for treating him out there. I was pretty concerned about him right after it happened."

"Me too. I thought about it all night. Next time, we have to go at first light, so we have a better chance of catching them off guard."

The line was quiet for so long that Jason looked at his phone to see if he had dropped the call. "You still there?"

"Yeah, I'm here. There won't be a next time."

"What do you mean?"

"Captain Selah doesn't want you involved in this case anymore. He said if he finds you on tribal land again, he'll arrest you for trespassing."

"Can he do that?"

"He's the captain."

"I guess I won't be seeing you in Whiteriver, so keep me posted after you see Spencer tonight."

"I actually called you for another reason," Luna shared.

"Oh, so there's more bad news?"

"The feds are involved. The FBI called yesterday after they received news of an officer-involved shooting on the reservation. Captain Selah had them talk to me, and after I told them about the evidence of a cartel, they referred the case to the DEA. I spoke with Special Agent Holland from the DEA's Phoenix division office on the phone a few minutes ago. He's on his way to your house to speak with you right now. Before he knocks on your door, I wanted you to know."

Jason looked out of his bedroom window but saw no new vehicles in the driveway.

"I appreciate the heads up on the DEA special agent and the ban from Fort Apache Reservation. However, I can't promise I won't sneak in and phone in an anonymous tip if I find them again."

Luna chuckled. "I expected that answer from you. Just don't get caught. Captain Selah is not happy about another officer-involved shooting, and he will not hesitate to arrest you."

Jason heard the crunching of gravel from a vehicle pulling into his driveway. "I think I have company. Thanks for the call."

A few minutes later, Jason heard his father shouting for him.

"Jason, you have someone here who wants to speak with you."

Jason took his time packing the rest of his stuff. When he reached the kitchen, he saw a man that looked to be in his early thirties sitting at the kitchen table with a cup of coffee. Jason guessed he was a gym rat with blue eyes and a square jaw to complement his buzzed blond hair.

"Hi, Jason. I'm Special Agent Holland. Can we go somewhere private so I can ask you some questions?"

Jason scanned the room. "It's still cool outside. Let's go out on the back patio."

Holland followed Jason outside. They each selected a chair around the square fiberglass patio table.

"Your dad said you're leaving soon, so I won't take too much of your time."

Holland placed a notepad on the table and found a new blank page.

"I've already spoken with Lieutenant Luna, so I need your account of what happened yesterday. Please share everything you remember."

Jason recounted everything from the initial phone call until Sergeant Spencer departed in the helicopter.

"Thank you for all the detailed information. Lieutenant Luna also shared that you found blotter paper with fentanyl and the potential evidence of a cartel from Central America. Where did you find this?" Holland asked.

"I searched a fire tower they were using as a lookout and noticed some trash that seemed out of place. I found a Pepsi can from Guatemala and an empty cigarette package from El Salvador. Then when I searched the area, I found men in military fatigues pulling security with AK-74s."

"Interesting. Is that everything you've found?"

"Yeah. Everything else in the tower was just empty beer cans and fast food bags."

Special Agent Holland wrote a few lines of notes when Jason put up his hand. "Wait. There was something else."

Jason opened his wallet and handed Special Agent Holland the Canadian hundred-dollar bill. He flipped the bill over and examined it for several seconds.

"I don't know if it's related to a cartel, but Canadian money in an abandoned fire tower felt strange to me."

"Oh, it's related and most likely from an organized syndicate. They like to trade in Canadian Dollars since it's easier to launder. This points to an organized crime organization. It's definitely not some local guys. The organization may or may not be a Central American drug cartel, but it's something we need to investigate further."

"Will the DEA go after these guys?" Jason asked.

"I'll submit my report to the Phoenix division office, and they'll assign a team. We're drowning with cases now, but we'll get someone on it soon."

Jason shook hands with Holland and took his card. After the DEA agent left, he moved to the outdoor lounge chair and stared up at the cloudless indigo sky. A million questions swirled around in his head.

Why did a cartel choose a forest in rural Arizona? Could he trust the DEA to apprehend the cartel? Should he re-enlist or pursue Josh's killers full-time?

Jason pulled out his phone and sent a text.

His dad stepped out onto the patio. "Are you about ready to leave?"

It was harder to leave every time Jason came home, especially after Josh's death. He wanted to stay and help, but his team at JLBM in Tacoma also needed him.

"I'll grab my bags."

Jason found his mother on the couch in the family room and kissed her goodbye. As he returned to the patio, his phone buzzed. Jason read the text and smiled.

"Good news?" Phillip asked.

"Yes. Excellent news," Jason replied.

Two days later, Jason skipped his morning run on base because his stomach was in knots. He rarely felt this nervous, but the meeting with Sergeant Hopkins to review his new contract was in hours. Jason was sure he'd re-enlist up until a month ago. Even last week, he assumed he'd sign a new contract, but the text from

Clay two days ago changed everything. He confirmed the Air Force Reserve 943rd Rescue Group at Davis-Monthan Air Base in Tucson had an open pararescue position. Open slots for PJs in the Air Force Reserve didn't open up often and it wouldn't be available for long. Jason called the commander of the 943rd the day he returned to JBLM, and he confirmed the open slot and his willingness to consider Jason. A new opportunity Jason wasn't even aware of three days ago was suddenly a real possibility. He could remain a part-time PJ in the Air Force Reserve and still dedicate himself to finding Josh's killers. It would require him to walk away from his team and a career he deeply loved.

Once the meeting with Sergeant Hopkins started, Jason's knee bounced under the table like a stallion trying to buck off a rider. His nervous bouncing grew worse as she carefully reviewed the details of the contract with him. Finally, when she turned to page two, Jason's knee went still. It was like she flipped a switch. He understood what he had to do. Jason held up his hand to stop her.

"I'm not signing a new contract," Jason interrupted.

"I'm sorry. You're not going to sign?"

"That's correct."

"Are you sure?"

"Yes."

Hopkins crossed her arms and tilted her head. "You told me in the past that you wanted to retire as an Air Force pararescueman."

Jason didn't respond. He was 99% sure of his decision, but that one percent of doubt did not want to go away without a fight.

"Can I ask why?"

Jason pursed his lips and cleared his throat. "I love the Air Force, my squad, and being a PJ, but I can't do it full-time anymore. I've already spoken to the CO at the 943rd Air Force Reserve and they have an open slot for prior service, and I plan to take it."

Jason wasn't sure who was more surprised with the words leaving his mouth, Sergeant Hopkins or himself.

"You know it can be difficult to come back if you change your mind later. It's not impossible, but it's unlikely you'll retire as a PJ if you don't extend now." She fixed her eyes on Jason, but he couldn't return the gaze. Instead, Jason focused on all the pages of a contract that determined his long-term future.

"If you're sure that's what you want, I'll rip up this contract."

Jason looked up and locked eyes with Hopkins. He swallowed hard and nodded.

"In that case, I wish you luck on your final weeks as a full-time PJ."

Jason ambled out of the office and into his truck. He looked around the parking lot before turning the ignition. In a week, he'd have to pack up and move from JBLM. Leaving his temporary home for the past year wouldn't be easy. He'd miss the Pacific Northwest and JBLM, but most of all he'd miss his team.

He sat for another minute pondering the path he chose at such a critical crossroads in his life.

Was this the right decision?

The engine roared to life as resolve smashed all remaining doubts. Jason had another essential job ahead of him. He would transition from full-time Air Force pararescueman to full-time cartel hunter. His new job wouldn't be complete until they were all behind bars or buried six feet below ground.

CHAPTER 18

Jason loaded the last items from his apartment at JBLM onto the yellow moving truck. His current bed was in better shape than the old one in Payson and he had a lot of personal tactical gear. He also had to tow his truck home.

The goodbyes to his team at the squadron took over an hour, and then Jason drove south on Interstate 5. The next evening just before sunset, Jason pulled into his driveway in Arizona. Noah was sitting at the kitchen table scrolling through his phone over an empty dinner plate.

"Did you hear the news about the hunters?" Noah asked when Jason entered.

"Now? Hunting season isn't for another five months."

"Okay then, future hunters. Anyway, a father and his sixteen-year-old son got lucky and were drawn for an elk tag by White Mountain Apache Tribe Game and Fish Department this year. Their tag is for the self-guided west-end hunt, so they went out to scout the area over the weekend and never came home. WMAT PD found their truck about twenty miles southeast of Cibecue forty hours after the wife reported them missing."

"I'd bet they're lost. People get lost all the time in a forest the size of New Jersey."

"I know, but the father is an experienced hunter and searchers found gear and water piled up against a tree on the Fort Apache Reservation. No way anyone ditches their water and gear out there without a good reason. I think they ran into some trouble."

Noah didn't even have to say what trouble they may have encountered. Jason already knew and understood the dire situation.

"Do you think you can help look for them?" Noah asked.

"I'm not allowed on the Fort Apache Reservation."

"The boy went to the same school as Josh. I don't think this town can take another loss of a high school student."

"I'll see what I can do."

Jason found his mom and dad and then went to his old bedroom. He sat down on his bed and typed out a text he'd thought about for the last thousand miles. It contained three words, but each letter felt heavy. Jason's thumb hovered over the send button for several seconds until he finally punched it.

Can we talk?

The lime green umbrella outside Pinetop Coffee House and Roasting Company in Pinetop-Lakeside, Arizona shaded Jason and his coffee resting on the picnic table. He intentionally arrived early and selected a seat facing the parking lot to watch his coffee date arrive.

Ten minutes after securing his position in the outdoor seating area, a white Kia SUV pulled in and Jason recognized the silhouette of Shanna at the wheel. She tossed and straightened her hair several times in the mirror, not knowing she was under surveillance.

Shanna stepped out of her vehicle, put on dark sunglasses, and slung a brown leather bag over her shoulder. Her ebony hair slung over her other shoulder and bounced off her breast as she crossed the parking lot. She wore a loose blouse with a tight, knee-length pencil skirt that looked professional for her therapy sessions but revealed her athletic figure.

"Damn, she's beautiful," Jason whispered.

Shanna didn't appear to notice Jason sitting outside as she approached the front door.

"Hey, do you know where someone can get a good cup of coffee around here?" Jason asked.

Shanna turned to see the question come from Jason and returned a wide smile.

"You didn't have to drive all the way over here. I would have come to Payson," Shanna said. She placed her bag on the table and sat down across from Jason.

"I know my inconsiderate brother may make you do that, but I won't."

"Noah isn't inconsiderate. He's just busy with work."

"Is that what he told you?"

Shanna tilted her head and stared at Jason.

"What would you like to drink?" Jason asked after he'd finished flirting.

Shanna looked at Jason's cup. "I'll take what you're having."

"You sure? It's just black coffee."

"I'll take a little cream."

When Jason returned, Shanna had her laptop and a notepad on the table.

"Are you ready to talk about how you're doing?" Shanna asked.

Jason stared back without responding.

"Do you not want to talk about what happened to Josh and your mom?"

"Not really."

Shanna pinched her eyebrows. "Why did you ask me to meet you?"

"I'm hoping you can help me with something."

"I'll try."

"The captain of the White Mountain Apache Tribe Police Department banned me from the reservation. He said he'd arrest me for trespassing if I'm caught on tribal land, but I still need to investigate what happened to Josh. I'm hoping you know someone who can get me in and out of the Fort Apache Reservation without being detected by the police."

"Why did you get banned?"

"You know Sergeant Spencer, right?"

"I do. I was with his wife yesterday. How do you know him?"

"I was with him when they shot him. He came with Lieutenant Luna to investigate a lead I provided on the people that killed Josh."

Shanna opened her mouth to talk, but wrote something down in her notebook. After she finished, she put the pen down and leaned toward Jason.

"Why do you feel you're uniquely qualified to find the people that killed Josh?"

Jason exhaled. "I've had a lot of related training in the Air Force. I've been hunting, fishing, and hiking in some parts of this forest since I was ten. I can find the people that killed Josh."

Shanna smiled. "Why search for the killers by yourself? Why not go as a group so it's safer? The forest can be very dangerous."

"Right now, it's just me, so I have to work with what I have."

"Noah would help you if you asked."

"Did he tell you that?" Jason asked.

"You know I can't tell you what we talk about."

Jason kept his gaze on Shanna until he realized she would not slip and say any more.

"He doesn't have the necessary training or experience. I've already seen what the cartel will do to a trained police officer, so I don't think it's a good idea for Noah to get involved. I know he may want to help, but I'm only trying to protect him."

Shanna nodded and jotted more notes in her notepad. "Do you think that's why you're having nightmares about Josh?"

Jason leaned back and stiffened. "I don't follow."

"You're protective of your family and said you were having nightmares about Josh. Is that what they're about? You weren't able to protect him?"

Jason felt exposed. He didn't meet with Shanna to bare his deepest thoughts and feelings, so he looked at his watch and stood up.

"I'm taking my mom to physical therapy today to give my dad a break, so I have to get back. Thanks for meeting me for coffee."

Shanna grabbed Jason's hand before he could bolt to the parking lot. "I'm sorry if I pushed too far today. I would like to know more about your nightmares so I can help you understand them. It's hard for people to navigate grief and feelings of immense loss alone."

Jason stared at Shanna but did not respond.

"Could we meet somewhere private? Would you feel more comfortable talking then?" she asked.

Jason looked down at his hands and shrugged. "I don't think talking about Josh is what I need right now. What I need is to find the people that killed him and bring them to justice. That's the therapy I'm looking for. I was hoping you could help me."

"I may be able to help. Give me a little time."

"Thank you."

The next morning, instead of going east to Show Low or Young, Jason drove west through Payson. He turned north a mile outside of town and drove until the Mogollon Rim, a 7000 foot high escarpment, filled his windshield. After he passed a few cabins hidden in the tall pines of the Whispering Pines community, Jason pulled over and parked his truck in knee-high grass. He paced the property in a Z-pattern back to a flowing stream. He slid down the embankment and hopped over the water splashing across bowling ball-sized rocks to the other bank and back several times. A vehicle pulled up and parked behind Jason, so he climbed up and saw a burly man in his fifties sauntering toward him. Jason walked across the lot to meet him.

"So, what do you think?" the man asked after they shook hands.

"Does the property go all the way to the creek?"

"That's a river."

Jason turned back to the narrow body of water he'd recently jumped across. "The East Verde River?"

"Yep. The headwater is less than two miles upstream. The property is two acres, so you have over two-hundred and twenty feet of riverside access."

Jason turned slowly and examined the ring of towering pine trees surrounding the clearing. It would make the ideal home base for life after the Air Force.

"Does it have electricity and water?"

"Electricity, yes, but you'll have to dig a well and put in a septic tank. No cable or phone lines, and cell service is spotty."

Jason smiled.

"What's to the north?"

"Tonto National Forest and then the rim."

"And the south?"

"Another two-acre lot."

Jason looked across the river and pointed to a cabin a quarter mile away.

"Is that the nearest neighbor?"

The man looked across the creek and grinned. "Yep, that's Larry Pratt. Retired from the Navy and bought that lot seven or eight years ago. He's really quiet."

Jason turned toward the river and then back to the lot owner. "I'll take it."

Jason left his new property, rolled down the truck windows and tapped on his steering wheel like a drummer. Over the last six years, he'd saved almost all his Air Force pay to buy land somewhere secluded to build his off-grid home. The first domino in a long line had just fallen into place.

Jason stopped playing the air drums and continued driving past Payson until he was at Young Highway again. He couldn't resist taking another look at the area where Josh and his mom were pushed off the road. Before long, Jason was back on the ridge, where he'd found Josh's plant identification pamphlet. This time he walked to the area the police said was a poachers' camp. He found evidence of a fire pit and a couple of footprints but not much else. Jason began his walk back to his truck when a small object caught his eye on the edge of the clearing. It was more blotter paper that looked like a watercolor painted postage stamp of a black sun.

Jason took a picture and walked back to his truck. He drove deeper into the Fort Apache Reservation when he noticed a growing plume of dust on the road ahead. It was coming toward him.

"Could that be them?" Jason asked himself.

He pulled over, parked, and took cover in the forest. A minute later, three Polaris side-by-side off-highway motor vehicles that looked like evolved dune buggies blew past Jason and his truck. No cartel. Just some locals enjoying their off-road vehicles. Once the dust settled, Jason left his cover in the woods, and that was when an SUV with the emblem of the White Mountain Apache Tribe Police Department stopped in front of his truck.

"Shit," Jason muttered to himself. He hoped it was Lieutenant Luna, but a shorter, older man emerged from the police vehicle. Jason leaned against the side of the truck as the officer approached.

"You with those guys in the off-road vehicles?"

"No, sir."

"What are you doing all the way out here?"

"Just looking around."

The officer eyed Jason for several seconds. "I need to see your driver's license and reservation permit."

Jason opened his wallet and handed him two cards.

The officer looked at his driver's license and then at his permit.

"This day pass expired weeks ago."

Jason stared back at the officer but did not offer a rebuttal.

"Wait here while I call this in."

Jason remained near his front hood while watching the officer call in on his satellite phone. He wondered if Captain Selah put something in the system officially banning Jason. Five minutes later, the officer returned with a dire look. Jason noticed the strap over his service pistol was unbuttoned. He knew what was coming next.

"Turn around and put your hands on the hood."

"What's the problem, officer?" Jason asked.

"You're under arrest."

CHAPTER 19

A man in his upper twenties with shoulder-length raven hair slept on the sole cell bed inside Whiteriver Police Station. Jason slid down the wall as far away as possible from the man and sat on the cool concrete floor. He hoped the arrest, cuffs, and drive to Whiteriver were all a misunderstanding that would soon be resolved. Thirty minutes into his detention, the charge of interfering with an investigation became real.

Jason made his one phone call and pondered his next move. His cellmate rolled over in bed and coughed several times. The smell of stale beer filled the tight cell, making it feel even smaller. Jason was sure the guy would throw up, so he pushed his back against the steel bars to get as far away from the man as possible when Lieutenant Luna arrived through a side door.

"Lieutenant Luna, over here," Jason said with a wave.

Luna did a double take and walked over to the bars separating him from Jason.

"Tell me you didn't."

"Didn't what?" Jason asked.

"I told you Captain Selah said he didn't want you poking around the reservation. What were you doing?"

"It doesn't matter. How do I get out of here?"

"You know an attorney familiar with tribal law? I'd start there."

Luna received a call from dispatch and left Jason alone with the man gagging and burping before an imminent explosive eruption of vomit. Jason tensed all his muscles as he retreated into the corner farther from the man. He didn't relax until the man stopped coughing.

Ninety minutes later, two visitors arrived. It was Shanna with a blond woman who looked to be in her forties. Jason hoped the woman with Shanna was a lawyer.

They spoke with the officer at the front desk for a minute, and then another officer that looked like a sergeant joined them. Ten minutes later, the blond woman left and the front desk officer, with Shanna by his side, walked back to the cell.

"Hey, Jason. How are you doing?" Shanna asked.

"Better now that you're here. Thanks for coming so fast. Was that other lady an attorney?"

"Yeah, I know her from work. She has a practice in Show Low and she's helped a few patients who've had run-ins with the White Mountain Apache Tribe Police Department."

The front desk officer unlocked the cell and Jason walked out. He hugged Shanna and twisted his torso in both directions to stretch out his back. "Thanks for coming so fast and bringing an attorney. What did she say to get them to let me out?"

Shanna turned to the officer standing next to the open door and then to Jason. "How she got you out is not important. Just don't let it happen again."

The officer smirked and returned to the front counter.

"Be sure to tell her I said thank you next time you see her," Jason said.

"I will."

Jason took several steps from the cell and turned back to ensure Shanna was behind him. He was eager to leave the police station, but Shanna remained beside the open cell door.

"You coming?" Jason asked.

Shanna didn't respond. She walked into the cell and tapped the sleeping man. He didn't respond, so she shook him harder, and then he opened his eyes.

"Come on, Tarek. Let's go."

Jason's jaw dropped. He shuffled back to the cell while the man sat up.

"You know this guy?" Jason asked.

"Yeah, this is Tarek. He's my cousin. He's the guy that we talked about that can help you."

Jason didn't say a word until they dropped Tarek off at a small house with peeling paint, missing shingles, and knee-high grass a couple of miles from the police station. After Shanna helped Tarek into the house through the back door, she returned to the SUV.

"That's your cousin?"

"Yeah, he's had a rough night. A pretty rough life, actually."

"I'd say. What happened?"

"It's a long story, but the bottom line is that he hit rock bottom after our grandpa died. They were very close, and Tarek struggled with his death. Eventually, he turned to meth and got hooked on it. After a year or so, my aunt got him into rehab. Tarek got clean in rehab and has been doing better the last few years but occasionally has setbacks. He's not supposed to drink, but still does when he gets stressed or depressed. Tarek lost his job last week, so I was afraid something like this would happen."

"Wow, I'm sorry to hear that. Where did he work?"

"He worked for a logging company for the past couple of years. They let several guys go last week, and it's not easy to find jobs around here."

Jason nodded. He asked what was weighing on his mind.

"You said he was the guy that could help me. How could he help me?"

Shanna looked through the windshield toward Tarek's house. "Tarek used to be a hot shot for the fire service and a hunting guide, but his real skills came from our grandpa. He taught Tarek all about the land. So, if you need someone to guide you through every inch of the forest on the reservation, he's the guy."

Jason turned to the house that looked like it could blow over in a storm and then back to Shanna.

"That guy?" He pointed toward Tarek's home with his thumb.

"Yep."

"Is he always like that? Drunker than a skunk?"

Shanna laughed. "He'll be fine tomorrow and won't drink again for a while."

Shanna backed out of Tarek's driveway, put her SUV in drive, and looked over to Jason. "Where to?"

"Can you take me back to my truck?"

"Where is it?"

A sheepish grin formed on Jason's face. "About an hour away."

It came out sounding more like a question than an answer.

Shanna looked up as if she was mentally calculating how much that would mess up her day.

Jason didn't want to risk a negative response and quickly added, "I'll tell you about my high school girlfriend. The one that died in a crash similar to Josh."

"Let me see if I can move around my afternoon appointments."

A minute later, Shanna looked up from her phone. "I moved my appointment so I can take you." She removed her foot from the brake, and ninety minutes later, they arrived alongside Jason's truck covered in dust.

"I'm sorry it was longer than I thought. Can I at least buy you dinner?" Jason asked.

"Dinner? I'm not dressed to go out for dinner."

"I'm not either. Follow me to this barbecue joint I know in Forest Lakes. You can park there and we'll grab takeout and go somewhere to talk."

Shanna agreed, and an hour later, Jason backed his truck up to the edge of the Mogollon Rim overlooking millions of acres of pine forest a thousand feet below. The setting sun cast orange and purple swatches in the sky behind the silhouette of the dark, rolling mountain peaks. Jason opened up two of the four folding chairs in the bed of his truck and turned over a five-gallon bucket for a table. Together, they enjoyed beef brisket with the best views in the state. They ate in close quarters, which led to unavoidable encounters of shoulders, arms, and legs in the back of his truck. Each brush of Shanna's bare silky skin on his sent an electric shock through Jason's body, and he didn't want it to end.

The stars appeared after they finished eating, and Shanna turned to Jason. "Do you feel comfortable telling me about your high school girlfriend?"

Jason nodded and took a deep breath.

"Gaby and I started dating the first semester of our junior year. We did all the things high school couples do. Dances, parties, sporting events, and all that stuff. During our senior year, we got pretty serious and agreed we'd go to the University of Arizona together. She planned to get her degree in nursing, and I would get one in biology in the BioMed department. Our future was set.

After graduation, we went out with our friends to celebrate the end of high school. My friend Jeff was driving his dad's GMC Yukon XL with a moon roof on those winding roads north of town. We were driving around and jamming to music when Gaby took off her seat belt and stood up through the moon roof. She extended her arms and laughed while the wind whipped her hair. It was fun until she started yelling 'faster' over and over to Jeff."

Jason paused and gulped down a quarter of his soft drink.

"At first Jeff drove normally, but he sped up after Gaby yelled for him to go faster. Then Jeff punched it, and I grabbed onto Gaby's legs as we entered another sharp curve. She looked down at me and said, 'stop worrying about everything all the time. Sometimes you've just got to live a little.' Those were the last words I heard from Gaby. I still remember them like it was yesterday."

Jason paused and stared straight ahead as if he was watching the scene again on a movie screen. Shanna sat silent and waited for Jason to resume his story.

"A second later, the right wheels of the Yukon went off the road, and Jeff overcorrected and yanked the wheel left. The SUV rolled two or three times. I can still remember the feeling of her legs slipping through my arms."

Jason swallowed hard and continued.

"Jeff and I had our seatbelts on, so we were still inside the SUV when it came to a rest on its wheels, but the front passenger, Lucas, and Gaby, were missing. I couldn't get out of my door because it was smashed in, so I crawled out the broken window and found Lucas a few yards away. He was conscious and moaning as he held his left arm, which I knew, even back then, was badly broken. I left Lucas and searched for Gaby, but I couldn't find her," Jason said as his voice cracked.

Shanna moved her hand over Jason's and he took it. She maintained eye contact with him and gestured with a slight nod that she was still listening.

"Finally, I saw a dark object on the road under the moonlight around fifty yards away. I prayed it wasn't Gaby as I sprinted over and found her unconscious. She had so much blood on her face that it was hard to recognize her. Blood soaked her curly black hair."

Jason moved his fist to his mouth like he was blowing into his hand to warm them on a cold day and exhaled.

"I called 911 and hung up after I gave them our location. The only first aid I knew at the time was CPR from my lifeguard training, so I began chest compressions. Tears flowed down my cheeks and onto hers as I prayed for some sign of life. When the paramedics arrived, they pushed me aside and tried to save Gaby. I couldn't do anything. I just watched her die."

Jason stopped talking and let his head drop until his eyes were on his boots.

Neither spoke for a half minute until Shanna broke the silence.

"I'm sorry for the horrible tragedy you witnessed and the sudden loss of a loved one," Shanna said with a squeeze of her hand.

"I felt completely helpless and hated it. That night I vowed to never feel that way again, which is why I ultimately became a PJ. I'm driven to rescue and protect people, especially the people I care about most. It's become part of my DNA."

Jason maintained his gaze on the bed of his truck.

"Over time, the more people I helped in the Air Force the better it got. I was doing what I had to do, and I thought I was doing it well, until Josh died."

Jason let go of Shanna's hand and curled his hands into fists. His voice deepened, and his face was sullen when he turned to Shanna.

"Josh's eyes in my nightmares still haunt me, and I can't shake the feeling that I should have been able to protect him. Josh needed me and I failed."

It was quiet again. This time for over a minute.

"I know it won't bring Josh back, but I have to find the people responsible for his death. I need justice for Josh."

Shanna nodded and their eyes met.

"I've never told anyone outside my family about Gaby."

Shanna grabbed Jason's hand again.

"I'm glad you told me," Shanna said.

Chapter 20

The following morning, Jason wiped the sweat off his face and neck after finishing his six-mile run. He could feel the increasing humidity in the air as the weather pattern that brought seasonal monsoons inched closer to Arizona. It felt odd that he didn't have to report to the squadron after his morning run like he'd done hundreds of times over the past six years.

Jason showered and noticed he received a text from an unknown number when he checked his phone.

Call me if you want to meet.

Jason didn't know what to make of the cryptic text. Was it someone from the Air Force? Was it one of his old friends from high school?

Who is this?

The phone was silent for several minutes, so Jason continued to get dressed until the phone buzzed again.

Tarek.

Jason stared at the text for several seconds, dropped the phone onto his bed, and started pacing.

Did he really want help from a man he didn't know? Could a person with such a checkered past really help him?

Despite all the warning signs, the need for someone to help him navigate his way in and around the Fort Apache Reservation was strong. Jason hit the call button on his phone.

"Yeah," a man answered.

"This is Jason Mulder. I just got your text."

The man did not reply.

"Shanna said you know your way around the forest."

"Yes. I know it well."

"Did she say why I need your help?"

"She just said it had to do with the boy from Payson that died in the accident over by Canyon Creek."

Jason bristled at the description of Josh's death as an accident but let it go.

"Can you help me find a small group hiding in the most remote parts of the forest?"

"Yeah, I can do that."

"Can you do it today?"

Silence for several seconds.

"I have nothing else going on."

"Great. Where's a good place to meet?" Jason asked.

"At my house."

"In Whiteriver?" Jason asked.

"My truck isn't running right now, and that's all I have to get around."

Jason ran his fingers through his hair and paced again. Going all the way to Whiteriver and back to the west end of the reservation would add at least two additional hours of drive time. Four if you included dropping Tarek off after the search. After twenty seconds of pacing, Jason replied.

"Fine. I'll be there in two hours, so be ready to leave when I pull up."

"How much will I get paid for the day?"

Jason hadn't thought about payment but knew it was fair to pay Tarek for his help.

"How about fifty dollars for the day?" Jason asked.

Tarek laughed on the other end of the line. "I got ten times that as a guide during the trophy elk hunts. You've got to do better than that."

Jason wanted to remind Tarek this wasn't a trophy hunt but opted for a slightly higher offer to complete the negotiation.

"I'm not exactly rolling in the dough myself, so I can't go that high, but how about $150 a day?"

"I'll see you in two hours."

Jason pulled into a driveway with freshly cut grass. He double-checked the address to be sure he had the right place. Seconds later, Tarek strutted out of the side door and joined Jason in his truck. After their previous encounter in the jail cell, Jason barely recognized the man in his passenger seat. His shoulder-length straight black hair was shiny and pulled back in a ponytail. His previously bloodshot eyes were clear, and his clothes were freshly laundered.

Jason extended his hand, and the two men shook.

"Where should we start?" Jason asked.

"Wasn't a team searching for some hunters over by Cibecue?"

"Yeah, but they didn't find anything over there."

"The people you're searching for will need a source of fresh water. Cibecue Creek is where I'd start if it was my search."

Jason had the same thought about water since visiting the old fire tower. A water source was nearby when Josh and Celeste accidentally ran into them. They were next to a tiny man-made pond the fire service put in decades ago when he found their black truck concealed in the woods. Accessible water deep in the forest was limited as Arizona neared the end of the June dry season. The rainy monsoon season would start soon, but until then, targeting sources of fresh water allowed them to narrow their search area.

Jason nodded. "Okay, I'll head towards Cibecue. Let me know the best place to start our search."

An hour later, Jason transitioned from a graded forest road to what he considered a path for off-road vehicles. Tarek guided him to the best place to park and transition to searching on foot.

Jason snagged his backpack with a full water bladder from his back seat and slung it over his back. He turned to Tarek and noticed he had a single bottle of water in his hand.

"Is that all you have?"

"Yeah. I don't need all that," Tarek replied, pointing to Jason's gear.

"It's pretty hot out here. Shouldn't you take more water?"

"I drank a lot of herbal tea this morning, so I'll be fine."

Jason didn't know enough about Tarek or his herbal tea regimen to argue with him. Before they departed, Jason looked him over and concluded that Tarek was only about five feet eight inches and one-hundred and fifty pounds if he had to carry his dehydrated ass out of the forest.

"I'll follow you," Jason said.

Tarek didn't move. He stood and stared at Jason. "Why does my cousin want me to help you? Is she your girlfriend?"

It was the first time Tarek had looked Jason in the eye since they met, and the question caught him like an unexpected slap. "Ah—um—we're friends and she's trying to help me find the people that killed my brother. Why?"

"She has a good heart."

Jason nodded. "I've only known her for a few weeks, but she seems like a good person. I'm grateful she is willing to help me."

Tarek studied Jason and then looked back to the ground. After ten seconds of silence, Jason asked, "Are you still willing to help me?"

"Yeah. I can help you find those people. I'll find their trail and lead you to them."

Jason was skeptical of Tarek's claim, but his red hot desire to find the cartel was too powerful to resist. He followed Tarek into the unpredictable and unforgiving forest.

Chapter 21

Two hours and four miles later, they arrived at the bank of Cibecue Creek. Jason removed his backpack and sat on a flat boulder in the shade. He opened a protein bar and took a bite while Tarek walked along the creek.

"Do you think you'll find their trail?" Jason asked.

"I'm following it now," Tarek replied without looking up.

"What?"

Jason jumped up and rushed toward the creek, but Tarek held his hand up to stop him.

"Wait. I'm trying to see how many men were here."

Jason looked at the same ground as Tarek but saw nothing that looked like a crowd of men had been there. Moments later, Tarek waded into the shallow creek and continued to examine the area. After ten minutes, Jason interrupted him.

"I don't see any sign of the cartel operating around here. What are you seeing that I'm not?"

Tarek looked up from the creek and waded back to the shore. He pointed to wild grasses growing ten feet up the bank. "You see how that patch of grass is lower than the grass around it?"

Jason squinted and tilted his head in the direction Tarek pointed. "I guess some of it is an inch or two lower than the rest."

"They placed something on that grass for a couple of days. It recovers within a day or two after rain but takes up to a week during the dry season. People were here in the past few days."

Tarek moved closer to the muddy bank. "See this flat rock?"

Jason looked at the rock about the size of a deck of cards and nodded.

"Someone flipped it over recently. It's in direct sun most of the day, but you can see the dark underside exposed compared to the lighter rocks around it. The sun bleaches rocks quickly this time of year, so that rock was also disturbed in the past few weeks. The prickly pear cactus next to you is another clue humans were here."

Jason looked down at the lime green cactus with a dozen areoles that looked like flat mittens without a thumb covered in spiny thorns. Blood-red buds the size of large grapes clung to the desert succulent.

"I don't see any broken pieces or missing thorns," Jason said.

"You see how the buds on the west section are slightly smaller than the other half?"

Jason bent over and looked closer. "It's not real obvious, but they are definitely a little smaller on this end."

"Those buds should be the same size or larger than the other side because this is their blooming season. They placed something large nearby that shaded the prickly pear during the high sun, so those buds are maturing up to a week behind the rest of the plant."

Jason gazed at the cactus and then over at Tarek. He would never have noticed any of the things Tarek found. Instead, Jason would have looked for disturbed soil or footprints and, without finding any, assumed the cartel was never in the area and kept walking.

"Could you tell how many men were here?"

"I don't know how many have been here, but I know which direction they traveled."

"Where?"

"I found a partial boot print in the mud heading downstream toward Cibecue Falls."

"Great. How long will it take for us to hike to Cibecue Falls?"

"Probably a couple of days."

"Days?"

"Yeah. It's close to thirty miles from here, and it gets more rugged as the creek drops into Lower Cibecue Canyon. They could have followed several tributaries into the creek near the falls."

"We don't have days. They could kill again anytime. I've rucked over thirty miles in a day, so if we push hard and limit our breaks, we can make it today. I have a water purifier and will share my water with you." Jason started downstream and expected Tarek to follow, but he didn't. "You coming?"

Tarek leaned against the trunk of a cottonwood tree. "Your problem is that you're in too much of a hurry. You want to solve a problem so it will disappear, and then you rush and miss many clues. The forest reveals her secrets if you slow down long enough to look, listen, and feel what she is telling you. Try it sometime, and you will see for yourself."

Jason was used to being called prepared and obsessive but too rushed was a first. He studied maps, memorized intel, and took meticulous notes before every mission. Jason turned away from the creek and moved away from the bank.

"I'm going to look around for more clues up here."

Steps into the canopy of trees near the creek, the temperature dropped ten degrees. It cooled down Jason's skin and anger. He needed a minute to regain his composure, so he walked twenty yards downstream parallel to the creek. Jason sat on the cool soil overlooking the creek and sipped water from his hydration pack, when he heard a noise that sounded like a branch snapping downstream. Crows called from the trees and Jason knew something spooked them. He unbuttoned his shirt to easily access his weapon and turned over into a prone position in one fluid motion. Jason low crawled through the thorny brush to gain a one-hundred-and-eighty-degree view of Cibecue Creek. He saw nothing when he arrived and lay motionless to listen for any new sounds. He pulled his binoculars out of his cargo pants and slowly looked up and down the creek.

Movement caught his eye, and his body stiffened. A person pushed through the undergrowth toward him, but Jason couldn't confirm whether the individual was a cartel member or had a weapon. He didn't look like the men he saw from the cartel, but that didn't mean he wasn't part of the murderous group. They were undisciplined, just like this guy, so he may have been out on patrol.

After a few seconds of deliberation, Jason determined he had to go back to Tarek and confront the man. He didn't have a plan beyond making initial contact, but the desire to know if the unidentified person was part of the cartel was too strong to resist.

Jason rushed back to the bank waving his arms. He motioned wildly for Tarek to come out of the water, but the former hunting guide stared back at Jason with a blank look on his face.

"Get out of the creek and get down!" Jason growled between gritted teeth.

Tarek didn't move, and Jason wished he'd never hired him. Any man or woman that wore a military uniform knew to seek cover when a threat appeared, but Tarek didn't budge. If it was the cartel, he'd get himself and Jason killed.

Jason took cover behind a cottonwood tree and opened his shirt to access his SIG Sauer P226 9mm pistol in his shoulder holster. Jason felt his pulse beating faster in his neck as the shuffling sounds from the man grew louder. He steadied himself to draw his weapon when the man cleared the dense band of trees and marched toward Tarek. He closed the gap between them in a few strides. Jason moved his right hand onto the pistol grip and inched over for a better firing angle when he saw the white logo with White Mountain Apache Tribe Game and Fish on his polo shirt.

Jason moved from the tree to behind a waist-high cactus so he wouldn't look suspicious hiding from the ranger.

"White Mountain Apache Tribe Game and Fish," the ranger announced.

The ranger strode down to Tarek, and they began talking. Jason exhaled, buttoned up his shirt, and walked over to join the conversation.

"What are you two doing out here?" the ranger asked.

Jason slammed his hands in his pockets and rocked back and forth on his heels. Now he regretted arguing with Tarek. He didn't want to go back to jail. This time, Jason was sure he wouldn't get out hours after arriving.

Tarek shot Jason a quick glance that he didn't know what to make of it.

"I said, what are you doing out here?" The ranger's tone contained hints of irritation in his second question.

"I'm helping scout the area for elk season," Tarek said.

"Are you a guide?"

"Just trying to help a friend bag a big bull this year."

"What's your name?"

"Tarek Dosala."

The ranger scribbled on a small notepad and turned to Jason. "Your name?"

Jason turned to Tarek and then back to the ranger. He swallowed hard. "Jason Mul—"

The ranger held up his hand to stop him. "Wait. Tarek, were you a guide for the trophy elk hunt five or six years ago?"

Tarek nodded.

"You helped my father-in-law take down a nine-hundred-pound bull with a nice 6x6 rack. He still talks about it."

"I remember. That was a good day," Tarek replied softly.

"You're one of the better guides out here, so I'm sure you'll help Jason be one of the lucky hunters this season."

"I hope so," Tarek said.

"Me too," Jason replied. He hoped his confirmation added more believability to the ruse.

"You two be careful out here. A father and his son are missing after scouting elk earlier this week. We still haven't found them, so let us know if you see them or anything that may help us find them."

Jason looked at Tarek from the corner of his eye to see if he would reveal their recent find.

"I haven't seen any signs of people out here, but I'll contact you if we do," Tarek replied.

"Thank you."

The ranger turned downstream until he vanished from view.

"That was close," Jason said.

Jason exhaled and let his cramping shoulders relax. The defensive anger vanished, and now Jason just wanted to get out of the forest and regroup. As he neared his truck, the gravity of their encounter hit him.

What if he had encountered two or three armed cartel members with AK-74s instead of a game and fish ranger? Would we have retreated? Would we still be alive?

A two-person team wasn't enough, even with Tarek's elite tracker skills and Jason's pararescue and SERE training. It would be impossible for the two of them to find a dozen men in a forest larger than several US states. They needed a force multiplier to hunt down the cartel. Jason and Tarek needed help soon before the cartel murdered again or vanished forever deeper into the forest.

CHAPTER 22

Jason turned up the air conditioner in his truck up to the maximum as he exited Show Low. He felt unusually warm even with the artic cool air blasting his bare arms. Jason had talked to Shanna on the phone every night since he opened up about Gaby, and now he was minutes away from picking her up for their first proper date.

Driving to pick up Shanna in Whiteriver added an hour to an already long drive, but Jason wanted to do it. She offered to meet him in Show Low, but he wanted to learn more about her. Shanna knew Jason's entire family and was aware of the most painful moments in his life, but he knew little about her.

Jason entered the town of 4,000 people on the Fort Apache Reservation for the third time in his life. He passed the Indian Health Service hospital complex on the north edge of town and then, a mile later, he passed the police department he'd visited during his two previous trips. Jason continued south and turned after the high school and before the only grocery store. He crept along the broken asphalt pavement in his truck, taking in the new sites. The modest homes reminded Jason of parts of Payson, but that changed once he turned at the T in the road. First, he noticed many residents stop and turn to watch the strange man in their neighborhood. Next, Jason observed block after block covered in identical-looking single-family homes. They were the same size, shape, and color. A concrete driveway led up to each garageless beige home with three windows and a white front door surrounded by a grass front yard. Some yards had chain-link fence dividers in various states of disrepair. Two blocks later, the homes' sizes, shapes, and colors changed slightly, but they gained the valuable addition of a carport to shade their vehicles. The color options expanded from one shade of brown to dark green, maroon, and white, giving the entire block a fresher look. Jason assumed a homebuilder came in and built multiple homes at a time with one model to keep costs down for the community with lower incomes than surrounding towns.

Jason pulled in front of one of the white carport homes and parked his truck. The sounds of children playing outside in front yards caught his attention when he opened his door. He exited his vehicle and turned around to appreciate the 360-degree views of the mountains surrounding the Whiteriver Valley. Every front and backyard on the block had a majestic mountain view.

Jason sauntered up the driveway to the front door. It had been nearly eight years since he had to knock on a door for a first date. He'd had his fair share of dates at the various bases he'd been stationed at, but he met the local ladies at clubs and bars. Either because of his crazy schedule, lack of interest, or both, Jason never got serious enough to visit the people he dated at their home. He was rusty in the dating scene, and Jason hoped that if he walked slow enough, Shanna might come out and spare him the uncomfortable feeling of meeting a new family for the first time. Shanna never appeared, so Jason stood on the concrete porch, took a deep breath, and tapped on the aluminum door. Half a minute later, a young male opened the door that Jason estimated was around twenty. He wore wire-rimmed glasses with his curly black hair tucked in a gold beanie. His thin frame was practically swimming inside his loose T-shirt with the letters NAU in gold over the navy-blue T-shirt. Jason concluded from his age and apparel that he was a student at Northern Arizona University.

"Hi, I'm Jason. I'm here for Shanna."

The college student smiled, nodded, and then walked away from the door.

"Shanna, some guy is at the door for you."

Jason stood by himself at the open front door, so he moved inside a few steps and shut the door behind him. He arrived in a family room that flowed into the kitchen. Jason saw long black hair with streaks of gray on a short woman standing at the stove with her back to him. He assumed it was Shanna's mom, but she never turned around.

A minute later, Shanna emerged from the hallway containing all three bedrooms and the only bathroom in the house. Jason smiled at the sight of his date and gave her a quick hug.

"Mama, this is my friend, Jason. We're going up to Show Low for dinner tonight, so I'll be home later."

The woman turned around with a scowl and shuffled over. She stood barely over five feet and wore a loose white top accented by a turquoise bead necklace with a black flowing skirt and boots. She maintained a sour look, looked Jason up and down, and then returned to the kitchen without saying a word. Shanna shrugged when Jason looked at her.

They found a simple burger joint with outdoor seating to take advantage of the pleasant temperatures after sunset. After dinner, they played cornhole against another couple.

After a toss, Jason turned to Shanna. "I don't think your mom likes me."

"She takes a while to warm up to new people."

"If looks could kill, I'd be in full cardiac arrest now."

Shanna didn't respond.

"Was that your brother in the NAU shirt?"

"Yeah. That's Kai. He'll be a senior this fall."

"That's cool. What about your dad? Was he home?"

Shanna focused on her beanbag and tossed it onto the rectangular platform with a hole cut out near the top twenty-seven feet away. "He died of a heart attack when I was fifteen."

"I'm sorry. That must have been hard on you at that age."

"It was, but it was even harder on my mom. She had to support my two brothers and me, so she went back to school to become a Licensed Practical Nurse. Fortunately, she got a job as an LPN right away at Whiteriver Indian Hospital, but times were still tight. I had to take care of my two brothers and still live at home today to help my mom out with the bills and the boys. Kai was easy. He's smart and driven, but the youngest, Evan, liked to push the limits with me, teachers, or anyone in authority. He has a good heart but lashed out for years after our dad passed. Nobody helped him manage the loss of a parent at seven years old, so that's one of the reasons I chose to become a victim and grief counselor. All of us had to grow up faster than—"

Shanna's voice cracked, and she stopped talking. She turned away, so Jason took a little extra time with his next toss.

"Are you still trying to find the cartel?" Shanna asked, changing the subject.

Jason tossed his bag through the hole.

"Tarek reached out to me, and he took me to some remote parts of the forest. Thank you for giving him my number."

"I'm glad he's helping, but I don't want either of you putting yourselves in danger," Shanna said.

"I won't let him get close enough to get hurt."

"The same goes for you."

Jason nodded.

Shanna turned, aimed, and tossed her bag through the hole to win the game. She raised her arms in victory, and Jason picked her up and spun her around. Inches separated their lips, but Shanna pulled away when he set her down.

Jason checked his watch. "I have to drive to Tucson tomorrow for my first reserve weekend, so I can't be too late tonight. How about a drink before I drive you home?"

"Sure," Shanna replied with a smile.

"I found a bar and grill online with a great outdoor patio in Pinetop. The reviews are great and it's right on the way to your house."

Shanna's smile disappeared. "Can we go somewhere else?"

"Um, I guess. Where do you want to go?"

Shanna turned her eyes skyward, and Jason could tell she was thinking. "You know what, let's go to that bar and grill you found online."

"Are you sure? You seem hesitant."

"Yeah, I want to go. I just don't want to stay too long though."

"No problem. We'll just have one drink, so we'll be in and out," Jason assured Shanna.

"Fine. Just one quick drink."

The outdoor patio was nearly full as residents from Phoenix flocked to the cooler climate of the White Mountains from the heat in the Valley of the Sun. They were lucky to find an open table near the entrance, so Jason jogged ahead to snag it for them. After they sat down and received their drinks, Shanna appeared to relax. She reached across the table and grabbed Jason's hand while he told her how he transitioned from full-time to the Air Force

Reserve. Jason began to share his story about his off-grid home when Shanna let go of his hand. Her face turned ashen, and her body stiffened. Jason looked over his shoulder and saw a man in his mid-twenties wearing jeans, boots, and a western-style shirt with the top half unbuttoned. He had a round face and long, straight black hair parted in the middle.

"Who's that?" Jason asked.

"That's my ex-boyfriend. He comes here all the time."

Jason felt his own muscles tighten every time Shanna looked over his shoulder.

"Hey, we don't have to stay here if he makes you uncomfortable."

"That's all right. We can leave after you finish your beer."

Jason saw Shanna's eyes rise as her ex stumbled to their table.

"Who's this?" the ex-boyfriend slurred.

"This is my friend, Jason."

"This is your new boyfriend? You're kidding, right?"

Shanna looked at Jason and started to say something, but the ex-boyfriend interrupted her.

"Let's go out to the parking lot. I want to talk."

"I don't think that's a good idea. You've had too much to drink, and I'm here with somebody else."

The ex-boyfriend's face hardened. "I said, let's go. I need to talk to you."

Shanna returned an obvious forced and fake smile. "Not tonight."

The ex-boyfriend stepped closer and grabbed Shanna's arm above the elbow. He yanked on it for a split second and Jason jumped up from his seat.

"Did you hear her? She said no!" Jason roared inches from his face. Nearby patrons rose and moved closer to break up the skirmish, while Shanna tugged on Jason's shirt near the small of his back.

"Let him go. I don't want any problems with him tonight."

"He won't take no for an answer from you, so I want to be sure he heard it loud and clear from me."

"Please, Jason. I don't like fighting. I just want to go home."

Jason didn't turn to face Shanna, but could tell by her voice she was upset, so he took a step back. The ex-boyfriend swayed from side to side, flashed a grin, and swung at Jason. He slid a step to his right and grabbed the ex's arm before his fist contacted Jason's chest. Jason secured his arm and used his momentum to spin him around until Jason was behind him with his right hand on the back of his head. He pushed forward and slammed the ex's face on the table. Silverware rattled and Shanna's water tipped over from the impact.

The former boyfriend straightened and looked like a toddler taking his first steps. He shook his head, wobbled over to a barstool, and leaned on it. The ex moved his fingers to examine the growing bump on his forehead. Shanna saw this and turned back to Jason.

"Why did you do that?"

"I don't like bullies," Jason replied. He was proud of his quick response and his restraint when he could have easily put the ex-boyfriend in the hospital.

"I want to go now," Shanna said. She grabbed her purse and turned toward the exit. Jason pulled cash from his wallet and tossed it on the table. He caught up with Shanna in the parking lot. Despite his six-inch height advantage, he could barely keep up with her determined march.

"Slow down."

Shanna slowed and Jason arrived at her side.

"I didn't mean to upset you, but I was taught to never let a man treat a lady like that."

Shanna stared back at Jason. "Can you please take me home now?"

"Okay, let's go."

Jason drove Shanna home and the only sound in the cab of Jason's truck was the white noise from the road until they reached Whiteriver. Jason broke the silence when they turned into Shanna's neighborhood.

"In case you didn't notice, I was only trying to help."

Shanna turned toward Jason. "I know you were, but it's how you helped that bothers me. I could have handled the situation without violence, but you slammed his head into the table two seconds after you stood. You didn't have to do that."

Jason rubbed the back of his neck. "I saw the way he grabbed your arm. Guys like that won't stop until someone stands up to them."

"You just don't get it. For you, it's about punching first and asking questions later."

Jason shook his head. "Not true. Guys like that only understand one language. Good people have to meet their aggression with greater force. Fortunately, I speak that language well."

"That's the problem, Jason. You think using force is the only response to every problem."

Jason pulled in front of Shanna's house and parked. He turned toward Shanna, and she scooted closer to the passenger door. Jason tried to make eye contact, but Shanna wouldn't look at him.

"If you let aggression go unchecked, it grows. I understand you don't like fighting, but sometimes violence is the only option to stop violence. That's why I do what I do."

Shanna opened the door and slid out. "Thank you for the ride home," she said as she shut the door behind her.

Jason watched her stomp up the concrete steps to her front porch and fumble with her keys. The door opened and shut quickly behind her. Jason stared at the closed door for several seconds wondering if he'd ever see Shanna again.

CHAPTER 23

The Show Low grocery store cashier slid a twenty-pound bag of dried beans, ten pounds of rice, and canned chicken across the scanner. Victor Romero yanked the beans and rice off the conveyor.

"Let me help you with that."

He put them in his cart and flashed a bright smile at the young lady next to the cash register. She returned the smile as her cheeks flushed a dull pink. Victor had visited the same grocery store for food and supplies over the past three months. He always selected a lane staffed by one of the young twenty-something female employees. While they scanned his groceries, Victor complimented them and tried to be funny. He spoke with a heavy accent, but his English was good enough to evoke giggles and shy smiles from all the cashiers. Although he was married, Victor loved to flirt, which was a much-needed ego boost for the former ladies' man while away from home. It was also an excellent tactic to divert suspicion of his purchases and presence in a new community.

Victor pushed his cart to the pickup truck he'd parked several rows away from the other vehicles in the parking lot. His top two lieutenants waited for him in the back cab, obscured by dark tinted windows. Victor always brought along two men and had them duck down in the backseat to look like he was driving alone. He didn't want to attract unnecessary attention. Cartels from El Salvador tended to stand out in small towns in the United States.

The trio left the grocery store parking lot and drove to the city park several blocks away. The heavily wooded park had an area cut out for baseball and soccer fields as well as dozens of picnic tables arranged under dark green metal canopies throughout the park. Once again, Victor selected a parking spot as far as possible from any other vehicles, which was an easy task at three in the afternoon on a warm day. Once he parked, the two backseat passengers left the truck to find a table in the shade to give Victor maximum privacy for his weekly call to El Jaguar.

Victor dialed Orlando's number from heart on the burner phone he'd use for this single call. His boss answered and immediately launched into important business.

"How much QE2 do you have in your possession?" El Jaguar asked. He referred to the Canadian twenty-dollar note featuring a portrait of Queen Elizabeth II.

Victor's forehead wrinkled as he pondered the question. "I would have to count it all to be sure, but close to half a million."

"Good. I need you to leave tonight and bring it home."

"My plan is to stay another month before I return. We're selling more than I expected up here. Can I bring it at the end of June?"

"No!" the cartel boss roared. "We need it now. You can return to your current operation as soon as I have all the queens."

Victor sensed Orlando's anger and didn't want to throw his boss into a rage, but he had to know why he was being pulled away from his successful operation.

"Okay, I will bring it. Why so urgent?"

The phone was quiet for several seconds. Victor could hear El Jaguar breathing heavily into the phone, so he waited for a response.

"Because they stole our large shipment to our friend in Texas outside Texcalco," El Jaguar snapped.

Nothing more needed to be said. Texcalco was a choke point along La Palma's preferred smuggling route sixty miles east of Acapulco, Mexico. Rival Mexican drug cartels had harassed and stolen La Palma shipments countless times over the years. La Palma was too small to retaliate against an established Mexican cartel, so they utilized speed and deception along alternate routes to avoid losing their cargo. The alternate routes cost more money and took more time, and after six months, they thought the more direct route might be safe to use again. The substantial La Palma shipment ran into the same fate near Texcalco. The material and monetary losses were immense, and the shipment was destined for their largest US buyer in Texas, compounding the problem. It was another reason Victor was in Arizona.

Victor knew his boss was likely spitting on the phone in anger. A pit grew in his stomach as he knew they'd still have to produce and ship hundreds of kilos of fentanyl blotters while he was away. Victor had visions of El Jaguar praising him for his success in the United States, but now the stolen shipment would overshadow all his positive contributions in Arizona. Disobeying the cartel boss was not an option, so Victor chose to travel back to El Salvador as fast as possible.

"I'll be there in a couple of days with all the queens."

Victor hung up and snapped the flip phone in half. He tossed it into the trash and waved for his men to return to the truck. Victor was quiet while driving to the other side of town to the only independent gas station in Show Low. The seventies-era gas station still used vintage pumps, and the owner refused to take credit cards. With no payment at the pump, customers had to go inside to prepay, which meant the station was never busy, and the station owners did not need cameras to monitor the pumps. It was the ideal location to hold a quick, secretive meeting with his local contact.

Right on schedule, Victor's contact parked his car on the opposite side of the pump. They met twenty minutes later each week to prevent the appearance of a pattern. Victor and his contact began fueling their vehicles and appeared engaged in neighborly banter typical in small towns. The local ran his fingers over the top of the pump until he closed his hand into a fist. He secured a key and discretely put it in his shirt pocket. Two minutes after they started whispering updates, they finished fueling and parted ways.

The local contact shared new information with Victor that should have pleased him, but his sudden return trip to El Salvador spoiled his mood. He considered several methods to maintain a productive Arizona operation while in El Salvador. Victor's mind was elsewhere when he passed a popular fast food chain off the main highway in Show Low.

One of the men in the back cab noticed the error and tapped Victor on the shoulder.

"Are we going to get food?

"Oh, yeah. I'll turn around."

Victor did a U-turn and returned to the fast food chain. They drove through twice to get enough cheeseburgers and fries for all twelve men. Victor was always careful not to tip off the size of his crew while in town.

The hearty meal was a treat Victor provided his men when he went into Show Low for his weekly check-ins. He was less interested in the food but reveled in the only opportunity to escape the forest each week. Although he grew up in poverty and lived on the streets as a teenager, he'd enjoyed the finer things in life since joining the La Palma cartel. He owned a mansion by El Salvador standards and missed the simple pleasures of running water, flushable toilets, and a soft bed. Victor was not a fan of camping.

Once he had food in his stomach, his mind returned to his plans for the operation while he was out. After some thought, he decided to hedge his bets in case one of the crews was captured. He shared his plan with his men as they left Show Low.

"I have to make a quick trip back to La Palma for about a week, so I need to split up operations while I'm gone. Carlos, take half the equipment and move twenty miles farther south down near Cibecue Falls on the reservation. Rafael, you take the other half and move east of a town called Heber. There's a heavily wooded area a few miles off Highway 260 called Wildcat Springs. Find a place away from any trails and set up your operation, but don't go any farther than Wildcat Springs. We need to stay in Navajo County. Build up inventory and we'll combine operations when I return."

Victor repeated the plan to the rest of the men at the camp about his short trip to El Salvador. Then, under the full moon later that night, Victor departed. He returned to the spot one hundred and twenty miles west of El Paso, Texas, and snuck across the border on foot with a suitcase full of Canadian currency. As the sun rose above the mountains in the east, he arrived at the cluster of farmhouses where he'd prearranged for transportation back to El Salvador.

Victor planned to return as soon as possible to ensure his men continued to produce and ship enough fentanyl to make up some of the losses of the stolen shipment. He also wanted to act on the new information his local contact shared across the gas pump. It was a heist that could launch Victor to the top ranks of the La Palma cartel. He shook with excitement in the back of the truck at the career-defining opportunity that awaited him on his return to Arizona.

CHAPTER 24

Jason arrived at his new Air Force Reserve squadron on Davis-Monthan Air Force Base in Tucson, Arizona late Friday night. He parked near a sign containing a Pegasus image with 943rd Rescue Group written in a scroll underneath the winged horse logo. Jason wanted to be on time for his zero seven hundred formation on Saturday, so he completed the three-hour drive the day before. As the new PJ in the unit, he wanted to be sure he brought his A-game on day one.

Saturday morning, once he'd buttoned up his finely pressed airman battle uniform, he headed to the assembly area for morning formation. He caught a glimpse of himself in the mirror, stopped, and returned to the reflection. Jason adjusted his collar and nodded at the man in the mirror. This was the longest he'd gone without wearing a US Air Force-issued uniform, and it felt great to don his ABUs again. He practically floated to the assembly room.

For two days, Jason and his fellow PJs in the 943rd conducted training like he'd done for years. The camaraderie was like a cool drink on a scorching afternoon. He'd forgotten how much he missed it. After final formation Sunday, Jason bumped into Clay Landry from the Oregon water rescue mission in the locker room.

"You survived your first weekend," Clay said with a slap on the back.

"Yeah, getting back out there with the guys felt good. I wish I didn't have to wait an entire month."

"The squadron usually has opportunities for work between weekend drills. I come in sometimes since I'm still looking for full-time work around here."

"I saw you working with the unmanned aerial vehicles. You're a real pro with those UAVs. You should find a job doing that for a living."

Clay laughed. "It took hundreds of hours to fly like that. When I'm not playing with drones here on drill weekends or at home, the dream is to land a job doing something with UAVs."

It was Jason's turn to pat Clay on the back. "I've got to get rolling. I'll see you next time."

Jason left the locker room and climbed inside his truck, but instead of leaving, he waited. He'd learned new information about Clay that intrigued him. Because of his training in Special Reconnaissance, Clay was an expert operator of small UAVs. Drones were the best way to cost-effectively search a large area, and that was what Jason needed to find the cartel. Plus, he found out that Clay was not working full-time, so he might have time to come up to Northern Arizona for a day or two to help in the search.

Jason rolled down his window and intercepted Clay as he strutted toward his black lifted pickup truck.

"You got a minute?"

Clay looked around as if he was checking to be sure he wasn't being followed. "Sure."

"Hop in. I want to buy you a beer for helping me in Oregon."

Clay perked up and smiled. "I have a rule to never turn down a free beer."

Ten minutes later, Jason and Clay sat at a high-top table in the bar area of a local Mexican restaurant. They caught up on past deployments and assignments until the server brought them each a plate of tacos and a beer.

Clay inhaled a carne asada taco and downed a pint of beer before Jason finished his ancho chili shrimp taco. Jason concluded it was best to eat and then talk. Once they'd both finished four tacos and two beers, Jason leaned toward Clay.

"How long have you lived in Tucson?" Jason asked.

"Four months now. After my last deployment, I thought about moving back home to Louisiana, but I wanted to try Arizona and this squadron."

"Louisiana? What part?"

"I'm from Cajun country. I grew up outside Alexandria in Bentley. It's a really small town. Are you familiar with Louisiana?" Clay asked.

"I've been to Barksdale Air Base outside Shreveport once and New Orleans a couple of times, but that's it. Heat hits different here than Louisiana, doesn't it?"

Clay whistled. "You ain't lying about that. It's an oven here, but it's a sauna back home. I'll take this over the hurricanes and mosquitoes, though."

Jason nodded. "You mentioned you like to play with UAVs between drill weekends. Do you have personal drones here in Arizona?"

"I have four in my apartment. What size do you want?"

"I'm not looking for me, but I want to see if I can hire you for a day or two to come up and help me look around the forest."

"Look around the forest? What for?"

Jason didn't want to get into his personal story, but he had to be honest with Clay. He exhaled and spoke just above a whisper. "I'm looking for someone."

"They've got dating sites for that," Clay said with a snort. "You don't need a drone to find yourself a honey."

"Okay, let me rephrase that. I'm looking for the people that killed my brother. They're hiding in millions of acres of forest east of Payson. That's why I need a drone."

The smile on Clay's face vanished. He pulled the straw out of his mouth. "Are you serious?"

Jason's unblinking stare answered Clay's question.

Clay put the straw back in his mouth. "I'm in."

"It's a drug cartel from Central America."

"Still in, and I'll bring my friends HK and Glock with me."

Jason smiled and filled Clay in on the rest of the details. They agreed to meet at Jason's house in Payson in two days to start the search.

Two days later as promised, Clay pulled into the Mulder family driveway and parked his truck. Jason strolled outside to greet him. He extended his hand, but instead of shaking it, the six-foot-four Cajun pulled Jason in for a hug.

"Thanks for inviting me up here. It's beautiful."

"I'm glad you could come up here for a few days."

Jason reached into the truck's bed and pulled out Clay's overnight bag. "Follow me. I'll introduce you to my family and show you where you'll be staying for the next couple of nights."

Once inside, Jason introduced Clay to his mom, dad, and Noah. He led Clay down the hallway past Josh's bedroom, which had remained untouched since the day he died, until he reached Kevin's former bedroom. The oldest brother's bedroom had become the default guest room for visitors since he moved out seven years ago.

They both geared up and secured water and snacks for the journey. Jason offered to drive, but Clay insisted since his drones were already in a secure Pelican case bolted into the bed of his truck. The duo departed Payson and drove to the Fort Apache Reservation south of Cibecue to start their aerial search. Jason got lost in the maze of forest roads and unmarked off-road vehicle trails. The last time he was in the area, Tarek helped guide him to the optimal location. Despite Jason's best efforts, they parked a few miles north of where Tarek and Jason found activity from the cartel.

Clay and Jason hiked a half mile until they reached a bluff overlooking Cibecue Creek. Fifteen minutes after they arrived, the UAV, guided by Clay, lifted off above the trees.

"I usually wear the goggles, but I also want you to see," Clay said. He turned the tablet slightly so Jason could view the image beaming from the drone's camera.

It took Jason a few seconds to adjust his eyes to the images on the screen, but he finally recognized the landscape forty feet below the camera.

The drone returned over their heads after its first pass across the creek.

"Based on what we discussed on the way here, I'll search two-hundred yards on each side of the creek in a grid so we don't miss anything. I'll start here and go south for as long as the battery will allow."

The two looked from the screen to the sky for the next ninety minutes as the UAVs scanned the forest. Clay covered a grid over four square miles with two of his drones. He finished packing the second drone away when the sky darkened, and the wind picked up. The former cotton-like white puffy clouds turned ominous as they grew taller and darker until they blocked the sun.

"Can you get the third drone up?" Jason asked.

Clay looked at the massive cumulus cloud billowing up over 40,000 feet into the air. A gentle rumble of thunder could be felt after flashes of lightning lit up the graphite gray clouds. It was the start of monsoon season in Arizona. Although Clay had never experienced a monsoon storm personally, he had heard about the destructive lightning, flash flooding, and strong winds accompanying a monsoon storm.

"Not in this weather. It's borderline too windy now, and it looks like it will get worse. Let's pack up and get out of here before we get caught in the storm. I've heard they can get pretty nasty."

They hiked back to Clay's truck and were back on paved Highway 260 for less than a minute when a torrent of rain engulfed their vehicle.

"Whoa, doggie, that was close. You sure know how to make someone from Louisiana feel right at home," Clay bellowed.

He flipped his windshield wipers to the highest speed. They were quiet for the next ten minutes while Clay navigated their way through the wind-whipped rain. Then it stopped as fast as it started.

Clay looked up at the blue sky. "Man, you've got some wild storms here."

Jason felt Clay look over at him for a response, but he didn't have one. Instead, he focused on their failed mission and was mentally devising a plan to improve their next search. Clay must have noticed Jason's mind wasn't on the weather.

"I know we didn't get as much as you wanted today, but I hope it was helpful."

"Unfortunately, we searched a place we already know the cartel has left, but that's not your fault, it's mine. I should have had Tarek come with us to make sure we find the best areas to search. I won't make that mistake again."

Chapter 25

The next morning, Clay and Jason joined Philip, Celeste, and Noah for breakfast. They drank coffee and gobbled up pounds of bacon and eggs.

Celeste attempted to stand up with her plate in her hand but fell back into her chair. All three Mulder men leaped to their feet to help, but Celeste stopped them.

"I can get it. My left leg is still a little shaky. I thought it would be better by now."

"You're doing great, Mom. A broken femur is a serious injury that takes months to fully heal," Jason interjected. "We're all here to help if you need it, so just say the word."

"I know you are. My doctor told me not to baby it, so I need to do as much as I can by myself."

The four men sat and watched Celeste slowly rise from the table and carry her plate to the stovetop, where she spooned herself another serving of eggs. Jason moved to the edge of his seat to spring into action if needed, but it wasn't necessary. It pained him to see his mom struggle for eight weeks to recover from the accident.

"Where are you guys going today?" Noah asked.

"We're going out to play with Clay's drones for a while," Jason replied. This was code for sneaking onto the reservation to search for Josh's killers, which Jason assumed Noah understood.

"You boys be careful out there. There are some bad people hanging out in the forest right now," Phillip replied. It was apparent that Jason was a better PJ than a spy because his sophisticated code language fooled nobody.

"Too bad I have to work today, or I could bring the new drone with the infrared cameras," Noah chirped.

"Clay is a pro UAV operator. Can we take it?

"I can't let that thing out of my sight, but I can go with you sometime."

Clay smiled approvingly. "It's a date."

Jason and Clay left Payson and swung by Whiteriver to pick up Tarek. He was waiting in his front yard when Clay's truck pulled into the driveway. Tarek climbed in and shook hands with Clay. He moved to the middle of the backseat to guide Clay to a site five miles south of where they last found evidence of the cartel.

They reached a dead end on the sparsely used trail and parked.

"I would never have found this place," Jason said.

"None of these trails are on maps, and they are barely visible on a satellite image of the area. I only know them from my time as a Hot Shot. We fought a large fire north of here five or six years ago."

"Where are we now?"

"We are getting closer to Cibecue Falls. A lot of people visit the area below the falls during the summer months, so I doubt the cartel would go south of there if they don't want to be detected. The area above the falls is secluded, with deep canyons and thick stands of trees, so there are plenty of areas to hide. We should focus our search here."

Each man carried a drone, and they hiked for twenty minutes to a plateau devoid of tall trees. It provided the perfect base to launch the drones and keep a visual on them while they scanned the banks of Cibecue Creek.

"Stand back," Clay ordered as he launched the first drone. The three men looked back and forth at the screen and the drone hovering hundreds of feet over the canyon. He resumed his grid-like search of the area south of the starting point until a beep indicated the battery level was getting low. They did the same with the second and third drones, covering every inch of the vast canyon above Cibecue Falls.

Jason grew more frustrated with each unsuccessful pass of the drone and stepped back from the tablet. "I can't stare at the screen any longer."

This allowed Tarek to get closer to the screen, and minutes later, he tapped Clay on the shoulder.

"Can you go back a little and go lower?"

"Sure. Let me know when to stop."

"Right there. Now get closer to the ground."

Clay dropped the elevation of the drone and moved his face closer to the screen. "I don't see anything down there. What are you seeing?

Jason smiled at the education he assumed Clay was about to receive.

Tarek put his hand up. "Hold it right there."

Clay pinched his nose and scratched his temple. Jason recognized the signs of confusion so he moved back to the group and stood behind Tarek.

"What do you see, Tarek?" Jason asked.

"They were here recently."

Clay tilted his head and squinted at the screen. "What in the hell are you seeing that I'm not?"

"See that grass over there that's pushed down in the middle? It looks the same shape as those small collapsible shovels campers and hunters use."

Clay stared at the screen. "Okay, I guess that could be a shovel, but it could also be a small boulder or anything. So, how do you know they've been here recently?"

"Go lower," Tarek commanded.

Clay moved the drone down until it hovered ten feet above the bank.

"Do you see that round puddle a few steps away from the creek?"

"Yeah, I see it," Clay replied. A hint of irritation crept into his voice.

"That's not natural. They must need drinking water, so someone dug a seep well to gather drinkable water."

"Yeah, yeah. I can see it now. That hole is almost a perfect circle, so it had to be dug with a shovel or tool. How can you tell it's new?"

"I don't think it's new because the dirt around the well is dry, but they used it recently because the water is murky with sediment and the level is down a few inches."

"I see now. If that well was left alone for a couple of days, the water would be clear and near the top."

"Exactly," Tarek replied.

"How long ago do you think they last used it?

"That's hard to say. Less than twenty-four hours, for sure. Probably in the last six to seven hours."

Jason looked over the canyon. "They're probably hiding in a dense cluster of trees up and away from the creek."

"I agree," Tarek confirmed.

The drone beeped.

"Sorry, guys. I've got to bring her back now, and that's all the battery we have for today."

The three men returned to the truck. They dropped Tarek off at his home in Whiteriver and continued to Show Low.

"Let me fill up your tank, Clay. I really appreciate you driving these past two days."

"You don't need to do that. I love this stuff. It's fun searching for these cartel characters."

"Yes, I do. Pull in right here."

Jason jumped out, inserted his credit card, and began pumping gas. He noticed the SUV on the other side of the pump had a Navajo County Sheriff's Office emblem on the side, so he took a few steps to see if he recognized the driver. It was Deputy Jarvis, so Jason stepped to the other side of the pump.

"Hi, Deputy. It's Jason Mulder. We met at the station a few weeks ago about my brother."

The deputy stared at Jason for a couple of seconds and then smiled. "Oh, yeah, I remember. You're one of the three brothers that came in. How's it going?"

"It's going okay. I may have some new information to share about the location of my brother's killers in the near future. I don't want to say anything until I am 100% positive it's them, but I expect to have that confirmation soon."

The smile on the deputy's face vanished, and his eyes turned cold.

"You need to leave that to law enforcement. That's a good way to get yourself killed."

Jason was laser focused on bringing the cartel to justice and mistakenly thought the deputy would be happy to receive a lead that could solve a crime. It was clear the deputy did not see Jason's information from his personal investigation as a positive development. Jason was at a loss for words. Before Jason found his voice, the deputy's pump clicked off.

"Sorry I can't stick around and chat, but you shouldn't be looking for any criminals in the forest. It's dangerous out there."

Jason watched the deputy speed out of the gas station lot and finished filling Clay's tank. He got back into the truck confused by the deputy's response. Jason understood he wouldn't want civilians to get injured trying to solve a crime, but he reacted overly negative at the potential good news.

"It's past dinner time, and I'm starving. Can we grab something to eat?" Clay asked. "I'm not one of you lean muscle PJs that need to watch your figure. I need my calories."

Jason snapped his attention from Deputy Jarvis to Clay. "Yeah, there are several restaurants up ahead."

"Where do you want to go?"

"I don't care. You pick the place, and I'll buy."

Minutes later, Clay perked up in the driver's seat when the fast food worker delivered a bag of four burgers and two fries through the drive-through window. Clay opened the bag, put his face inside, and inhaled.

He looked over to the teenage girl in the drive-through window that handed him the bag.

"Thank you for saving my life."

Clay handed Jason a burger and fries. He drove forward to exit the drive-through lane when a white truck left the highway and sped into the parking lot. Clay braked hard to stop one or two feet from a collision with the speeding vehicle. Jason noticed four Hispanic males in their twenties in the truck. The passenger stared Jason down while Clay yelled out the window. "Where's the fire?"

The passenger said something to the driver, and they backed up and pulled around Clay. Once they passed, Clay pulled onto the highway towards Payson.

"Stop! I think I know one of those guys," Jason shouted.

Clay pulled into an open parking spot. "You know those guys?"

"I saw that guy in the passenger seat somewhere recently." Jason stared straight ahead out of the windshield. Seconds later, he shouted. "He was one of the men that shot Sergeant Spencer!"

"What?"

"I remember that face. He came up behind their leader after they shot Sergeant Spencer from the White Mountain Apache Police Department. He's part of the cartel. Where did they go?"

"They're in line for the drive-through."

"Should we call the DEA or the local sheriff?" Clay asked.

Jason thought about the reaction from the NCSO deputy and concluded he needed more concrete evidence before he involved law enforcement again.

"I'm 90% sure that was the guy in the forest, but I want to be 100% positive before I call the sheriff. Let's move to the bank parking lot next door. Then, we can follow them when they leave, and maybe they'll lead us to the entire operation."

Clay pulled his truck into the back of the bank parking lot, so they could see all the vehicles leaving the fast food restaurant but were out of view from the white truck. Five minutes later, the white truck pulled onto Highway 260 and headed east toward Payson.

"Follow them, but not too close," Jason said.

"Did you forget what I do in the Air Force? Special Reconnaissance? I've got this."

Clay remained a quarter mile behind the white truck through town and stayed behind several cars on the open highway. The sun dropped on the horizon, so Jason kept an eye on the distinctive taillights of the pickup truck. Forty-five minutes after they started following the white truck, it suddenly pulled over onto the shoulder of the highway.

Jason was sure the men realized they were being followed. "Keep going!"

They passed the white truck, and Jason spotted a narrow forest road that he'd never noticed before in the one-hundred-plus times he'd passed through the area. He suspected that was where they were going.

Clay drove another two miles, turned around, and returned to the area where the white truck had pulled over. It was nowhere to be found.

"They had to go this way. Should we follow them down this road?" Clay asked.

It was almost dark, so Jason followed the beam of the headlights onto the narrow dirt path surrounded by pine trees standing tall three to four stories into the air. He knew the area was sparsely populated and secluded. Ideal conditions for a cartel to hide, but also perfect conditions for an ambush.

"Did you bring any weapons?"

Clay pointed to the glove box. "I never leave home without my Glock, but I left my rifles at home. What about you?"

Jason opened his shirt to expose the SIG Sauer in his shoulder holster.

"Nice," Clay replied with a wide grin.

Jason removed Clay's 9-millimeter Glock from the glove box and handed it to him. "If we go, we need to be prepared to use these."

"I'm always prepared," Clay replied.

Jason stared into the black forest, welcoming the adrenaline forming in his gut like soldiers lining up on the front line. He verified he had a round in the chamber and tightened his belt. "I'm ready."

Clay removed the straw from his mouth. "Let's go."

Jason understood the importance of Clay's response when the plastic straw temporarily left its home between his lips. The sight of the straw outside his oral cavity was the unspoken exclamation point for anything Clay said or did.

Jason turned his attention toward the dirt road that disappeared into the forest as they began rolling forward.

CHAPTER 26

The truck crept into the forest and stopped after a hundred yards. Clay turned off the headlights and turned to Jason. "We'll let our eyes adjust to the dark. Then, once we're ready, I'll drive slow as possible and only use the parking brake so we don't light up the forest."

Their eyes adjusted to the moonless night five minutes after they killed the headlights. Millions of stars, obscured only by a few lingering clouds, provided enough light to move through the forest.

Clay whispered to Jason. "What I wouldn't give to have our night vision goggles right now."

"That'd be ideal, but I doubt those cartel pricks have any light discipline. Let's use that to our advantage."

Clay took his foot off the brake and let the truck inch forward a couple of miles an hour at idle speed. Twenty minutes later, Jason slapped Clay on the shoulder and pointed at ten o'clock.

"I saw a flash of white light."

Clay switched to neutral, slowed to a crawl and then applied the parking brake to stop without creating a noticeable red glow in the dark forest. The truck windows were down, so they both listened and focused their gaze to the left of the hood. They didn't see or hear anything for another five or six minutes until a flame flickered for a few seconds. In the dark of night, it seemed to light up the entire forest. Jason chuckled at the thought that the cartel members couldn't resist smoking, even if it meant giving their position away.

Clay disabled the dome light before opening the door, and they slipped out undetected.

Standing behind the rear tailgate, Clay slid his Glock into his waistband. Jason started into the forest with Clay following silently ten feet behind him. Their footfalls were concealed under the cover of thousands of insects serenading their mates on the balmy summer night. They continued in the direction of the light until Jason put his fist in the air. They both dropped to a knee and observed the area. Jason heard voices and saw cell phones illuminate the faces of several men. He moved back to Clay and knelt beside him.

He leaned in within a few inches of Clay's ear and whispered, "I count four or five of them.

Although they followed the cartel members from Show Low and saw them in the woods with his own eyes, Jason was surprised to find them so quickly. The armed Central Americans had been elusive up to this point, almost as if they had received advanced notice that somebody was coming. Now they were easy to find. A little too easy.

"I see weapons, but I don't see anybody on security," Jason whispered.

Clay chambered a round. "So how do you want to do this?"

Jason watched the men huddled together around a phone laughing. They could be the same people that drove his mom and Josh off the road. A quick flash of revenge made Jason want to rush ahead shooting to make them pay for what they did to Josh, but the sensible side of Jason's brain kicked in. Calling the police with adequate resources to ensure the men were captured and arrested was the proper call.

"We need to go back and call this in."

Clay nodded.

Jason couldn't take his eyes off the men. Justice for Josh was close enough to taste. The cool satisfaction of capturing or killing the people that murdered Josh was difficult to resist.

A cartel member moving away from the group caught Jason's attention. He put his hand on Clay's shoulder, pushed him down, and motioned toward a cartel member walking in their direction.

Jason slowly lowered himself until his chest was on the cool forest floor. He locked his eyes on the silhouette moving toward them. The man stopped, unslung his rifle, and moved it to the ready position in front of him. He stepped carefully from the main camp area into the underbrush and stopped forty feet away from Jason and Clay. They breathed slowly as they watched the cartel member scan the woods and stop. He looked right at Jason and took another step toward him. Jason reached into his holster and removed his SIG Sauer P226. He'd fire if the cartel member got any closer. Hesitating too long could cost Jason and Clay their lives.

The other cartel members laughed in unison as they watched a video on a cell phone, and that distracted the man staring at Jason. He turned slowly and rejoined the group.

Clay and Jason remained motionless for another minute. Jason waved for Clay to follow him, and they left as quietly as possible.

Back at the truck, Jason whispered to Clay, "That was close. We better call now."

Jason retrieved his cell phone from the glove box. It had a weak signal, so he called the Navajo County Sheriff dispatcher and asked to be connected to Detective Caldwell. When she said he didn't pick up his cell phone, Jason asked for Deputy Jarvis and then Sheriff Kellerman. Nobody Jason knew at NCSO was available, so he shared the GPS coordinates from his Casio Pro Tech watch with the dispatcher. Jason hung up, and they waited. He checked the time and expected it would take an hour for the Navajo County Sheriff's Office strike team to reach the county's western edge. Eleven minutes after Jason hung up, three sets of headlights appeared on the fire road behind Jason and Clay, and they were coming fast.

"Oh, shit. The rest of the cartel is coming back! Into the woods."

Clay went left and Jason went right into the forest. Three black Chevy Suburban SUVs halted behind Clay's truck a minute later, blocking their progress on the forest road. Four men jumped out of the front vehicle and moved tactically toward the truck. Jason could see they all had rifles in their silhouettes, highlighted by the headlights.

Then Jason heard the unmistakable sound of a helicopter approaching. He looked up and saw a spotlight streaking across the treetops until it hovered over Clay's truck. Jason saw three bold capital letters in yellow across the back of the people in black uniforms around Clay's truck. It was the DEA.

Jason couldn't believe they got there so fast but was elated to see them. He put his SIG Sauer back in the holster and walked towards the DEA special agents.

The agents didn't hear Jason coming over the sound of the helicopter overhead, and he didn't want to surprise a bunch of DEA special agents holding weapons and expecting to encounter a Central American drug cartel.

"Friendly approaching," Jason shouted.

He was within twenty feet and didn't know what else to say, but it seemed like the best option. It got their attention. Jason stopped and put his hands high in the air when the DEA special agents turned and pointed their rifles at him.

"I'm the one who called it in. Can I approach and show you exactly where they are?"

The agents kept their weapons pointed at Jason.

"Turn around, keep your hands in the air and back up to us nice and slow," one of the special agents commanded.

Jason backed up, and thirty seconds later, he felt handcuffs go over one wrist while they pulled down both arms behind his back. They slapped cuffs over his other wrist and a man with his face covered stepped forward while the others kept their weapons trained on Jason. "Who are you, and what are you doing out here?"

"I'm Jason Mulder, and I called the cartel location into the Navajo County Sheriff. You can check with special agent Holland. He knows I've been tracking the cartel."

The special agent holding Jason by the arm whispered something to another agent, and everyone stood in place as the helicopter moved its spotlight from Clay's truck farther down the fire road. Two minutes later, another special agent arrived. "I talked to Holland. This guy fits the description and he said he's good. You can uncuff him."

Jason felt the cuffs unleash their grip from his wrists, and he turned around to face a half dozen DEA special agents ready for an ambush.

"They were over there about a half click away twenty minutes ago. I observed four or five of them and they're all armed." Jason pointed in the direction they came from earlier.

"I have another guy with me. I'm going to call him in, so you know everyone else out there is a bad guy."

"Call your guy in and stay by your truck."

Jason waved his finger in a circular motion above his head, and Clay emerged from the woods. They stood by Clay's truck while the DEA special agents fanned out and slipped through the forest like lions on a hunt. The helicopter circled overhead for what seemed like an eternity. Then several pops came from the direction of the cartel operation. Jason thought it sounded like the report from a Kalashnikov rifle, but couldn't be sure over the beat of the helicopter rotors. Clay and Jason scrambled to the other side of the truck to avoid being struck by gunfire. Jason hated sitting on the sidelines during the sting but knew he didn't have the gear or the right weapons to take on a cartel. He figured he could help anyone injured or shot and that made him feel better about not helping with the sting.

Half an hour after the agents entered the forest, the first cartel member restrained with zip cuffs appeared on the dirt path. The DEA special agent made the cartel member kneel in front of the first Suburban.

"They tried to run, but mostly stuck together so we got five. Get transport out here ASAP," one of the special agents yelled to another.

"All clear?" a masked special agent asked.

"Yeah, we got them all. All clear."

Jason heard the news, so he stood and walked to the other special agents exiting the woods. Soon, the headlights illuminated five kneeling cartel members.

"Did you get all of them?" Jason asked.

The special agent nodded.

"I thought there would be more," Jason said.

"We spotted five on our approach. They ran but didn't scatter like most do. One of them shot at the helicopter and that's when we swooped in. Not the brightest drug runners we've encountered."

A special agent took a statement from Jason and Clay while they waited for the transport vehicle to arrive. An hour after the DEA arrived on the scene, they left with the cartel members, and the forest was dark and eerily quiet again.

Jason was silent while Clay drove back to Payson. Instead of feeling a sense of accomplishment for capturing the cartel, his gut felt like it was trying to digest a prickly cactus. The cartel was too easy to find, the DEA arrived too fast, and then they were easy to capture. Nothing about the sting felt right.

CHAPTER 27

Jason sat silently in the kitchen drinking coffee as the shadows of pine trees receded like the tide, bathing the Mulder family home in sunlight. Halfway through his first cup, Clay shuffled into the kitchen with his overnight bag.

"Why are you up so early?" Jason asked.

"Why are you staring at the wall drinking coffee?"

"Touché." Jason snickered. "I'm just thinking."

"You must be pretty pumped about the cartel going to prison."

Jason took a sip of coffee. "I am. It's just that—"

Clay tilted his head while Jason stared at the wall. "It's just what?"

"I'm sure it's nothing, but I keep replaying everything from last night in my head, and something doesn't feel right."

Clay slapped Jason on the back. "That's normal. You've been chasing these guys for so long that it's hard to believe it's really over."

Jason nodded.

"Yeah, that's probably it." He pointed to Clay's bag. "You heading out now?"

"I have a meeting with Pima County Search and Rescue this morning. If all goes well, I'll get paid to play with my drones. I have to get rolling soon so I don't miss the meeting."

Jason stood and raised his hand. Clay cupped his hand, and they bumped chests.

"Good luck with Pima County, and thanks for coming up here to help."

"Anytime," Clay replied.

"You want to take a cup of coffee or something with you?"

"I'll take a bottle of water if you have one."

After Clay departed, Jason returned to the kitchen table. He noticed mail with his name on it and opened it. Jason snapped to his feet once he read the contents.

It was a building permit for his new lot in Whispering Pines. Now he had the perfect distraction from all his questions surrounding the takedown of the cartel. Jason filled his travel mug with coffee and loaded a shovel, spade, and rake into the back of his truck. Forty minutes later, he arrived at his lot while the air was still cool.

Jason planned to construct a home that was one hundred percent off the grid, and build as much as possible himself. He wasn't a carpenter, or even a handy person, but he was resourceful and always loved a challenge. He wanted to use this opportunity to learn new skills while putting his own sweat equity into his new home. Jason had the architectural drawings and materials list for the modest four-bedroom home a family friend that worked for an architecture firm in Scottsdale, Arizona, created for him last year. His first step was to prepare the lot for a concrete basement he contracted to be excavated and poured for him.

Jason used his measuring tape to sketch the thirty-three by sixty square foot structure. Once constructed, the home would have two thousand square feet of livable space. For the next five hours, Jason cleared small boulders, rocks, and ground cover from the area that would be his basement someday. He basked in the fact that he could stand on his future driveway and envision his home rising one story from the rocky Arizona soil. Like his childhood home in Payson, his future house would have a large backyard patio to optimize the views of the river and the spectacular morning sunrises over the sea of mountains to the east.

After Jason spent much of his day prepping his new lot, he drove home and practically passed out on the family room couch. He took a quick cat nap, showered, and stopped in his tracks when he entered the kitchen. Shanna was at the table with Noah.

Shanna looked up at Jason and then lowered her eyes to his shirtless chest. Jason saw her and quickly pulled on the t-shirt draped over his shoulder. They stared awkwardly at each other until Jason spoke.

"Hey."

"Hi, Jason," Shanna replied. She pulled strands of hair over her ears.

"I didn't know you were coming here today."

"I still meet with Noah every Friday."

Jason nodded.

"You look like you were busy today," Shanna said.

"I started on my off-grid home in Whispering Pines. Once I get some walls up, I'll show it to you.

"I'd like that," Shanna said in a whisper.

"I can go so you two can talk," Noah snapped.

"No, no," Shanna and Jason replied in unison.

"I was passing through on my way to the family room. I'll leave you two to finish your session."

Philip had the local five o'clock news on TV when Jason sat on the couch. The two watched the news anchors cover stories on a massive wildfire in southern Arizona, heat-related deaths in Phoenix, and flash flooding near the Grand Canyon from a monsoon storm. After the weather, the anchor teased the next story before they went to a commercial break.

"We're taking you to a press conference by the Navajo County Sheriff on a large drug ring his office broke up in the high country. Details after the break." The screen flashed video footage of Sheriff Kellerman standing beside a podium while shaking hands with eager citizens.

Once Jason had viewed six consecutive political ads, the news returned with a reporter live on the scene for the press conference.

"This is Ally Rutledge live in Holbrook for the press conference held by Sheriff Kellerman on the drug ring his office broke up in Navajo County. It's starting now, so let's listen to the sheriff."

Sheriff Kellerman stood behind a podium in Gillespie Park across the street from the Navajo County Sheriff's Office in Holbrook, Arizona. Behind him, a flagpole with the red, white, and blue of the United States flag perched at the top with the copper, blue, yellow, and red Arizona state flag waving in the wind below Old Glory. Two white folding tables were in front of the podium and were covered with four AK-74 rifles, six handguns, piles of fentanyl blotter paper, and stacks of Canadian and US currency. Four sheriff's deputies, with their faces covered, in full-tactical gear and M-4 rifles, guarded the contraband.

"Gotta love election season," Jason said to his father.

"Yeah, that's laying it on pretty thick."

The sheriff pulled the microphone up, so he didn't have to lean down, and began his prime time press conference.

"Ladies and gentlemen, Navajo County and all of Arizona are safer today because these thugs are no longer selling drugs to our kids."

The small crowd of citizens standing in attendance clapped.

"Last night, in coordination with the DEA, we arrested these five men and took them off our streets."

Kellerman pointed to the mug shots of the cartel members taped to a poster board supported by an easel next to him.

"They've hurt many people directly with physical violence and indirectly with the dangerous opioids trafficked into our great state from our southern border. As a former DEA agent, I know our communities are safer every time we lock up drug dealers. My team did just that with this international drug syndicate from El Salvador. You can see on the table in front of me that they were well-armed and active in distributing fentanyl around the state. In partnership with the DEA, this is another successful case closed by this office. As America's toughest sheriff, I can tell you that no criminals are safe in this county. Break the law in Navajo County, and you'll go to jail."

Jason leaped up from the couch. "I can't believe people believe the line of BS he's feeding everyone!" Jason shouted at the TV.

"I thought this was good news. Aren't those the guys that chased down Mom and Josh?" Phillip asked.

"It's only a few of them. Maybe not even half of them."

Jason started pacing in the family room.

Phillip leaned forward in his recliner. "I don't understand."

"Mom said she saw a dozen men, and I've found evidence supporting at least that many people are hiding in the forest. So, if they only caught five men, that means seven or eight are still on the loose, but the sheriff wants to act like the entire cartel is locked up and the case is closed."

Phillip stood and moved next to Jason. He put his hand on his son's shoulder. "Are you sure there are more of them still out there?"

"I wish that was all of them and this was over, but I'm positive there are more still hiding in the forest. Clearly, the sheriff wants to portray this as a victory for his political campaign, and we won't get any more support from NCSO. Now they have to pretend the case is closed. At least until after the election this November."

Jason continued to pace. He'd felt something was amiss with the DEA sting, and the press conference confirmed his suspicions. The notion that politics could obstruct the pursuit of justice for Josh's murderers was a bitter pill to swallow. Bile surged into Jason's throat as the growing rage churned within him.

The back door slammed shut, interrupting Jason from his thoughts. He looked out the family room window and saw Shanna's SUV pull out of the driveway. Jason hoped he'd get a minute to talk with Shanna alone and smooth things out. She must have heard his rant and now his best chance to reconcile with her vanished.

Jason felt like a shaken soda can, ready to burst at any moment. He had to escape the walls of the room closing in on him.

"I'm going for a run. I'm going to explode if I don't get out of here."

Jason changed and was a mile from home seven minutes later. His sore muscles from working on his off-grid home earlier in the day didn't slow him down. Jason welcomed the pain and used it as fuel to push himself harder.

After two miles, Jason's thoughts turned from Shanna and Sheriff Kellerman's press conference to how he'd find justice for Josh. He tried to play by the rules and do the right thing as much as possible, but it wasn't working.

Gaby is dead, Josh is dead, and others may die if I don't change something.

He couldn't rely on law enforcement to cooperate or lead a search for the cartel. There were too many political constraints. Jason had to switch tactics to find the rest of the cartel and bring them to justice. He understood his changes brought increased danger, but working with NCSO or the DEA was no longer an option.

After his run, Jason walked up his driveway full of resolve. He'd form a team of capable people and go on offense. It was cartel season, and Jason was ready to hunt.

CHAPTER 28

Eight days after he left his men in Arizona, Victor Romero followed a stream of people across a footbridge over the Rio Grande River. Although he was officially standing over US soil, he still had to get through the Paso del Norte Port of Entry in El Paso, Texas. He intentionally chose the second busiest pedestrian crossing into the United States since the border agents felt pressure to keep the line moving and spent a second or two less scrutinizing each passport. Victor, a citizen of El Salvador, had a Mexican passport in his possession. He purchased it during one of his scouting trips earlier that year from a man he met at a hotel bar in Ciudad Juárez. The younger man had the same height and weight as Victor, but more importantly, they had similar cheekbones and noses. Two things border agents like to check.

Victor paid a handsome ransom for the passport, but it was a worthwhile investment. The Mexican national had a clean record and agreed not to report it stolen for one year. Victor felt more at ease and preferred to enter the United States at an official border crossing versus using the services of coyotes like some of his cartel counterparts. Victor did not wish to walk across the Arizona desert for days and nights, only to be transferred from safe house to safe house. He did that once before and vowed to never do it again. He'd heard stories of teenage coyotes abusing the illegal border crossers and beating them for more money. Victor had little patience with such tactics and even less if it was from an eighteen or nineteen-year-old boy. He figured he'd kill several coyotes and upset the Mexican cartels receiving a cut from their activities. Victor wanted no more problems with cartels along his trade route from El Salvador to the United States.

He approached the U.S. Customs and Border Patrol agent with this paperwork, passport, and trademark toothy smile.

"What brings you to the United States?"

"I'm a welder on the I-10 construction project," Victor replied in his best English. He believed the better his English, the better the odds of getting through the checkpoint.

The slightly overweight CPB agent with white hair laughed. "That thing is a mess. How long before you are done?"

"Not soon enough," Victor replied.

"Amen to that."

The agent held the passport up and examined Victor's face. The cartel lieutenant tried to remain calm but felt himself swallow hard.

"How was the drive up from Chihuahua, Mr. Perez?"

Victor knew the CPB agent was testing him. "Chihuahua? That must be a mistake, sir. I live here over by the university."

The agent stared at Victor for a few more seconds and smiled. "Welcome to the United States, Mr. Perez."

Victor took his stamped passport and walked to the bus station.

One of Victor's men, Carlos, waited in his truck as he arrived in Tucson just after sunset. Victor jumped in, and they were out of the city twenty minutes later. As soon as the lights from Tucson were in the rearview mirror, Carlos told Victor about the arrest of the other team operating near Heber. Victor slammed his fist into the dashboard multiple times and yelled, "Those idiots!"

Neither spoke for several miles, and once Victor's anger dissipated enough for him to speak. He turned to Carlos.

"This is why I separated the two operations. At least half the crew remains. Times will get tougher for us because I was told by El Jaguar that he wants us to double our production during our final days in Arizona. That will be a challenge with fewer men."

"What about the opportunity from our local source?" Carlos asked.

Victor looked out the window into the dark night. A minute later, he turned to Carlos.

"I think that is the only way for us to succeed. First, I need to learn more about what happened to the other crew. I'll speak with our local source again in two days and find out what happened. I will also confirm the shipment is still coming."

Three hours after they left Tucson, Victor and Carlos arrived at their remote location on the Fort Apache Reservation. They parked the truck and climbed two hundred feet up a steep ridge to the new operation. The new location tucked underneath a granite overhang within a dense stand of pine trees impressed Victor. It was their best location since they had arrived in Arizona. The camp was invisible from the air, and they could see anybody coming from up to a mile below.

Upon his arrival, Victor called a meeting for the remaining six men. They all stood several yards away from Victor while he shared details of his journey back to El Salvador and his conversation with the La Palma boss.

"We will leave this awful place and return to El Salvador in ten days. Before we leave, we must increase our output and sell as much as possible. I'm also working on a major opportunity during our final days here. I need you to be as diligent as possible to avoid detection and put in the necessary long hours. Can I count on you to give 100% until we return to El Salvador?"

Victor looked at each man as they nodded and verbally committed to Victor's command.

"Carlos, come with me."

Carlos looked at the other five men and ambled to Victor. The lieutenant put his arm around him to guide him away from the rest of the group.

"I have another job for you."

Carlos nodded.

"I need you to take one guy and go into New Mexico and buy one hundred kilos of meth. Bring it back here, but don't buy it in Arizona. It's too risky. After you do that, find the people that bought our fentanyl that was stolen in Mexico. El Jaguar says the buyer is in San Antonio. Once you find the buyer, tell them we'll sell them meth at half price."

Victor removed his arm and sat down on a nearby boulder.

"I don't understand. Why would we give the people that bought the stolen fentanyl a deal?" Carlos asked.

"We are going to teach them a lesson."

Carlos stared blankly at Victor.

"Once the meth is here, we'll lace it with five kilos of fentanyl before we sell it to them."

"That will kill many people!"

"Exactly!" Victor hissed. "The authorities do little if one or two junkies die, but if dozens die, they will have no choice but to track down and arrest the culprits. The buyers will all go to prison, hurting the Mexicans who stole our shipment. We can't fight them in the streets, but we can still inflict excruciating pain."

The thought of exacting revenge on the Mexican cartel that caused him to leave his Arizona operation and, as a result, get half of his crew captured helped soothe his simmering fury. He bounced back to his tent set away from the others and sat on his cot. The plan for revenge was underway, but now he had to start working on his grand scheme. First, he had to talk to his local contact, and then Victor would finalize the plan for his extraordinary heist.

Two days later, Victor arrived at the old gas station in Show Low for his weekly meeting with his local source. During the quick, covert update, Victor learned the sheriff was publicly promoting the arrest of half of his operation.

"How is this possible? They were in Navajo County, no?"

"The guy that accused you of killing his brother tracked your guys down and called the DEA. They came in and arrested all your men," the local source replied.

"The tall American. Do you know his name?"

"His name is Jason Mulder."

"Jason Mulder," Victor repeated. He looked at his source, but didn't see him. Victor was picturing the revenge he'd unleash on Jason Mulder. His vision ended and he turned his attention back to the local man.

"You said this wouldn't happen."

"Relax, this is a good thing. The public thinks a major drug ring has been arrested, so nobody knows to look for you and the rest of your operation. They think everyone involved is in jail. This is a lucky break for you. You shouldn't have anyone else harass you before you leave."

Victor considered this possibility. He liked the idea of no more people looking for him before he returned to El Salvador.

"What about the large shipment of dance fever you told me about last meeting? Is that still coming?" Victor asked, using a common street name for fentanyl.

The cartel lieutenant's gas pump kicked off. Seconds later, the same thing happened to the local source. They had to wrap up the conversation soon.

"Yeah, a delivery truck with several pallets of Sublimaze will arrive in nine days. That's enough liquid dance fever to supply hundreds of hospitals on the West Coast. I'll confirm the exact time and location at our next meeting. I still have the key and expect to receive a little more this time for this premium info."

Victor bit his lip and tilted his head. "You'll get more, but it'll be in a new box with a new key that I'll share after I have possession of those pallets."

"Fine," the source barked. He strutted back to his vehicle and left the gas station. Victor returned to his truck but waited a minute before starting his engine. He'd finally received some good news, and now his objective was clear. He had to intercept the fentanyl bound for the hospitals and sell it to his top buyer in Houston before returning to El Salvador.

Victor left the gas station and pulled onto the main highway, but his mind was still on the steps required to pull off the heist. Much had to be done in a week. He needed a foolproof plan to snatch a giant shipment of fentanyl in broad daylight.

First, he had to eliminate his biggest problem. They had to find Jason Mulder and kill him before their heist. A sardonic smile appeared on Victor's face at the thought of sending another message to anyone meddling with the La Palma cartel. They wouldn't just kill Jason Mulder. They'd butcher his entire family.

CHAPTER 29

Jason remained on his back patio to cool down after his morning run. He considered his next move while watching the seasonal storm clouds multiply and expand above him. He checked his watch and noted it was a quarter past eight, then texted Clay.

How was your meeting with Pima County search and rescue?

Clay responded thirty seconds later.

Great. I'm on call for any future search and rescue operations.

You still open for another mission up here?

DEA didn't catch all of them?

Nope.

Didn't think so.

You in?

Clay didn't respond right away. Jason assumed he was thinking about whether he wanted to help or how to best say "hell no." Five minutes later, Jason's phone buzzed.

I'm in.

Jason pumped his fist and texted Tarek to complete the three-person team. After an hour, Tarek hadn't responded, so Jason called. He didn't answer the phone, so Jason left a voicemail.

Jason wasn't just impatient; he was concerned.

"Did he talk to Shanna?" Jason asked aloud.

Not knowing the reason Tarek wasn't responding was eating at Jason. Fifteen minutes after he left the voicemail, he called Tarek again, and this time, he answered.

"Hey, Tarek. How's it going?"

"I'm swamped," Tarek replied abruptly.

Jason waited for further explanation from Tarek, but after five seconds of silence, he revealed the reason for his call.

"Do you still want to help with my search?"

Another long pause.

"Yeah. I'll still help."

"We're going back out this week. Are you in?"

"I'm not sure."

Tarek was a man of few words, but he was quieter than usual. Jason was sure Shanna had said something negative about him. He bit down on his lower lip as he thought about it and decided to ask.

"Did Shanna say something bad about me?"

"Shanna? No, why?"

"You're quieter than normal. I can't tell if you're being evasive or if something is wrong."

Jason heard shuffling, and then the line went quiet again. "Tarek?"

"I have an interview today for a new job at Sunrise Park Resort. It's for a full-time ski lift maintenance mechanic, and I really want this job, but my truck isn't running. I have no way to get there, so I have a lot on my mind right now. I have to figure this out soon."

Jason could hear the shame and frustration in Tarek's voice. "What's wrong with your truck? Do you know?"

"The starter is shot. I can't afford to buy a new one right now."

"What time is your interview?"

"Two o'clock."

Jason checked his watch. He had enough time to get to Whiteriver and then back to Sunrise Park Resort, but he'd have to leave soon.

"I'll be there at 12:45, so be ready, and I'll take you."

"What?"

"I'll take you to the interview, but I have to leave soon, so be ready when I get there."

"I'll be ready," Tarek replied. Jason noted more strength in his voice.

Fifteen minutes later, Jason pulled into the junkyard he had visited a couple of months earlier to examine his mom's totaled SUV. Jason found the owner in a small shed with an air conditioner rattling in the front window. He asked the thin, gray-haired man if he had any used starters available for a twenty-year-old Chevy pickup truck.

"You can pull anything you need off any vehicle out back. I've got lots of old Chevy trucks."

Jason looked out the window at the sea of partially dismantled vehicles and then back to the owner.

"I know, but I don't have time. I'm trying to help a friend get to a job interview. He needs this job bad. Do you have anything faster?"

The man stroked his silver beard for a moment. "Follow me."

The owner left the shed and walked behind the junkyard corporate office. He stopped at a faded blue, forty-foot metal shipping container and swung open a rusty door. The musty air mixed with the aroma of old motor oil blasted Jason, causing him to take several steps back from the container. He remained outside while the owner rummaged through dozens of parts stacked on shelves. A few minutes after he entered, the owner emerged into the sunlight with a smile and a starter. Jason paid, placed it into the bed of his truck, and continued his journey to Whiteriver.

Two hours later, Jason pulled into Tarek's driveway early. After waiting a few minutes, he texted the interviewee. Tarek stepped from his side door clean-shaven with his shiny black hair pulled back into a ponytail. He wore freshly pressed khakis with a white long-sleeve button-down shirt. He looked like a different person.

Jason commented on his appearance after Tarek got settled in the passenger seat.

"Looking good, Mr. Dosala. I'd hire you."

He flashed a half smile and let his eyes drop to the floor. Jason felt for Tarek. He'd had a tough life as an adult and didn't seem accustomed to receiving compliments.

"You ready to go?"

"Yes. Thanks for taking me."

The cab was mostly quiet during the sixty-minute commute to Sunrise Park Resort. Jason assumed Tarek was nervous or thinking about his answers, so he didn't want to trip him up with questions that could wait until he was done. Tarek exited the truck at the resort front office, and Jason drove to the back of the half-full parking lot to wait for him to finish his interview.

The White Mountain Apache Tribe opened Sunrise Park Resort in the early 1970s and every year hundreds of tribal members work at the outdoor entertainment complex. The winter ski park rivaled some Colorado parks, with its three peaks reaching 11,000 feet in elevation. It was Arizona's largest ski resort with sixty-five trails and seven lifts. Sunrise Park Resorts attracted skiers from around the state, including the Phoenix area three and a half hours away by car.

Over the years, the tribe added many warm-weather amenities like mountain biking, horseback riding, scenic lift rides, and a zip line. It was the perfect place for Tarek to get his foot in the door, showcase his talents, and grow within the organization. He needed a break and an opportunity, and this could provide both for Tarek.

Ninety minutes later, Tarek emerged from the office building, and Jason picked him up.

"So, how was it?"

"I think I did pretty good. Three different people interviewed me for half an hour, and the last one in HR said she'd let me know in a couple of days."

Tarek's demeanor seemed more relaxed and upbeat.

"They're smart. I bet you'll hear good news soon."

During the return trip to Whiteriver, Jason was eager to question Tarek about Shanna. Once Jason turned south onto Highway 73, he knew he was down to thirty minutes of drive time.

"Has Shanna said anything about me lately?"

"I don't think so. Why?"

"We went out a week ago, and everything was going great until we ran into her ex at a bar in Pinetop-Lakeside. He was pretty drunk and got a little handsy with Shanna when he wanted her to leave for a talk. I may have overreacted a bit, and Shanna had me take her home early. We've only spoken briefly since that night."

"Did you hit him?"

"No."

Tarek raised both eyebrows. "No?"

"I mostly just slammed his head into the table."

"Ah. I think I know the problem."

Jason nodded and waited for Tarek to fill him in.

"Shanna's mom dated a guy for a while after her dad died. He was a heavy drinker and a mean drunk. The bully hit my aunt and the boys all the time. He may have even hit Shanna a time or two. We all hated him and were thrilled when he finally got tossed in prison in Nevada. After that, Shanna's mom stopped dating, but Shanna wasn't the same after him. She despises violence."

Jason's shoulders slumped. He felt like a complete idiot for making Shanna feel so uncomfortable. Her reaction made sense now. He also knew he'd struggle to mend fences with her while hunting down the people who killed Josh.

Jason changed the subject as he entered Whiteriver and asked another question weighing on his mind.

"I've been paying more attention to the opioid epidemic since I learned drug dealers killed my brother. It seems like so many people get hooked and can't get off. Was it hard for you?"

Tarek turned in his seat and stared at Jason.

"Shanna told me."

Tarek returned his gaze to the front and stared out the windshield. "It was the hardest thing I've ever done in my life."

Jason remained silent. He could tell Tarek was thinking back to darker times in his life.

"I went to rehab in Tucson for a while and relapsed a few times after I came home. I didn't think I'd ever give up meth until I spoke to one of the elders." Tarek looked out the window at the passing buildings. "He said in order to live, you must first die. After that, I never touched meth again."

The cab was quiet for a half minute until Jason spoke again. "I don't understand. What does that mean?"

Tarek cleared his throat, and his expression turned somber. "Old Tarek was lost to drugs. Meth took my entire body, mind, and soul hostage. The elders performed a ceremony to let old Tarek pass so I could be reborn into a new body without the curse of meth. Now I have a healthy soul. New Tarek doesn't touch meth or any drugs. Sometimes I drink too much, but I'll never be the old Tarek again. He's dead."

Neither said another word until they pulled into Tarek's driveway.

Jason jumped out and hurried to the bed of his truck. Tarek followed with a confused look as Jason held up a metal cylinder with thick electrical wires hanging from it.

"Can you install it yourself?" he asked.

Tarek took a step closer to the starter. "Yeah, I could install it if I had the right tools. I know someone that should be able to lend them to me."

Jason handed the starter to Tarek. He glanced at the critical part in his hand and looked up with a tear rolling down his cheek.

"I don't know how to thank you for all this."

"You've done so much for me, so no thanks are needed. Let's call it even now."

Tarek sniffed and nodded.

"I'm going to head out now, but I'll text you the details about our next search."

"Thanks, Jason."

As Jason put his truck in reverse, a familiar SUV pulled up next to his vehicle in Tarek's driveway.

Shanna waved through her open window, so Jason immediately braked.

"What are you doing here?" Shanna asked.

"I gave Tarek a ride."

"A ride? To where?"

"I'll let him tell you all about it."

Shanna stared warily at Jason.

After several seconds of awkward silence, Jason spoke. "I have to get back to Payson now."

"You can't stay for a few minutes?"

Jason wanted to say yes with every fiber in his body. Shanna's smile and touch were like a life preserver to someone adrift in the ocean. She made the world seem brighter, but Jason knew the odds were against a future together. Shanna's mother hated him, and she hated violence. Jason would not stop hunting the cartel until he brought them to justice. It wasn't a good fit.

"Not tonight."

Jason took his foot off his brake and reversed out of the driveway. It was harder than he had imagined leaving, but it was the right thing to do. His sole focus was to capture the cartel.

CHAPTER 30

"Help! Somebody help me!"

The cry for help came through Jason's open bedroom window. He rose and darted from his room toward the source of the voice outside. He recognized the call came from his mother. Jason pushed through the back door and saw Celeste lying at the bottom of the patio steps next to an empty serving bowl.

"Mom, are you okay?" Jason yelled.

A second later, Jason was at her side. He gently wiggled her foot from between two stairs and helped Celeste move to a seated position on the bottom step.

"What happened?"

"I was up early, so I thought I'd pick some strawberries from the garden and my leg gave out. I fell down the last two stairs and my foot got stuck. It's my bad leg, so I didn't want to force it."

"You did the right thing. Does anything hurt?"

Celeste pulled the skin on her elbow to get a better look. "I banged my elbow when I fell, but that's it. I'm okay now."

"Let's get you up to the patio."

Jason helped Celeste up the stairs and into a patio chair.

"Noah, Dad, or I can help you get strawberries if you want them. You just need to ask."

"You all have been helping me for months. I want to start doing some stuff by myself," Celeste responded abruptly, the exasperation evident in her reply.

"Fair enough. Are you sure you're okay?"

Celeste pushed herself up and limped toward the back door. "Just a bruised ego, but other than that, I'm fine."

She hobbled inside while Jason remained on the patio, arms crossed tightly in disappointment that he'd slept later than normal since coming home. That morning - the only morning he'd woken after 6:00 am - his mom woke early to forage for food in the garden.

Over the next two hours, Jason rummaged through all the maps in his closet and downed several cups of coffee. He moved to the back patio to wait for his first teammate to arrive.

Minutes later, Clay pulled in and Jason met him outside his truck. While Jason greeted Clay, a strange rusty white truck turned and lurched onto the driveway.

"What the hell is that?" Jason said aloud.

He leaned forward and squinted toward the oncoming vehicle until he recognized the face behind the wheel. It was Tarek, and he'd got his truck running less than forty-eight hours after Jason gave him the starter. The beaming smile on his face told Jason all he needed to know about whether it was worth the extra effort to provide the starter to Tarek.

Jason shook Tarek's hand, and Clay hugged him when he got out.

"Did you get the job?" Jason asked.

"Yes, they called this morning. I start next week."

"Congratulations, man. I'm excited for you. You deserve a fresh start."

"Thank you for taking me to the interview."

"It's the least I could do."

The three men proceeded up the back deck and into Jason's pseudo-war room on the kitchen table. Topographical maps of Gila, Navajo, and Apache counties, along with the Fort Apache Reservation, were laid across an oak, six-person table. Jason stood in the middle as he shared the areas he felt were the best places to search.

"Are you sure the DEA didn't catch them all? The sheriff is on TV saying he broke up the drug ring. Do you think more of them are still hiding?" Tarek asked.

"There's no way the cartel I've seen is only five men. I don't know how many more are out there, but I'm positive more cartel members are still somewhere in one of these forests," Jason replied.

Clay stepped forward.

"I would have left if part of my crew was arrested. Do you really think they're still out there?"

Jason took in a deep breath and let out a loud sigh. "Yeah, I do, but I don't think we have much time to find them. I'm sure they're spooked by the arrests and want to finish up around here and get out of town. Plus, the Fourth of July is next week, and these forests will be crawling with campers, hikers, off-roaders, and future hunters scouting the best spots for the elk season that starts in August. If they are still out there, which I believe they are, I'm afraid there will be more casualties if we don't find them soon."

"And the people that killed your brother will get away," Clay added.

"Exactly," Jason whispered.

Tarek and Clay stood next to Jason as he leaned over the maps to examine them.

"I think we should start here," Jason said. He pointed to an area along Cibecue Creek south of where they last searched with drones.

"I don't have any issues with that, but it's still a ton of ground to cover," Clay responded.

Tarek stepped forward. "I agree. Cibecue Creek is a good place to start. It has more water running through it now after the last monsoon storm, and we know the cartel needs to be close to a water source."

"I'd hate to lose all that time if we are wrong. Jason, doesn't your brother have access to drones with built-in infrared cameras?" Clay inquired.

"Yeah, but he said he would have to go with us to operate it."

Clay looked over at Tarek and then back at Jason. "I don't think either of us has a problem with him coming. How soon can he get the drone and head out?"

Despite Jason's new commitment to go on offense, he still wasn't comfortable bringing Noah into the forest to search for the cartel.

"He's busy with work right now," Jason lied. "We can ask him at lunch."

"Good. We need all the help we can get to find a handful of men in an area that massive."

They discussed starting the search near Cibecue Creek and formed a detailed action plan together.

Just after noon, Noah entered the kitchen and opened the refrigerator.

"Man, I'm starving. Anything good in here?" Noah asked anyone in the room willing to listen.

Jason maintained his gaze on the maps until Clay elbowed him in the side.

"Let's ask him now."

Noah looked up over the open refrigerator door. "Ask him what?"

Jason swallowed hard. He never wanted his search for the cartel to reach the point he had to involve family members.

"We're just wondering if we could use your drone with the FLIR cameras?" Jason asked. He hoped Noah had forgotten his requirement that only he could operate his new drone. It didn't work.

"I said you can use it, but I have to be the one to operate it. It's on loan from my company and if something happens to it, I'm responsible. I'm happy to help if you need it, but that drone and I are a package deal."

Noah dropped his head back into the refrigerator as if he expected the same pushback from Jason he'd received since Josh's death.

"How soon can you go out with us?" Jason asked.

Noah's head shot up above the refrigerator door and he quickly closed it. "Seriously?"

"Yeah. We're going out later today to take advantage of the heat differentials near sundown. We can cover a lot more ground that way. Can you do it?"

"Hell yeah, I can do it."

"Can we see this super-duper drone you have?" Clay asked.

"Sure. I'll be right back."

Noah jogged back to his room and returned two minutes later. He set a black, rigid case on top of the maps and opened it.

"Here's our new quadcopter with all the bells and whistles," Noah said. He removed the Unmanned Aerial System or UAS from the case and set it on the table. Then, Noah backed away to make room for others to get a closer look.

"This model has a forty-five-minute flight time, a range of three miles, and a payload of up to ten pounds. It has a second battery to provide a total of ninety minutes in the air. Plus, this baby includes a laser range finder, a 4K visible light camera with 16x optical zoom, and a 640 × 512 resolution Thermal Camera with FLIR image analysis software. It can cover several square miles in a single flight."

Noah shared the UAS specs like a proud parent bragging about a gifted child.

"I'm on the team that built the control and guidance system," Noah added.

Jason elbowed Clay. "I don't understand anything he just said. Is it good?"

"Yeah, it's good. I can't wait to get this thing in the air."

"Great, we have a plan. We'll leave at four, so we have plenty of time to get there and get the UAS in the air before it gets too dark," Jason said.

Noah darted out of the room with a wide smile and forgot about his hunger pangs. Although Jason was still uneasy about including his brother in such a dangerous operation, he loved seeing how happy Noah was to be included. He hoped he wouldn't regret his decision.

CHAPTER 31

The cab was silent as Clay gripped the steering wheel until his knuckles turned white to keep his truck on the highway in the blinding rain. An afternoon storm brought sixty-mile-per-hour winds, cloud-to-ground lightning, and sheets of rain to the forest above 6000 feet in elevation. A common occurrence in the Arizona High Country in late June as monsoon season gripped the region, but it made flying a drone impossible. The powerful, scattered storms became destructive as they fed on the summer heat of the Sonoran Desert.

"Do you think it will be storming when we get to Cibecue Creek?" Noah asked.

Tarek leaned closer to the windshield from his position in the front passenger seat. He looked right, left, and stared at the rain pelting the windshield.

"No. The storm will end soon, and we will have calm winds for the drone when we arrive at Cibecue Creek," Tarek responded. He maintained his gaze on the sheets of rain ahead.

"Wow, that's impressive. Did your ancestors teach you how to predict the weather like that?" Noah inquired.

Tarek turned to face Noah in the truck's backseat. His eyes widened, and his square jaw clenched.

Noah squirmed in his seat until a smile cracked the stern look on Tarek's face.

"No, I just checked the weather app on my phone before you asked."

Tarek held up his smartphone and everyone in the cab erupted in laughter. Jason leaned over and punched his younger brother in the arm. It was the perfect initiation for Noah. True to Tarek's prediction, the rain ended ten minutes later.

Clay parked as close as he could get to the section of Cibecue Creek they wished to scan, and the foursome hiked a half mile through the woods until they reached a clearing. Noah placed the drone case on the ground and carefully removed the quadcopter. Next, he performed several maneuvers to calibrate the drone with the operating software and conducted a quick test flight to ensure everything was in working order. Noah treated his drone during preflight as if he was about to pilot an F-35 fighter jet over a combat zone. Finally satisfied, Noah directed the drone into the blue sky with the menacing storm clouds moving away.

The sun dropped to a horizontal position behind the mountains due west as Noah completed the first search grid. He kept his eyes glued to the tablet to view the 4K color video camera and infrared thermal camera signal beaming from the drone hundreds of yards away. Tarek, Clay, and Jason took turns assisting Noah, so the team always had at least two sets of eyes on both displays.

Forty minutes after the initial launch, they hadn't detected any thermal anomalies or signs of human activity, so Noah brought the UAS back. They had less than an hour of daylight and the second battery provided forty-five additional minutes of flight time. It would be their last flight of the day.

Tarek put his hand on Noah's arm to stop him before he launched the drone.

"I think you should move another three or four hundred yards to the south and start your search there. A sharp bend in the creek down there provides deeper water and denser forest to conceal their location in that area."

"That will leave a gap in our search grid, and I'd hate to miss them by skipping areas," Noah replied.

Tarek did not respond, so Clay chimed in.

"Ordinarily, I'd agree with you, Noah, but we are getting short on time, and we need to target the most likely areas versus a comprehensive search. So, I'd start three hundred yards to the south."

Noah stared at Clay for several seconds. He looked as if he wanted to debate the recommendation but nodded and lifted the drone into the sky.

Twenty minutes into their new search, Clay leaned closer to the tablet screen.

"Wait! Back up. I saw something on the infrared camera up on that ridge."

This announcement attracted the attention of Jason and Tarek. Seconds later, all four crowded around the tablet beaming the infrared images.

"Go back to where the densest batch of trees rises along the bank just north of the bend in the creek."

Noah moved the drone with a steady hand.

"There it is again. That heat signal looks human," Clay said.

Noah zoomed in on the image and estimated the dark red blob on the screen was about three feet high and two feet wide.

"It has the heat signature of a person, but that seems too small to be a man. It almost looks like a little kid," Jason said.

"Do you think that's one of the lost hunters?" Noah asked.

"Give me a sec," Clay said. He zoomed in as far as the tablet screen allowed. He stared for several seconds and then zoomed back out.

"That's a view from somebody's back. I think the person is sitting down. They could be eating or reading. Could be taking a dump."

Just as the words left Clay's mouth, the image on the screen doubled in size. The person stood and shuffled off camera.

"Follow him!" Jason barked.

It took a few seconds, but Noah found the target and followed until it came into contact with two new red and white figures on the screen. More humans. They were under thick layers of trees, shrubs, and undergrowth, and the 4K color camera couldn't easily detect the men in camouflage but were clearly visible on the infrared screen.

The images caused the hair on Jason's arms to prickle. He knew what three men together in that part of Fort Apache Reservation meant before anyone uttered a word.

"That has to be the cartel," Clay said.

"It is," Tarek responded.

Noah noted the drone coordinates while the others kept their eyes on the infrared feed. They watched the three engage in what looked like an animated discussion or argument. One waved his arms wildly at the others. Next, they saw two men with rifles turn toward the drone. Seconds later, they saw muzzle flashes and heard gunshots coming from a quarter mile away on the other side of the ridge.

"They're shooting at me!" Noah shouted.

Noah pushed the drone away from the shots so fast that he tilted his entire body to will the expensive drone out of the shower of lead aimed toward the quadcopter. The drone arrived with only three working rotors. The AK-74 slug hit it and broke off one rotor, but the drone returned to its home base.

"Shit! They shot off one of my rotors. My boss is going to kill me."

"We better get out of here or the cartel may kill you first," Jason chirped.

The rotors stopped spinning, and Noah jogged to the drone. He returned it to the case as quickly as possible while Clay helped pack the rest of the drone equipment.

Once again, the truck was quiet on the return trip to the Mulder's home in Payson. Jason was deep in thought while Noah mumbled under his breath. After listening to Noah for twenty minutes, Jason turned to him.

"What's wrong with you?"

"What's wrong? They shot up a twenty-thousand-dollar drone, and I'll have to pay for it. I don't have that kind of money."

Jason started to respond, but Clay put his hand up to stop him. He looked at Noah in the rearview mirror.

"You're looking at this the wrong way, bro."

"How am I looking at this the wrong way?"

"You took the drone out for a test flight, and some disgruntled hunters put multiple rounds of high-powered ammo into your UAS. And it returned! Do you know how important that is to Game and Fish, Law Enforcement or Military accounts?"

Noah shrugged.

"Pardon the pun, but it's the first bullet point I'd put on your sell sheet. As special reconnaissance in the Air Force, I've flown many UASs; some of them wouldn't make it back from a direct hit. You just helped the company sell more drones."

Noah stared at Clay for several seconds. Jason couldn't tell if Clay convinced him that the new three-rotor quadcopter was actually a benefit, but he stopped mumbling the rest of the way, which pleased Jason.

All four men stood outside Clay's truck after they returned to Jason's driveway to discuss the next mission.

"They know we've spotted them, so they're going to be on the move soon," Jason said. He pointed to Clay and Tarek. "The three of us need to gear up to get back out there again before dawn. We need to catch them before they disappear again."

"Now you're excluding me after I helped with the drone! What's up with that?" Noah protested.

Jason exchanged a glance with Clay and then walked next to Noah.

"We appreciate your help. We wouldn't have found them without you, but this next mission will be on a different level."

"I still want to go. In case you forgot, my brother died too."

Jason spun toward Noah. "Are you prepared to take a life?"

Noah took a step back from Jason but didn't respond.

"The men in the cartel are cold-blooded killers, and you can't hesitate for a split second. You have to be willing to pull the trigger, or they will kill you. It's a decision I hope you never have to make. The chances you'd be confronted with that decision during our next mission are high."

Noah stared at Jason for several seconds, turned, and walked toward the back door. Jason waited until he was inside and then exhaled loudly.

"How about both of you? Are you in?"

Clay and Tarek nodded.

"Good. Clay, did you bring everything we talked about?"

"Yeah, I brought everything and a little more."

Jason extended his fist and bumped it with Clay's fist.

"Let's see what you've got."

CHAPTER 32

The padlock opened with a click, and Clay swung open a metal utility storage box bolted to the bed of his pickup. Tarek's eyes widened, and Jason leaned over for a closer look at the goods illuminated by the truck bed LED lights.

"Is that an HK416 A5 rifle with red dot reflexive optics?" Jason asked.

"Sure is," Clay responded like a proud father. "I have two HK416s with fourteen-and-a-half inch barrels and two Smith & Wesson M&P 15-22 rifles, all with red dot optics. We have an extra M&P 15-22 if you want your brother to come."

"He won't be joining us on this mission."

Clay handed the HK416 to Jason and then the M&P 15-22 to Tarek.

"You okay with that?" Clay asked Tarek.

Tarek turned the matte black Smith & Wesson rifle on its side, raised it to eye level, and peered through the optics. "Never shot this before, but I've been hunting with rifles since I was seven years old. I feel comfortable with it."

"Great. Jason, look at what's under that black duffel bag to the right. I brought more essential gear."

Jason moved the bag and then looked back to Clay. "Where did you get these?"

Clay smiled but didn't respond. Jason continued to look at Clay until he answered.

"Let's just say that I know some guys in Louisiana who are ready for the next civil war, and they have more equipment than they need. But since bullets weren't flying last time I was home, they were willing to part with some of it for a reasonable price."

Jason handed Tarek a set of night vision goggles and showed him how to put them on.

"It takes a few minutes to get used to NVGs, but I'm sure the cartel doesn't have any thermal imaging or night vision technology, so this will give us the element of surprise."

Tarek put them on and walked into the forest at the end of Jason's yard. Two minutes later, he returned.

"It's a little hard at first with all the green, but I could see trees and boulders. They work fine."

"It sounds like we're all set with gear. What's the plan?" Clay asked.

The trio sat on Clay's lowered tailgate and discussed their plan to capture the cartel before sunrise.

Five hours later, Jason, Clay, and Tarek returned to the area just south of where they spotted the cartel. During the drive to the location a mile north of Cibecue Falls, Jason explained the hand gestures they would use to move through the forest without speaking. Clay and Jason secured their HK416 rifles and Tarek removed his Smith & Wesson M&P 15-22 from the utility box.

Each man loaded their magazines and chambered a round. After they affixed their NVGs and tested them, Clay led the three men in a single-line formation into the dark forest. They crept silently through the trees, down into a valley, and then up a ridge until they were a hundred yards outside the cartel camp. Clay gave the hand signal for Tarek to go left and then Jason to go right, as they discussed.

Jason wiggled his body through the underbrush and settled into the prone position with a view of his sector. The predetermined plan was for Clay, Tarek, and Jason to take one of the three sectors. Tarek took nine to eleven, Clay, the best shooter of the group, took the point from eleven to one, and Jason had one o'clock and everything to the right. Each would recon their sector to identify their first target and then move to a second. This plan allowed them to take out up to six cartel members before they could mount a counterattack. The team assumed this was around half of all the cartel members.

It took them longer than expected to traverse the woods, and the sky turned turquoise and lightened in the east.

Jason removed his NVGs and looked up at the stars before they disappeared. He remembered Josh's giggle as they'd laid inside their sleeping bags and admired the Milky Way when camping. Jason pretended to know all the constellations but just made them up.

"That's Taurus," Jason had lied as he pointed to random stars. "That's Zeus. That one over there is Thor, and that one in the far distance is Pokémon." He kept up the act until Josh was laughing so hard that Jason was afraid he'd hyperventilate. He longed to hear that laugh one more time.

Jason snapped out of his thoughts of Josh and focused on his sector as he scanned it from left to right. After five minutes, he identified one man that appeared to be on security detail for the camp. Jason watched him sit for several minutes, then occasionally stand up, walk fifteen yards to his left, and then return to his stump for a seat. He unknowingly volunteered himself to be Jason's first target. Jason continued to search for target number two. He didn't see the second body in his sector until the sky turned gold and his night vision goggles lost their usefulness. The second man walked back and forth from an area behind the other man pulling security. Jason couldn't tell exactly what he was doing but guessed he was gathering supplies based on his movements. He appeared to be preparing his station like a worker in an assembly plant, but this wasn't cars, refrigerators, or widgets. This man prepared to start his day with more production of dangerous fentanyl that would wreak havoc on thousands of Arizonans.

Jason looked twenty yards to his left and saw Clay looking through the optics on his rifle at his sector. Clay raised a few inches every five minutes to communicate with the team. They agreed that once they identified their primary and secondary targets, they'd hold up two fingers, their thumb and index finger, to indicate they had locked in two targets. Once Clay confirmed all three were ready, he would hold up five fingers to be prepared to fire. Jason and Tarek would fire immediately after Clay's initial shot. They would neutralize the primary targets without knowing what hit them, and then moments later, the second targets would meet the same fate. After the first two targets per sector were eliminated, they would wait. They'd hold their positions, react to any counterfire, or chase down any remaining cartel members who fled. It was all dependent on timing, teamwork, and communication. If any of those vital functions broke down, the mission would fail.

Jason raised two fingers toward Clay as soon as sunlight illuminated the scene. Clay responded with two fingers and a thumbs-up sign to show he had also identified his first two targets. Next, Clay held up one finger and pointed toward Tarek to signal he was still searching for his second target. Clay responded with two fingers and a thumbs-up sign to show he had also identified his first two targets. Next, Clay held up one finger and pointed toward Tarek to signal he was still searching for his second target.

It seemed eerily quiet to Jason as he waited. The night insects stopped their calls, and now Jason could hear his own breath entering and leaving his lungs. He felt his heart beating faster against the sandstone rocks pressing against his chest. Jason was eager to engage the enemy while they still had some element of surprise.

The first rays of sunlight penetrated the trees and warmed Jason's face. Now he was concerned their original plan may have to be aborted and held his palm upward toward Clay the next time they made eye contact. Clay understood Jason was questioning the reason for the delay and answered by shaking his head. He also did not know what was holding up Tarek.

Jason turned back to his sector when he heard a commotion coming from Tarek's position. It sounded like somebody throwing rocks at first, but then it turned into a full rockslide.

Jason looked toward his primary target and saw the noise attracted his attention. Jason slowed his breathing, turned his weapon from safe to fire, and guided his finger over the trigger. He kept his HK416 trained on his primary target and debated whether he should initiate the firing sequence with the first shot. Jason did not want them to escape again. He closed his eyes, took a deep breath, and prepared to fire.

CHAPTER 33

The red dot hovered over the target's chest and held steady. Jason's lungs emptied, and he applied additional pressure on the trigger. Just as he braced for a light recoil, Jason felt vibrations through the ground and into his chest. Someone to his left was running. He took his finger off the trigger, raised his head above the vegetation, and saw Tarek dart away from the cartel camp.

Jason slammed his fist into the dirt. He knew they had to abort the original plan but wasn't willing to retreat without taking a shot at the man that killed his brother. He peered through his reflex optic sight and counted a half dozen armed men moving toward him.

"Six men at ninety yards. One round in the chamber and fourteen in the magazine. You've got this," Jason whispered to himself.

He moved the red dot from one target to another. He'd eliminate the closest man and then move to the others as fast as he could.

When they reached within seventy-five yards of his position, Jason knew it was now or never. He had seconds to commit to firing at all six men or leaving to catch up with Tarek. His desire to strike was strong, but his odds were bleak. Further delay dropped his probability of survival close to zero. Retreating now meant Josh's killers could walk free forever.

Jason considered his options and smiled. Clay was still in position. He assumed Clay would know to fire upon the report of his HK416 and together they could take out the six cartel members. Jason took a small breath of air, found his target, and moved his finger over the trigger.

"Killing my brother was a big mistake," Jason whispered.

Jason took his eye off the target again when he sensed new vibrations. He pushed himself up and saw another man running away from the camp. Jason could tell it was Clay. He followed Tarek's path along the ridge.

The cartel goons were only sixty yards away. Jason figured that two special forces operators against six hastily trained cartel members with the element of surprise was a winnable scenario. Now, one on six seemed like suicide. Jason didn't have time to consider his next move. It was made for him.

The report from Kalashnikov rifles echoed off the canyon walls. The cartel had spotted both men running from their camp and made contact. Jason leaped from his position and dashed toward Clay and Tarek. He had to catch up so all three could get out of the line of fire. As the most athletic of all three men, Jason reached Tarek and Clay a minute later. Tarek and Clay didn't acknowledge his presence when he arrived. Everyone knew they had to keep moving or die.

They hurried along a game trail as cartel members fired in their direction. The trail provided little to no cover but allowed for the fastest escape from gunfire. They needed to put distance between themselves and the shots fast.

Nobody uttered a word or broke stride as they navigated the rocky dirt path hundreds of feet above Cibecue Creek. The only sounds Jason heard over his heavy breathing were boots rapidly smacking the trail and the pop of gunfire.

During the next half mile, Tarek, Clay, and Jason put four hundred yards between themselves and the shooters. They reached a safer distance from the incoming fire but went in the opposite direction of Clay's truck. The best option for escape was blocked by the cartel.

They continued moving along the game trail until it reached a T at the edge of a cliff. Going left took them down closer to the creek and right took them higher up the canyon and around the summit.

"Let's go right," Jason yelled. "We can't give them the higher ground, or we'll never get out of here."

They turned right in unison and climbed the trail as it hugged the side of the steep canyon walls. Sounds of gunfire grew muffled as they put craggy granite walls between themselves and their pursuers. Jason hoped the trail would lead up to a plateau and back down another side allowing them to skirt past cartel members back to Clay's truck with the safety of a mountain between them. His hopes were dashed when the trail took a sharp turn at an even higher cliff overlooking Cibecue Creek. The trail went in one direction, down toward the creek.

Each man panted as they executed 360-degree turns, scanning the landscape for an alternative route.

"We don't have a choice now. We have to go down toward the creek," Clay said between breaths.

Jason moved next to Clay and followed the trail with his eyes toward the creek that grew wider with less tree cover. Tarek left the group and walked back toward the oncoming cartel. He gazed up along the nearly vertical canyon walls while Clay and Jason looked down.

"I don't like that, Clay," Jason said. "Going down that steep part of the trail will slow us up and we'll be easy pickings from here once the shooters arrive."

"I don't like it either, but we have to do it. What other option do we have?"

"We can go up," Tarek shouted.

Jason turned toward Tarek and saw him looking at what appeared to be a small cave opening.

"Is that a cave?" Clay asked.

"I think so."

"Does it go back far enough to hide from the cartel?"

"I hope so," Tarek replied.

"Hope is not a plan," Clay barked.

Jason didn't like the idea of hiding in a dead-end cave like a rat, but it was better than dropping down into a canyon completely exposed to the cartel shooters.

"Standing here waiting to get shot isn't a good plan either," Jason added.

A pop broke the relative quiet, and granite fragments fell from the ridge above them. The cartel was almost around the ridge and with no cover in the area for the three fleeing men.

"Let's go!" Jason yelled.

Clay and Jason followed Tarek as they climbed over small boulders and thorny shrubs up the steep incline. Tarek entered the cave first, followed by Clay. When Jason pushed off to reach the entrance, the rocky earth gave way, and he slid down several feet. Smaller rocks skidded down the side while larger stones tumbled down, crashed on the trail, and continued hurtling toward Cibecue Creek hundreds of feet below. Jason knew those stones could be him and took action to slow his descent. He quickly spread his arms and legs out so that he looked like a six-foot

X on the side of the ridge. It worked, but when he looked down at the trail forty feet below, he saw shadows approaching. He turned, found some traction with his boots, and low-crawled up to the cave entrance. He lunged inside just as the cartel shooters appeared on the trail below.

Jason, Clay, and Tarek moved to the end of the visible cave and took defensive positions facing the entrance. Now they could only pray the cartel missed them entering the cave and continued to follow the trail down to the creek. It may have worked until Jason launched several rocks from their position. If the cartel discovered they were in the cave, the armed band from El Salvador could surround it and trap them inside. Jason, Clay, and Tarek steeled themselves in the shadows of the cave and prepared to respond to the imminent siege of a larger force.

Jason's heart slammed against his chest harder with each passing second. His gut was sending him signals again. A fight to the death was near.

CHAPTER 34

Sunlight illuminated the cave forty feet from the entrance. Clay moved to the right side, took a knee, and motioned for Jason and Tarek to go left. Seconds after entering the cave, they were in defensive positions. Their weapons aimed toward the opening and ready to fire.

"What the hell happened back there?" Jason asked between gasps for air.

Clay and Jason maintained their gaze on the entrance while waiting for Tarek to answer. Tarek put a hand on the granite wall and leaned forward as his chest heaved. He opened his mouth, but no words came out.

"Well, what happened?" Clay snapped.

"Dead. Bodies."

"Dead bodies?" Clay and Jason asked in unison.

Tarek inhaled deeply and caught his breath. "I was lying on loose rocks while scanning my sector for a target. They were sharp and jabbed me in my ribs. After I moved a few rocks out of the way, my hand brushed up against something strange. It was softer than rocks or wood but harder than the earth. It felt like a beaver's tail, so I moved more gravel and that's when I found the fingers."

"Human fingers?" Jason asked.

"Yeah. I rolled to my left side and pushed more material away until I found a hand. That's when the smell hit me, and I started breathing through my mouth. I wanted to know what was under me, so I quietly moved material until I uncovered the arm and shoulders, and finally, a boy's head appeared. By that time, it was lighter out. I'll never forget seeing his blond hair with dried blood on it."

Jason noted that Tarek was looking toward the entrance, but could tell his mind was elsewhere. He looked like he was watching the horrific scene in his mind again. Tarek continued.

"In the light, I noticed I was on top of a shallow grave and saw two more similar piles. I moved over a couple of feet, and under a flat boulder, I found the head and neck of a man. It looked like they cut his throat, and there was—" Tarek's voice trailed off, and he stopped talking.

"How old was the boy? A young boy or a teenager?" Jason asked.

Tarek looked toward Jason, and his eyes regained focus. "Um, hard to say. He was bigger than a young boy, so probably a teenager."

Jason nodded. "I think you may have found the missing hunters."

He thought about the unbearable pain the family would experience once the hope of their safe return was crushed.

"That boy went to the same high school as Josh. That's two high school kids murdered by the cartel now," Jason added.

"Oh, yeah. I heard about them on the news," Clay said. He didn't turn to look and kept his weapon pointed at the entrance.

"Is that what caused the rockslide?"

"No, it was the last grave."

"A third person?"

"I wanted to leave because the smell was horrible. It got so strong I thought the cartel might notice, but I had to know who was in the third grave. A couple minutes later, I found a girl. After I moved some sandy earth from her face, I recognized she was from Whiteriver and jumped away. That's when all the rocks started rolling. I didn't mean for it to happen."

"Did you know her?" Jason asked.

Tarek nodded. "Her parents own the auto repair shop in town. Her dad is the one that lent me the tools to put the starter in my car."

Tarek's voice cracked. "They are good people. I saw their daughter around town all the time."

"What's her name?"

"Her name is Annie. They reported her missing a few days after the hunters."

"Wow, I'm sorry. I didn't hear about that."

"You never do. Missing Native Americans, especially on reservations, never make the news."

Jason considered the claim, and despite Arizona having the third largest Native American population in the US, with twenty-two tribes living on nearly a quarter of the state, he couldn't recall ever hearing news about a missing person from a reservation on the local news. He'd heard a story or two of a political scandal, more news of natural disasters like floods and fires, and extensive coverage of every proposed new casino, but that was it.

"Now her family can give her a proper burial."

Tarek nodded and dropped his eyes to the cave floor. Jason turned his attention to the threat lurking outside.

"Are they out there?"

"I heard movement, so I think they're coming up to investigate, but nothing to shoot at yet," Clay replied.

"Hang on a sec." Jason lowered his night vision goggles and entered the darkness behind him. He returned thirty seconds later.

"It continues as far back as I can see with the NVGs. Do you know where this goes?" Jason asked Tarek.

"My grandpa took me through caves like this when I was young. Some are mines, and others are carved from water over millions of years. The mines and most caves run into a dead end pretty close to the entrance, but some go through the mountain to another entrance, while others can drop hundreds of feet without notice. He warned us to never go beyond what we could see in the caves while growing up."

Voices outside the cave entrance grew louder.

"How many do you think are out there?" Jason asked Clay.

"I'm guessing a half dozen. Maybe more if they brought reinforcements."

"Let's head deeper into the cave. Maybe we'll find another entrance."

"What about those hundred foot drop-offs?" Clay asked with concern in his voice.

"We have the NVGs. We'll be fine."

"These aren't the high-tech devices we're used to in special warfare. They're at least thirty years old and were available at the right price. I'm not sure these will work in complete darkness."

Jason heard the crunch of gravel from multiple men near the cave entrance. He reached down into a cargo pocket and held up a chemlight. "I have this."

"How long will it last? I don't want it to go out somewhere in the middle of the mountain."

"I don't know. A couple hours, I think," Jason replied. He recalled past training missions where he used chemlights. Jason thought they usually lasted three hours, but he wasn't sure.

A silhouette of a body with a rifle appeared at the end of the cave. "Hold your ears," Clay yelled.

A second later, a hive of slugs raced toward the entrance. The silhouette fell to the ground as the thunderous clap of the HK echoed throughout the cave. After the firing ended, the cartel member got up and darted away from the cave.

"We have no choice. We have to go deeper into the cave," Jason shouted. His ears were still ringing.

"All right. They know we're armed now, so that should buy us a few minutes while they regroup."

Jason ignited the chemlight and handed it to Tarek.

"Go in another twenty feet and wait for us. Clay and I will lay down some suppressive fire and then catch up with you. Got it?"

Tarek and Clay nodded.

Jason observed the chemlight floating waist-high in the dark a minute later. He could faintly make out Tarek's face.

"Okay. Three, two, one."

Clay and Jason sent hot lead through the cave entrance to deter the cartel shooters from entering anytime soon. A high-pitched whine filled Jason's ears, and he jogged with Clay back to Tarek's position. Jason affixed the chemlight to his chest, lowered his night vision goggles, and took the lead.

"Let's go. We have to keep moving."

The trio followed the serpentine cave at a snail's pace. Although they had NVGs, they had to be careful since depth perception while wearing NVGs was below average at best. As Clay, Jason, and Tarek traversed the tomb-like shaft, they experienced every defense the belly of the mountain threw at them. They passed through spacious caverns filled with bats, corridors with ceilings full of dagger-like stalactites, and claustrophobia-inducing sections that required them to squeeze through like they were being birthed a second time.

An hour after leaving the cave entrance, Jason felt the ground below him slope downward.

"Be careful. It's getting steep here," Jason warned.

"Is this one of those hundred-foot drop-offs?" Clay asked.

"I don't think so. Let's keep going, but be careful."

As soon as the words left Jason's mouth, he heard a thud behind him and then felt someone brush by him. They tried to grab onto his ankle to prevent him from slipping to the bottom but failed. He froze and waited until the cave was silent.

"Clay? Tarek? Are you okay?"

"I'm still behind you," Clay said.

"Tarek, are you hurt?"

The cave was as quiet as a tomb. Jason turned his feet sideways and slid down the slick slope like a snow skier.

"I'm okay," Tarek yelled. "I just banged my elbow when I fell."

Jason exhaled loudly, and he took the chemlight off his shirt.

"Hang on, I'm going to drop this down so you can see until we get there."

Five minutes later, the three men were united.

"Are you sure you're okay? That was some fall."

"Yeah, I'm fine. It levels off again, so that's good."

Over the next half hour, the trio walked in near silence. The cadence of brushing nylon and labored breathing were the only sounds detected by Jason. A lack of sound waves penetrating his inner ear was more disorienting than complete darkness.

"You see anything up ahead?" Clay asked. He was in the rear position while Jason was in front.

"Not yet."

"What if this is a dead end? We're only making our trek back up the way we came even longer. I doubt those guys are still waiting by the entrance. Let's turn around," Clay said.

Jason stopped moving to allow Tarek and Clay to catch up with him.

"Tarek, do you think this will open up somewhere else?" Jason asked.

"It should, but I don't know for sure."

"Not the reassuring answer I was hoping for," Jason said to himself. "Let's keep moving and see if we find another exit."

Clay flicked the dim green light on Jason's shirt with his finger. "Your chemlight looks like it's dying."

"We don't have much time left, so we need to speed up. We'll never get out of here if this light goes out."

Chapter 35

Jason picked up his pace and the other two followed. Twenty minutes later, Jason found it harder to see with his NVGs. He looked down and noticed his chemlight went dark.

Maybe Clay was right about going back.

All the movement in the cave ceased as Clay and Tarek also noticed their only light source was out.

"What do we do now?" Clay asked.

"I don't know. Give me a minute," Jason snapped.

His stomach turned queasy, and his chest tightened.

Instinctively, Jason looked at his watch. He guessed that he looked at his wrist a hundred times a day. Sometimes he wanted to know the time, temperature, or GPS coordinates, but mostly it was just a habit.

"What did you just do?" Clay asked.

"I checked my watch. I can't get a GPS signal in here, but I know we've been in the cave for over ninety minutes."

"Check the time again!"

Jason did and the tiny light in the watch cast a dim glow in the cave for ten seconds.

"I can see with my NVGs when your watch is lit up. Can you keep doing that until we get out of here?"

"It'll drain the battery pretty fast, but I'll keep doing it as long as I can."

Jason pressed the button on the right side of his watch every ten seconds, allowing the three men to continue navigating the cave. He noticed the light was getting a little dimmer with each button press, but he continued. Fifteen minutes later, he pressed the button on his watch and the corridor lit up. Jason stopped and noticed he could see well even after the watch went dark. He took a few more steps forward and saw a bright white light in his green night vision screen after rounding a corner.

"I see an exit."

A few steps later, Jason removed his NVGs and saw the cave open into a lofty cavern with a wide exit. It was twice the size of the entrance opening. Jason stopped twenty-five feet from the bright sun outside and let the others catch up with him.

"Tarek, hang tight while Clay and I move up to get a look outside."

Similar to approaching a door in urban combat training, Clay went left, and Jason took the right side until they reached a jagged line of shade separating the cave from the intense sun outside. They remained hidden in the shadows as they examined the area. Outside the cave, Jason observed they'd moved from the north side to the east side of the mountain and descended roughly two hundred feet from where they entered. The cave exited to a flat ledge overlooking a narrow canyon.

Without warning, Clay lunged back into the cave and Jason followed. It was a reflex now for Jason to react quickly without thinking.

"The cartel is up on the ridge. They're still looking for us, but I don't think they know we're down here."

Clay and Jason shuffled back to Tarek and told him what they found.

"Do you know where we are?" Jason asked.

Tarek nodded with a smile. "I know exactly where we are. We are on the ledge above Cibecue Creek a few hundred feet north of the falls."

"Great, so how do we get down from here?" Clay asked.

The smile disappeared. "We can climb down, but it is very steep and we'll have to descend slowly. It will be easy for the cartel to see us."

Jason paced in the cave as he pondered their next move. He returned to Tarek.

"How far down is the drop to the creek from the ledge outside the cave?"

"I think it's at least thirty to forty feet."

Jason ran his fingers through his hair. He walked near the cave opening, stared into the canyon, and returned.

"How deep do you think the creek is if we jump off the ledge?"

"It gets deep in some spots before the falls, but you don't know if there's a boulder or a log or something else you can't see under the water. Plus, you don't want to drift downstream and go over Cibecue Falls. That's another thirty-foot drop with water pounding on top of you. I've heard of people dying that have gone over the falls."

Jason gazed toward the rust-red canyon walls on the other side of the creek for several seconds.

"We have to go for it. It's about twenty yards from the cover of the cave to the cliff. Once we're over the side, the cartel won't be able to see us until they get to the edge of the cliff which will take them at least ten minutes. We can work our way past Cibecue Falls along the bank downstream and call for a ride at the campground."

The cave was quiet as looks were exchanged.

"Clay, are you in?" Jason asked.

"I'm not a big fan of heights, but I'll do it."

Tarek was more apprehensive. "I don't like to jump into water when I can't see what's below the surface. Is this our only option?"

Jason didn't even respond. He assumed this was Tarek trying to process the situation in his head and he gave him time.

"If I don't make it, will you be sure to find Annie's parents and tell them she is back with the Creator? They deserve to know."

Jason tilted his head. "You'll be able to tell them yourself. Where's this coming from?"

"I never assume I'll see tomorrow. I've cheated death many times before and I know my time will come. No matter when it happens, I'll be at peace with it. Just promise me you'll let Annie's family know."

Jason nodded. "I will."

"Okay. I'm ready."

The three men moved to the edge of the cave. Clay stuck his head out to see if the cartel member was still up on the ridge.

"Oh, shit! There's more of them and they're heading this way."

"We have to do this now. On three, run as fast as you can to the ledge and do not stop until you've jumped off!"

Jason rotated his neck and exhaled loudly. He stared at the jump off point for several seconds and began the countdown.

"Three, two, one, go!"

Jason emerged in front while Clay and Tarek followed close behind. Their movement attracted the attention of the cartel members bounding down the mountainside toward the cave. One of them raised their rifle and shot at the cluster of men darting toward the cliff.

At first, it was a couple of quick pops and then the canyon erupted with gunfire. He saw Tarek turn and raise his weapon toward the cartel out of the corner of his eye.

"Tarek, no!" Jason yelled.

"Hurry," Tarek responded.

Jason couldn't stop and a second later, his arms waved wildly as gravity pulled him toward the creek. Before impact, Jason heard the report from Tarek's Smith & Wesson. He tried to turn in the air to see what had happened, but he hit the water feet first with such force that it almost knocked the wind out of him. When he surfaced, he saw Clay entering the water feet first and then surface. Jason stared at the ledge until he saw Tarek appear.

His first reaction was relief, but that only lasted a nanosecond. Tarek fell awkwardly and was hurtling backwards toward the creek. There were only a few reasons Tarek would fall like that and none of them were good.

CHAPTER 36

The angle of Tarek's contorted body and his violent collision with the creek confirmed the worst-case scenario. Cartel gunfire had struck Tarek.

He remained submerged in the muddy stream and out of view for several tense seconds and then surfaced face down. Jason dove in from his position near the bank in the waist-deep water and quickly reached Tarek. He flipped his wounded friend over so his mouth and nose were skyward and tugged him from the grip of the current. On shore, Jason opened Tarek's eyelids and placed his fingers on his neck to check for a pulse.

"Is he alive?" Clay asked.

"He has a weak pulse, but he's not responsive. We need to get him to a hospital ASAP!"

Jason looked around for the best way to extract Tarek. They were on a sliver of a rocky bank clinging to the cliff they had just jumped off. The other side of the creek was below an even taller cliff. After concluding he had no good options in the immediate area, Jason floated Tarek downstream until they reached a flat, sandy area. The rumble of cascading water reverberated through Jason's body only twenty-five yards away from where they pulled Tarek ashore. He recalled Tarek's warning not to go over the waterfall, and now he understood why. Clay helped move Tarek out of the water and onto a level area. Jason started a blood sweep with both hands to find the entry and exit wounds. He stopped just above Tarek's left ankle when crimson stained his gloved hands.

"They shot him in the calf. It's a nasty through and through," Jason shared as he continued to examine Tarek.

The area of concern grew clear before Jason's blood sweep reached Tarek's abdomen. The blood-soaked shirt just above his left hip foreshadowed the gaping wound lurking beneath it. When Jason ripped Tarek's shirt apart, he observed mangled muscle and intestines intertwined in a rising pool of blood splattering outside the wound like water spilling over a dam. Jason did not see an exit wound. His new friend would die on the spot if he didn't treat and pack him for transport to a hospital.

"Why didn't you keep running?" Jason asked his unconscious friend.

The reserve PJ wiggled a pack off his back and removed a medical kit from his dry bag. It didn't have much, but contained iodine, blood clotting bandages, and two gauze rolls. Jason quickly wrapped Tarek's calf and then moved to his midsection.

"Slowly and carefully lift him up so I can get this wrap around his waist a few times," Jason instructed Clay. "On the count of three."

Clay helped lift Tarek so Jason could wrap the bandage around his mid-section twice. Then, Jason retook Tarek's pulse.

"I've got a stronger pulse but that will not last long. Plus, the cartel may still get a shot off at us until we get below the falls. Give me a hand with Tarek so we can get him some help!"

Although Clay was a couple of inches taller and had twenty more pounds of muscle than Jason, he did not have the training to transport a patient without a gurney. Clay raised Tarek to a standing position while Jason dropped to a knee to secure Tarek in a fireman's carry over his neck and shoulder.

Jason followed Clay down a path with his one-hundred-and-fifty-pound friend over his shoulder. He felt the warmth of Tarek's blood penetrating his shirt. After following a rocky path around the falls, they worked their way toward the parking lot at the Cibecue Falls trailhead. Thirty minutes after the cartel shot Tarek, Jason and Clay found a couple in their twenties wading up the creek toward the falls.

"Go see if they have a phone," Jason barked.

Clay ran ahead to the couple. They had a phone but no signal. They said a White Mountain Apache Tribe Game and Fish ranger was at the parking lot checking day permits. Jason picked up his pace and reached the parking lot five minutes later.

The ranger sauntered toward them and pulled his notepad out of his breast pocket. Jason laid Tarek down gently on the crushed granite of the parking lot. The ranger took one look at Tarek, and without saying a word, he broke out in a full sprint to his SUV. He was on a satellite phone when he returned.

"I just called for a medevac. Is he a member of the White Mountain Apache Tribe?"

"Yes. This is Tarek Dosala."

"I thought so. What happened?"

"He was shot by members of a drug cartel hiding above the falls. He's losing a lot of blood," Jason replied.

"A cartel? On the reservation?"

Jason regretted telling the ranger a detail that would distract him from the urgent task of helping Tarek.

"Captain Selah from the WMAT PD knows about it. Let's focus on stabilizing Tarek before the helicopter arrives."

The ranger rushed to his vehicle and returned with two blankets. They folded one under Tarek's head and put the other over him. He was shivering from all the blood loss.

Forty minutes after placing the call, dust swirled around the parking lot as the air ambulance landed. Jason helped the flight medics load Tarek onto the gurney and roll him to the helicopter. One medic put an oxygen mask on Tarek while Jason yelled to share his condition over the deafening rotor wash.

"He has two GSWs with a lot of blood loss. One in and out through the left calf, and another in his lower abdomen. No exit wound in the midsection. Abdominal wound packed with blood clotting bandages; no medications given."

Jason watched as the second flight medic hooked up the blood pressure, oxygen, and heart monitors. He wanted to jump in and start an IV right away.

"He needs blood ASAP."

The second flight medic gave Jason a thumbs up and tried to shut the door, but Jason stopped it.

"Where are you taking him?"

"The level 1 trauma center at Maricopa Medical Center in Phoenix," the medic shouted back.

The door closed as the engines revved, and the helicopter departed two minutes later.

Jason turned to ask the ranger if he could give them a ride to Clay's truck, and that's when he noticed Lieutenant Luna standing behind him. His eyebrows pinched and jaw clenched. Jason swallowed hard, expecting to receive a scolding or even get hauled back to jail in Whiteriver.

"What happened?" Lieutenant Luna asked.

Jason turned to Clay and then back to Luna.

"It's a long story. Can you take us back to my friend's truck a few miles upstream?"

"I'm not a taxi. A member of our community was shot, and I need to know what happened," Luna demanded. The veins in the lieutenant's neck popped out as his voice grew louder.

Jason took another step closer to him. "I'm not trying to be disrespectful, but we need to get to my friend's truck, and it really is a long story. I'll tell you everything on the way to his truck if you can give us a ride."

Luna stared at Jason for a few seconds. "Let's go."

Jason shared the full story during the one-hour drive. He knew it might get him in trouble, but Jason didn't care at this point. He wanted every local and federal law enforcement resource to focus on the cartel and take them out for good.

The WMAT PD SUV stopped behind Clay's truck. Luna said little during the commute to their vehicle. He listened and nodded until they parked. Clay got out while Jason shared more details.

"We also found the bodies of a man and a teenage boy that I believe are the missing hunters. Tarek said he found the body of a missing teenage girl that everyone hoped ran away. They're killing—"

"Is it Annie?" Luna interrupted.

"Yes. Tarek said her parents owned the repair shop in Whiteriver."

"That's Annie."

Luna stared out the windshield, so Jason continued.

"Nobody else is going after these guys. NCSO and DEA think they've already put the entire drug syndicate behind bars, and I don't know if the FBI is even on the case. I want justice for the innocent people those shitbags keep killing."

Luna continued to stare straight ahead. Jason wasn't sure he was listening, so he pulled on the door handle to quietly exit the vehicle. But, before Jason got one cheek off the seat, Luna slammed his fist on the steering wheel.

"Damn it!"

Jason jumped and turned to lieutenant Luna. His fiery red eyes were filled with tears.

"I went to high school with Annie's dad and saw her in the shop right before she vanished. She had some trouble in the past but was getting her life back on track. This has gone too far, and I will personally make sure those men pay for what they've done. I'm heading back to Whiteriver and going directly to Captain Selah," Luna said through gritted teeth.

Jason put his hand on Luna's shoulder. "I'm sorry for your loss. Don't give up until Captain Selah agrees to go after them." He exited the SUV, and Luna rolled down the window.

"Where are you going from here?"

"I'm going home to shower and then drive to Phoenix to check on Tarek."

"Call me tomorrow and let me know his condition and I'll fill you in on my conversation with Captain Selah."

During the drive back to Payson, Jason spoke fewer than a half dozen sentences to Clay. He had two questions constantly looping in his mind. Would Tarek be okay? The other question begged for a clear and concise answer. How could Jason make the cartel pay for all the pain they'd caused?

CHAPTER 37

The ten-story stucco and glass tower loomed large in Jason's windshield as he neared Maricopa Medical Center just east of downtown Phoenix. He turned into the parking lot and drove around for five minutes until he found an open spot. Once inside the hospital, the front desk attendant told him that Tarek was still in surgery and that he'd have to wait in the fourth floor waiting room.

Jason found the waiting room and flipped through an outdoor living magazine when his phone buzzed.

"Where are you?" Noah asked when Jason answered.

"I'm in Phoenix."

"Are you at the courthouse?"

"No. Why?"

"Today is the day those cartel members arrested by the DEA have their pre-trial hearing at the Federal courthouse. They all pled not guilty at their arraignments, so I assumed you'd want to know how the case was going. It is scheduled to start after lunch, and I wasn't sure how long a pre-trial hearing would last."

"I haven't followed their cases as closely as I should, so I didn't know that was today. I'm at the hospital with Tarek. They shot him during our mission this morning."

"What? I heard you come in and leave right away. What happened?"

"It's a long story and I can't get into all the details right now, but he's in surgery now. He didn't look good when he left in the helicopter."

The line was silent for several seconds.

"I hope he's okay," Noah whispered.

"Me too."

Jason checked his watch. It was a quarter after three, and he assumed he had little time to get to the courthouse.

"The doctor said Tarek will be in surgery and recovery for another hour or two, so I'm going to run over to the courthouse and see if I can catch the tail end of the hearing."

Twenty minutes later, Jason walked through the cavernous lobby of the contemporary Sandra Day O'Connor United States Courthouse in downtown Phoenix. The six-story glass and steel structure covered an ocean of marble making the room feel even grander. Once Jason found the correct room, he couldn't enter because court was in session. He found a black pleather chair bolted to the floor nearby and took a seat. He noticed other people mingling in the area and suspected they were waiting to get news of a verdict. Jason wondered if any of the men and women waiting near him were friends or family of the cartel members on trial for drug trafficking. He scanned the people milling around in the lobby but saw no familiar faces.

A door to the courtroom opened and a man exited. Jason stood and walked over, hoping the judge had adjourned for the day, but it was just an excused witness. Jason recognized the man's face when he looked up. It was special agent Holland from the DEA.

Jason hustled through the lobby to catch up. "Excuse me, sir."

The DEA special agent stopped and turned to face Jason. His eyebrows pinched and wrinkles spread across his forehead.

"I'm Jason Mulder. You interviewed me at my home in Payson about the cartel hiding in the forest."

The wrinkles disappeared.

"Oh. Hi, Jason. Are you also testifying?"

Jason shook his head. "I haven't heard from anyone since the night of the arrest, but I was in the area and wanted to see how the case was going."

Holland nodded. "I think we'll get convictions. Their public defender wants to negotiate a plea deal, but our attorneys are trying to tie in more information on their bosses, operations, and customers."

"They share anything yet?"

"No, they've clammed up, but we found a key and a ton of Canadian currency on them after we brought them in. They wouldn't say what the key is for, but our investigators believe it's for a box at one of those retail shipping centers."

"One of those UPS or FedEx stores?" Jason asked.

"Something like that. They don't know which one and what's inside the box yet, but our investigators will eventually find out."

Jason thought about the shipping stores along the main highway he'd passed by during previous trips to Show Low.

"I'm sure they'll find the store, and hopefully, the attorneys will get more info from them before they cut a deal," Jason said.

"All five men say they're just friends who got together to make fentanyl once in their life. They insist they have no ties to any of the cartels in Central America, Mexico, or South America, but all of them have palm tree tattoos in the shape of an X on their necks. We traced the ink to the La Palma cartel in El Salvador. They're a small cartel that peddles a fair amount of fentanyl and meth. Our legal team will keep pushing more, but I'm glad we took another cartel off the street."

"That's not all the members of the La Palma cartel in Arizona," Jason said.

Holland widened his stance and crossed his arms. "Why do you think that?"

Jason considered telling him about the cartel camp they found near Cibecue Falls from their attempted ambush but stopped himself. He'd received support from Lieutenant Luna and special agent Holland so far, but felt the mission earlier that morning that resulted in Tarek getting shot may push the federal agent beyond what he could accept.

"I think it's the same armed group that killed my brother and put my mom in the hospital. She said she saw about a dozen guys, so I figured there'd be more."

"It's a relatively small cartel. I doubt they have that many men to spare, and if they did, I bet they are back in El Salvador now."

Jason nodded and redirected to the other question on his mind since the sting that took in the five men on trial.

"I'm still surprised your team arrived minutes after we called. I'm glad you did, but I was shocked when I first saw the DEA vehicles coming our way. Did we catch your team geared up and out to dinner together in Heber?" Jason asked, partially joking.

Holland laughed. "I wish we were that fast. These guys have been on our radar for a couple of weeks, but just after noon that day, we received a tip of their location and spent a few hours planning our sting. We were already en route when your call came in."

Jason tilted his head to be sure he heard him correctly. "We'd just followed them back from Show Low. Who provided the tip?"

"It came from the Navajo County Sheriff's Office. I guess they were also tracking them."

"Did it come from Detective Caldwell?"

"The name sounds familiar. I think that's the guy that provided the tip."

Jason left the courthouse without waiting to get the results of the pre-trial hearing. He'd been suspicious of Detective Caldwell since he met him. The NCSO detective was not happy with Jason or Noah from the first moment he laid eyes on them. Jason found his behavior rude and unprofessional but never suspected he was up to something more sinister. The new information from special agent Holland changed everything.

CHAPTER 38

The glass door at Maricopa Medical Center automatically slid left when Jason approached, and he entered the lobby. The solemn gray-haired woman behind the counter confirmed Tarek was out of surgery and recovering in the ICU.

"Visiting hours for the ICU end at five, and only one visitor at a time. The family has priority over non-family," the front desk attendant informed Jason.

Jason looked at his watch. He only had fifteen minutes, so he shuffled to the bank of elevators at the far end of the lobby. The elevator doors shut, and Jason shuddered when a wave of cold enveloped him with the realization that Tarek was in intensive care. The conversation with Tarek on the ledge over Cibecue Creek replayed in his mind. Tarek felt something was wrong, and Jason dismissed it as nerves. He wished he'd listened more.

Jason remained confident Tarek would make a full recovery, even after he loaded his unresponsive friend into the bay of the helicopter. But now Jason had his doubts.

An ICU nurse at the station outside the elevator on the third floor informed Jason that a family member was currently in with Tarek and directed him to the waiting room. When Jason entered, he saw Shanna.

She didn't see Jason enter, which gave him time to study her face. He wasn't sure how she'd react to the man that got Tarek involved with the cartel that put him in the ICU. Several steps into the waiting room, Shanna looked up, and Jason caught her tear-filled eyes. Her lower lip quivered and Jason couldn't tell if it was extreme sadness or anger. She stood and drifted toward Jason. He braced for a slap but saw her arms reach for his waist and embrace him in a hug.

Jason held her tight for a full minute. He didn't want to let go but he finally took a step back.

"How is he?"

Shanna wiped away a tear. "His mom is in with him right now. The doctor said they removed the slug and stopped the bleeding. He's in serious but stable condition now."

Jason bit down on his lower lip. Internal bleeding is a major concern in an abdominal injury. He was pleased Tarek was in the ICU, where the doctors and nurses would monitor him around the clock for any dangerous effects from the gunshot wound.

"How are you doing?" Jason asked.

"Not good. When I got the news about Tarek, I also heard about Annie. I was with her family last week, and everyone still had hope she would return home. Our community has had so much bad news lately, and I'm not sure how much more we can take."

Before the mission that led to the shooting, Jason questioned whether he should include Tarek in a military-style ambush. Tarek was a capable marksman and excellent outdoorsman, but he didn't have the military training required to survive a firefight. He let his need for Tarek's knowledge and expertise bias his decision to include him in the mission. Further introspection revealed that Jason wanted Tarek there for more than just his skills. Jason respected Tarek and enjoyed his presence on the team. Tarek taught

Jason more than he expected about the forest and life in a short amount of time.

"I'm sorry I got Tarek involved in all this," Jason said. "I should have stopped inviting him after he helped me find the cartel the first time."

Shanna looked up at Jason. Her face hardened and her tears stopped. "Don't you dare apologize for including him," she growled.

This was the anger Jason had expected to encounter when he arrived.

"He considered you a friend. When he needed a ride to a job interview, you didn't have to help him, but you did. He got the job, and I haven't seen him this happy in a long time. His confidence and sense of purpose have exploded since he met you. You didn't pull the trigger, Jason. Those animals in the forest did. He was in a dark place when you met him in jail, and you helped him turn his life around. There is no need to apologize."

Shanna's response was less than ninety words, but those eight sentences lifted what felt like a hundred elephants off Jason's back. He was concerned Shanna blamed him for Tarek's condition and was relieved to learn that wasn't true.

"I wish there was more I could do for him."

"There is," Shanna said. Red streaks crisscrossed her eyes like bolts of lightning. "You can find those thugs and make sure they pay for this."

Jason's eyes widened. "Are you sure?"

"Yeah. A wise man once told me that sometimes it takes violence to stop violence."

Jason stood up straight and pulled his shoulders back. Shanna's vote of confidence reignited the fire in his belly. He looked at the clock in the waiting room and noted it was one minute past five. Visiting hours were over and they'd all have to leave soon.

"I'll find them and make them pay."

Jason kissed Shanna on the cheek and left the waiting room.

He walked out of the hospital, oblivious to everything around him. Jason had only one thing on his mind: wiping out every single member of the cartel.

CHAPTER 39

Victor watched the Oxford White Ford F-150 leave the hospital parking lot and his lips curled skyward. He'd raced from his camp on the Fort Apache Reservation to Phoenix after they failed to kill the intruders earlier that morning. He arrived at the federal courthouse in downtown Phoenix and waited in the lobby until they escorted the five detained members of the La Palma cartel into the courtroom. Although Victor was confident nobody would identify him, he couldn't risk sitting inside the secure room during the hearing, yet he accomplished his objective merely with his presence. The five cartel members saw Victor when he briefly walked in and out of the courtroom while they waited for the judge, and they knew what his presence meant. Their families would be safe and provided for as long as they did not speak a word of the cartel. If they revealed information about the La Palma cartel, they would face a gruesome and painful death in prison and their families in El Salvador would meet a similar demise.

While Victor waited in the lobby to send a final message to the five detainees, he saw the tall American strut across the threshold.

"Jason Mulder," Victor whispered to himself. He moved to a new bank of chairs farther away and concealed his face underneath a ball cap. The La Palma cartel member blended into the crowd like a grain of sand on a beach. Victor watched Jason speak with a man that testified during the hearing and then left with little warning.

When Jason rushed to the elevators for the attached parking garage, Victor had two options. He could stay in the lobby and reinforce his message of silence to the five cartel members, or he could follow Jason. It was an easy choice. Jason Mulder was responsible for the five men on trial and had been a disruptive nuisance to Victor and his operation for over a month. He could not waste an opportunity to eliminate the American thorn in his side.

After Jason drove to the hospital and went inside, Victor removed a cheap magnetic GPS tracker from his pack and placed it under the rear bumper of Jason's truck. It fell to the pavement, so Victor pushed the tracker up to his elbow deep inside the bumper. He knew the tag could fall out again, so he'd follow him home today.

Forty minutes later, Victor confirmed the GPS tracker was moving east on the freeway, so he exited his vehicle and walked toward the hospital's front desk. He hoped he could learn more about Jason based on the person he visited. Victor stood outside the doors, counted to three, and rushed into the lobby.

"I'm here with Jason Mulder. We brought in an injured man, and I need to see that he's okay!"

Victor spoke rapidly in his best English. He sounded like many worried friends arriving at the Phoenix trauma center before him.

The same woman that helped Jason two hours earlier looked up over her glasses at Victor. "Who are you looking for?"

"I don't remember his name. My friend Jason Mulder brought him here a couple of hours ago. I think he may have been shot."

The front desk attendant pecked a few keys on her keyboard and quietly examined the screen.

"Tarek Dosala was admitted by air ambulance five hours ago. Is that him?"

Victor flashed his winning smile. "Yes, that is the name my friend Jason Mulder used. Can I see him?"

"He's in the ICU, and visiting hours ended ten minutes ago. Come back after noon tomorrow."

Victor put his hands together as if praying and bowed. "Thank you."

He left the lobby and checked on the location of the tracking device. It was eight miles away. Victor slid his phone into one pocket and yanked the car keys from the other, but someone caught his attention before he departed for his vehicle. A stunning young lady in her twenties with long black hair and tear-stained cheeks exited the elevator and ambled through the lobby toward the parking lot. The urgency to follow Jason Mulder melted away at the sight of a beautiful woman in distress. Victor fumbled in his pocket to retrieve his phone and pretended to be on a call.

The woman exited through the automatic door and stopped underneath the covered hospital entrance. She opened her purse and rummaged through the contents while muttering something Victor could not hear. After a few beats, she pulled out a tube of lipstick, slammed it back into the purse, and burst into tears.

"Are you okay?" Victor asked.

The woman jumped at the sound of his voice, sniffed, and turned toward him. "Um—I'm just having a bad day. Visiting hours are over, and I just want to get home, but I can't find my car keys."

"I'm so sorry. Is the person you visited, okay?" Victor asked sincerely.

"We're not sure yet. He was shot and just got out of surgery. He's resting in the recovery room now."

Victor's interest in the woman turned from romantic aspirations to ruthless revenge in a split second. Was this woman here to visit Tarek Dosala? Does she know Jason Mulder?

"I'm sorry to hear that. Can I help you with something?"

The woman shook her head. "No. I just need to find my keys."

While the woman investigated the bottom of her purse again, Victor tapped his pocket to confirm his Ravencrest Tactical knife was there. Four inches of razor-sharp hardened steel that released instantly with a push of a button waited in his pocket.

Victor took two steps toward the woman. He was close enough to touch her.

"Found them!"

The woman dangled her keys and flashed a brief smile for the minor victory as tears continued to race down her cheeks.

Victor looked around and stuck one hand into his pocket with the knife.

"You seem very upset. Let me walk you to your car."

"Thank you, but that's not necessary."

The cartel lieutenant wiggled the knife into his palm while his index finger hovered over the button to expose the killing end of the blade. He scanned the area and then let go of the knife when a small group of visitors exited the lobby. Victor waited until they were in the parking lot and took another step toward the woman, causing her to step away and look at his face.

"I think you should let me walk you to your car. Parking lots can be dangerous."

The woman stared at Victor without responding. He watched her throat constrict on a swallow. Victor had to know if she was here for Jason Mulder's friend before he made his next move.

"Were you here to visit Tarek Dosala?"

"How do you—"

The woman stopped talking, pulled her purse close to her body, and searched his face. Victor could see the fear in her eyes. Her tears stopped and her jaw tightened. When he reached into his pocket to retrieve his knife, the woman bolted into the parking lot.

Her decision to flee and the speed at which she moved caught Victor off guard. He took several steps into the parking lot toward her, but a sedan pulling in to drop off a patient cut him off.

Victor hated that he missed an opportunity to inflict pain on a friend of Jason Mulder but was satisfied that he was getting closer. Soon Jason Mulder would be sorry he crossed Victor Romero and the La Palma cartel.

CHAPTER 40

Victor turned off the main highway in Payson toward the location of his GPS tracking device. The device hadn't moved in twenty-five minutes, so Victor hoped Jason Mulder was at home. The cartel lieutenant drove through a dense neighborhood of modest two-story homes with attached garages and small grassy lots toward the motionless tracker. He bounced over a speed bump and immediately knew why his tracker stopped moving. Victor exited his truck at the next speed bump and picked up the GPS tracker from the side of the road. He scanned the area and noted that the road continued toward a different community with spacious lots and larger homes wedged among a sea of trees. He'd lost the exact location of his prey but felt he was close.

Victor's heart beat faster with every rotation of his tires as he rolled slowly down the narrow road. He crept past every driveway looking for the late model white Ford F-150 with a distinct bumper sticker. Ten minutes after finding the tracker, Victor braked when he saw a white truck parked in a driveway. He stopped and pretended to look at his phone like a lost tourist to prevent suspicion from neighbors. Once Victor was satisfied no neighbors were paying attention, he leaned out of his window to get a better look at the ranch-style home. He noted two doors to the house and two additional vehicles parked in front. He backed up a couple of feet to get a better look at the white truck and Victor smiled wide. It had the bumper sticker of the two jolly green feet. It was Jason Mulder's house!

Victor found the highway and returned to the secluded outpost near Cibecue Falls. Once he reached the camp, he was ready to execute the next phase of his plan. He moved to the rear of his truck, lowered the tailgate, and took a seat.

"Tell the new guys to come up here," Victor demanded.

A man pulling security near him scampered into the camp. Minutes later, Oscar and Mauricio shuffled out of the darkness and into the soft white light illuminating Victor on the tailgate. Oscar was a hair under six feet tall with shoulder-length black hair and a wiry build that made him look taller. He stood in stark contrast to the shorter, muscular, and fully tattooed Mauricio. The two men in their mid-twenties were rising stars as sicarios for the La Palma cartel in Central America. El Jaguar sent them to Arizona as a thank-you for delivering the much-needed Canadian currency the previous week. They were also sent to help Victor achieve his requirement of doubling their fentanyl sales before returning home. Now they could test their unique skills in the United States.

"I have a job for both of you, and it has to be done tonight. Have a seat."

The two sicarios sat on stumps while Victor remained seated on the tailgate.

"An American has been harassing our operation for months and he must be eliminated. I would have killed him weeks ago, but I just found out where he lives today. His name is Jason Mulder."

Victor hopped off the tailgate and moved next to Oscar and Mauricio.

"He's responsible for the five men sitting in court today. The critical shipment arrives in two days. We can't have any surprises, so you need to go to his home and kill him tonight."

Oscar and Mauricio looked at each other and then back at Victor. They nodded in unison.

"No problem," Mauricio replied.

Victor laughed.

"Don't be so sure. He's not like any man you've faced in El Salvador. He has military weapons and gear and moves like a highly trained commando. Killing him will not be easy."

"Okay, we will prepare for a hard target. Does he live alone?"

"I believe he has a family. I counted three cars in the driveway, and there could be more, so prepare for more people."

"What should we do with his family?"

"Stand up!" Victor roared.

Both men rose to their feet, and Victor drifted next to the hitmen. He stopped once his nose was a foot from Mauricio's forehead and Oscar's chin.

"I want you to kill everyone in that house and burn it down once you're done. Everyone must learn not to mess with the La Palma cartel."

Oscar and Mauricio arrived in Payson an hour before sunrise. They drove past the target home several times and pulled into a semi-secluded spot a hundred yards from the Mulder property. They each carried an AK-74M rifle with Hexagon suppressors and subsonic rounds to conceal their assault as much as possible.

They entered the forest at the end of the driveway. The sicarios didn't have night vision or thermal imaging devices, so they carefully crept through the woods with only the light of the waxing moon. Once parallel with the house, the two hitmen scanned the building for all exits.

"I counted three doors. One on the south, another on the west, and the back door facing east," Mauricio whispered to Oscar in Spanish.

Although they were technically equals, Mauricio assumed the leadership role.

"We'll set up on the southeast and southwest corners of the house, and they won't have a choice but to run right into our trap."

Oscar nodded.

"Find your position to cover both the back and side door. I'll do the same for the front door and then meet back here in five minutes."

Each found a spot ten feet into the woods with a clear view of their sector. Mauricio set down his satchel next to Oscar's when they returned. He removed a glass bottle that used to contain a fifth of legendary Tennessee whiskey but now was filled with a blend of gasoline, hand sanitizer, diesel fuel, and liquid dish soap. Next, he removed a cotton rag cut into strips and a lighter. Oscar did the same, and they assembled their Molotov cocktails.

"Do you remember the plan?" Mauricio asked.

Oscar nodded, but Mauricio wasn't convinced.

"We'll each grab a large stone on our way to the house. Be sure to light your cocktail first, throw the stone through the window, and then throw the bottle so it explodes deep inside the house. I'll throw mine through the big front window, and you throw yours through the window near the south side door. That should be their kitchen," Mauricio said with his eyes locked on the target.

"Right after you throw it, run back to your position and be ready to shoot anyone that comes out of those doors."

Mauricio pulled his gloves tight and flexed his hands. "Are you ready?"

"Yes!" Oscar replied.

Each man crept up to the house and lit their Molotov cocktails. Oscar threw his stone first, and Mauricio followed a second later. Once the glass was out of the way, they launched their homemade firebombs deep into the house.

The house still seemed asleep when Oscar and Mauricio took their positions staking out all exits. The flickering light inside the front window was small and Mauricio wondered if their Molotov cocktails had failed. A minute later, he received his answer when flames grew visible, and smoke began to waft from the broken plate glass. He heard shouting from the burning building and knew they were seconds away from their targets appearing in their sights. The sicarios prepared for Jason Mulder and his family to emerge from the burning structure where the La Palma cartel assassins would swiftly gun them down. They readied their rifles and waited for their victims.

CHAPTER 41

The first crash woke Jason, and the second blast of shattering glass sent him rushing down the hallway into the kitchen. He stood motionless in his boxer shorts for several seconds as the orange glow of the growing fire flickered off his face. The fire was silent, unlike the crackling and pops he was used to from burning pine wood in the fire pit. Jason followed the trail of fire to the remains of a whiskey bottle broken into several pieces. The top portion contained a rag stuffed inside, resting underneath the kitchen table.

Jason searched for something to grab the source of the flames, but the fire doubled in size every few seconds. He could no longer reach it without getting burned.

Phillip arrived in the kitchen. "What happened?"

"Somebody hit us with Molotov cocktails. Get the fire extinguishers," Jason barked.

The kitchen had three fire extinguishers thanks to Jason's oldest brother Kevin and his job as a firefighter. His dad grabbed one from under the sink and sprayed the flames turning the carpet, table, and chairs into black carbon. The small fire extinguisher ran out of sodium bicarbonate, so Phillip ran to the pantry, removed the largest fire extinguisher in the house, and continued battling the flames as they charred the kitchen walls.

Jason flew into the living room and found the coffee table, couch, and carpet in flames. He pulled a throw blanket off his mom's chair and tossed it on the broken bottle that ignited multiple throw pillows on the couch. Jason bundled up the bottle pieces and ran out of the room. The front door was closer, but it was near dry brush and trees, and Jason didn't want to start a forest fire along with his house fire. Instead, he ran through the kitchen with the throw blanket that ignited and out the back door. He passed his mom and Noah as they stood frozen staring at the firestorm growing in the kitchen.

"Grab a fire extinguisher, water, or anything and help Dad put this out!" Jason yelled.

He passed through the door and tossed the fully engulfed bundle at the end of the patio into the fire pit area. Jason darted back into the house, and that was when he was hit. Splinters from the wood doorframe inches above his head rained down on him, and a half second later, he heard a noise like a large branch cracking. He dove to the floor out of habit but wasn't sure what had happened. Jason looked at the fire climbing up the nearby wall and assessed that it couldn't have splintered the wood across the room. He looked back to the door frame and saw the quarter-size hole about head high.

"Oh, shit!"

Smoke rose and filled the top two feet of the nine foot high ceiling when Jason shot into the family room.

"Nobody go outside and stay away from the windows!"

"Why?" Celeste screamed. She fought the flames with a fire extinguisher while Noah pushed furniture around to give her a direct shot at the burning carpet.

"Someone is outside with a rifle. They already shot at me. I don't know how many there are, so stay low and don't go outside."

"A rifle?" Phillip asked.

"They may be waiting for us to run out of the house. Do not go outside right now!"

Jason sprinted to his bedroom and tossed on his tactical pants, boots, and shirt lying over his chair from the previous day. Next, he holstered his SIG Sauer P226 9MM pistol and texted Clay to come over as soon as possible. He didn't have time for anything else. Instead of heading to the kitchen and family room to help with the fires, he went the opposite direction until he was in Josh's old room on the north end of the house. Jason wasn't sure how many people were outside but hoped they'd only be staking out the doors. That was what he'd do if it was a small team. He slowly opened the window and dropped to the floor in case someone was on that side of the house. When he drew no gunfire, he removed the screen and slid outside. Once his boots hit the ground, Jason froze. He allowed his eyes and ears to adjust from the bright fire and yells from inside the house. He noticed the eastern sky was transitioning from the blackness of midnight to turquoise as the blue hour approached. Jason did not have any gear to give him a tactical advantage over the shooters lurking in the woods. He would have to go old school this time.

The porch light near the back door bathed the patio in soft white light but cast dark shadows on the woods behind the house. Jason calculated from the hole in the door frame that the shot originated somewhere near the southeast corner of the backyard. Jason dropped to the grass in the yard and low crawled to the tree line. Once he had some cover in the woods, Jason continued toward the southeast corner. He took two gentle steps and then stopped. His ears were his best asset until the first rays of sunlight reached the woods, so until then, he'd listened for any signs of movement. Hearing none, he continued. Eighty steps later, he reached the middle of his backyard. He was parallel to the back door and verified again that the shooter must be in the corner covering the back and side doors. That was when Jason heard the unmistakable human sound of metal clinking metal from that direction. He estimated his first target was fifty to sixty paces away.

The porch light was less effective as twilight brightened the forest. Thirty silent paces later, Jason made out the silhouette of a man sitting on his butt with his elbows supporting a rifle on his knees. Jason dropped to a knee behind a tree and observed the shooter. The man wiggled his body and slid a couple of inches to his left while he maintained his gaze toward the house.

A wry smile formed on Jason's face. He knew the symptoms of a cold ass. The shooter's buttocks, legs, and lower back were probably cramping while he sat in the cold soil. Whenever he tried to find a new position to give him temporary relief, he gave Jason the break he needed. The shooter's metal zipper smacked the metal magazine of his rifle every time he adjusted his body. Jason saw him flip long hair out of his eyes, which generated the loudest sound of metal on metal yet in the quietness of the forest. Jason shook his head. That was why his clothing and tactical gear had plastic or hard rubber accessories.

The shooter never took his eyes off the house, so Jason continued in his direction, hoping for the element of surprise. Jason reached within six feet of the cartel sicario, or hitman, when he finally heard something. The hitman moved to his knees and swung the rifle toward Jason faster than he expected, but Jason's fist was already en route to the shooter's chin. The punch landed squarely, knocking the shooter back and the rifle out of his grasp. The Kalashnikov rifle landed several feet away with a thud. The shooter made it to his feet, shook his head and faced off with Jason.

"Jason Mulder. Uds. van a morir," the man growled.

A chill ran up Jason's spine. He understood the sicario said they would all die, but that wasn't what concerned him. They'd learned his name and found where he lived. One of his greatest fears had become a reality. Jason's family and friends were in grave danger. He didn't know how many shooters were hiding, but his objective was clear. Jason had to eliminate the threat by any means necessary. If he failed, everyone he loved could die.

Chapter 42

Searing heat replaced the sharp chill coursing throughout Jason's body. A cocktail of rage and intense focus fueled Jason as he moved into his fighting stance. He wasted no time waiting for the sicario to prepare and jabbed the man in the nose with lightning quickness. A river of blood immediately flowed from both nostrils to his lips. The shooter touched his lips, looked at the blood, and removed a four-inch knife from his cargo pocket. Jason took a step back and they moved around each other like boxers in a ring. They were sizing each other up, and Jason noted the man was not muscular, but he was tall and lanky. His long reach with a blade could be a problem.

The sicario jabbed several times, but Jason blocked each attempt. The sicario's eyes widened, and he rotated the knife from a slicing to a stabbing hold. Jason recognized that his next move would be a downward thrust with enough force to plunge the blade through Jason's flesh, bones, and organs. He considered reaching for his SIG Sauer to end the conflict within seconds but knew his unsuppressed fire could bring the other cartel members to assist him. Instead, Jason edged toward the man. His earlier battle with the Mountain Man from the cartel taught him to be more aggressive with his countermoves to end the fight as fast as possible.

The sicario raised his right hand over his head and came down as Jason expected. Jason met his forearm with his for a block, but due to the sicario's long arms, Jason missed his mark. The block was too close to the elbow and the blade grazed Jason's shoulder. He didn't have time to feel the sting of steel penetrating the skin because the sicario was already coming with his second stab attempt. This time Jason corrected his block and caught the assailant closer to his wrist while delivering a straight punch into his chin. Jason followed with a quick kick to the groin, bringing the knife down to waist level with Jason still holding onto his wrist. When he tried to disarm the sicario, the cartel hitman twisted his wrist and knife toward Jason making it impossible for him to reach the knife. Jason had to improvise, so he grabbed the knife with both hands, lowered his shoulder and slammed into the sicario causing both men to fall to the ground.

Jason landed on top of the sicario and felt warm wetness on his left shoulder. He hoped it was from the cartel hitman, but the sudden sharp sting from his deltoid confirmed the blade penetrated his flesh from the last stab attempt. He had to end the struggle soon, but neither man was willing to give up their grip on the knife dangerously close to both of their mid-sections. Jason thought of the enemy waiting to shoot his entire family and tapped into a final reserve of adrenaline to move to his knees and overpower the cartel member. The blade inched closer to the sicario's chest until the tip vanished and then the entire four-inch blade disappeared.

Jason peered down at the man and saw two wide, white ovals peering at him through a face covered in blood. The sicario gasped as he grabbed at his lethal wound with both hands.

Jason rolled off and observed the dying man. His medical training told him what was going on under his skin. The knife struck near his heart, so blood was pumping into his lungs and displacing all oxygen. He'd die from drowning in his own blood. The sicario opened his mouth to speak, but only gurgling noises emerged. A minute later, the man fell limp. His eyes remained open with a look of surprise plastered on his face for all eternity.

Once Jason was sure the man would not mount a counterattack, he moved toward the front of the house. His scuffle with the first shooter was anything but stealthy, and Jason figured that anyone else trying to kill him would be ready for his arrival. Jason removed his pistol from his waist as he skirted the driveway. He was slowed by his aching shoulder but continued toward the front of the house under the cover of mature pine trees scattered throughout the property. It was a good thing because Jason saw the second cartel hitman seconds before muzzle flashes from his rifle lit up the forest. The muffled sound of each blast sounded foreign to Jason. He'd never heard a suppressed Kalashnikov-made rifle before.

Once the firing from the AK-74 paused, Jason sent several rounds toward the second sicario and dove to the ground. He low crawled through the undergrowth and rose behind another sturdy ponderosa pine tree ten feet away. The La Palma sicario unloaded a full magazine into the tree he had just vacated. Jason heard a pause and the sound of switching out magazines. He considered jumping from behind the tree and firing, but the front door to the house swung open, grabbing the attention of both Jason and the shooter.

Phillip opened the front door, and smoke billowed out. He took a step through the doorway, bent over, and coughed on the front porch. Jason saw the shooter turn and aim his rifle toward his father.

"Dad!" Jason yelled. He emerged from behind the tree with his weapon at the ready. The sicario turned toward Jason but kept the rifle trained on Phillip. Jason squeezed the trigger in quick succession and fired three rounds. Two struck center mass in his chest, and the third struck above his left eye. A well-executed Mozambique Drill Jason heard the army rangers and Navy SEALs often discuss as the best way to instantaneously stop a bad guy.

The second shooter fell to the forest floor like a string puppet with its cords cut, and the forest fell silent again. Phillip dove back into the house, but Jason remained in the woods. He knelt and listened for several minutes before moving again. Hearing nothing, he moved toward the intersection of his driveway and the paved road with his SIG Sauer at the ready. Jason emerged from the woods as the sky turned blue and the sun's first rays hit the tree tops. He noticed a gray pickup truck parked down the road, so he slipped back into the forest. Jason assumed a getaway driver would have exited to help his comrades or left by now, but he wasn't taking any chances.

He reached the rear of the vehicle and moved to the tree line behind anyone that might have been in the gray truck. Seeing no silhouettes or movement in the cab, Jason charged toward the passenger door, ready to fire. Nobody was inside.

Jason exhaled and circled the vehicle. It was full of rust-colored mud, just like the area around Cibecue Creek, and that confirmed what Jason had already suspected. The cartel sent sicarios to his home to kill him and his family.

Jason marched on the pavement back to his house. A feeling of dread washed over him. He'd left his family fifteen minutes ago while combating flames, and he wasn't sure if they were alive or dead. Bile crawled up his gut and stung his throat as the gravity of the situation hit him.

"Please be okay," Jason said to himself. He sprinted toward the open front door, unaware of what he'd find inside.

CHAPTER 43

Smoke assaulted Jason's eyes and nostrils when he entered the living room. The fires were out, but smoke still clung to the ceiling as it slowly seeped out the open doors and windows. He saw Noah moving frantically in the kitchen and heard sobs to his right. His dad sat on the unburned loveseat while his mom lay in a fetal position with her head on Phillip's lap. He looked like he'd fought a twelve-round heavyweight fight as he stroked Celeste's curly black hair.

Sirens drew closer as Jason scanned the charred furniture his family used to sit in and share stories. The walls looked like someone splashed buckets of black paint throughout the living room and kitchen. Red and white strobes appeared and danced throughout the house.

"Is everyone okay?" Jason asked.

Nobody answered, but his father nodded. Jason moved into the kitchen and found Noah transporting items from a china cabinet next to a scorched table to the kitchen counter.

"What are you doing?" Jason asked.

"I called Kevin, and he said the fire department will check for hot spots and hidden embers, so we need to move all of Mom's valuables out of this china cabinet before they get here. The table and everything around it burned badly and they'll want to move it."

The amber cherry wood hutch had been a fixture in the kitchen since Jason could remember. The hutch contained a cabinet with two doors under four open shelves. It was more than a piece of furniture to store items. It was a time capsule of their lives. The top two shelves proudly displayed colorful holiday dinnerware passed down from Jason's grandmother, ornate nineteenth-century bottles of olive oil, and Mulder family pictures in antique pewter frames. A porcelain Spanish flamenco dancer doll made by an artist from Celeste's hometown in Santander, Spain and souvenirs from family trips and heirlooms passed down from Celeste's grandmother filled the next shelf. Jason identified several vintage school projects on the bottom and most prominent shelf above the cabinet doors. Handprints in plaster created in Mrs. Gilroy's third-grade art class were displayed from oldest to youngest for all four Mulder boys. Next to the handprints was a sorry clay coffee cup that looked like it melted under the sun. It was one of Kevin's less successful projects from the fifth grade. That was when it hit him. His parents and brother were almost killed. His chest tightened, and his entire body shuddered at the thought of one of them running outside during the fire. The overwhelming feeling of helplessness after Gaby's death entered his thoughts for the first time in seven years.

"Are you going to just stand there, or are you going to help?" Noah asked. "The fire department is outside and will be here in a minute."

The question jolted Jason out of his thoughts, and he got to work ferrying a lifetime of memories across the kitchen.

"Jason, are you okay?" Noah asked. He was staring at his shoulder.

Jason reached over with his right hand and touched the blood-soaked shirt. He seemed surprised to see the crimson on his hand. Jason didn't feel anything during the heat of battle, but now that Noah pointed it out, it immediately throbbed.

"I'm fine."

"It doesn't look fine to me. You'd better get that looked at."

By this time, firefighters and paramedics were inside the house. They tried to coax Jason into the ambulance and take him to the hospital, but he refused. Instead, the EMT gave him nine stitches while Jason sat on the back patio and answered the deputies' questions.

Two hours later, the firefighters and paramedics left, but an investigative team from the Gila County Sheriff's Office remained on the scene. They were still examining the dead bodies in the wooded lot adjacent to the Mulder property.

Clay arrived in the driveway and parked next to the yellow police caution streamer blocking off half the driveway. He went inside and found Jason walking into the kitchen.

"Whoa, is everyone okay?"

Jason dropped the charred couch cushion he was carrying and hugged his friend. "Yeah, everyone is shaken, but nobody is injured."

"Sorry it took me so long to get here. I stayed at a friend's house in Phoenix last night to be closer to Tarek. I left as soon as I got your text."

"Thanks for coming, man. The last forty-eight hours have been crazy."

"What did I miss here? Are those dead bodies in the woods?"

Jason exhaled and wiped off his hands. He pushed Clay gently to go outside to the back patio.

"I don't want them to hear all this. My mom is a wreck right now."

Clay nodded. Once outside, he crossed his arms as he leaned against the railing.

"The cartel came here to take out me and my family. Two guys tossed in Molotov cocktails and then staked out all the doors with Kalashnikov rifles to shoot anyone that left the house."

Jason stopped talking and looked into the forest. It all happened so fast that he was still processing the events from earlier that morning.

"That's brutal. They literally tried to smoke you out into an ambush. I assume you got out and eliminated them. How'd that go down?" Clay asked.

Jason looked down at the ground. "You know how it is. I did what I had to do."

"Tell me they're both dead."

Jason nodded.

It was quiet for several seconds until Clay spoke again. "I'm glad to hear those two will no longer be a threat. How do we pay back the rest of the pricks that ordered this hit on you and your family?"

Jason started to think clearly again after a massive adrenaline rush surged through every inch of his body. The clarity brought the strong sensation that he was sucker punched. He'd underestimated the ruthlessness of the cartel leader and his men. Jason always knew retaliation was possible but never thought they'd target his family while everyone slept in his boyhood home. For the first time since he started pursuing the cartel, a hint of doubt and fear crept into his thoughts. What if the cartel leader was too smart to be captured? If one of the sicarios had killed Jason, would the rest of his family have been murdered?

The last question sent a shudder through Jason.

"I don't know, man. Maybe we should just let the DEA deal with this."

"What?"

Jason put his hands in his pockets and shook his head. "I'm a civilian and a reservist and so are you. We can't just go after them like they're the enemy on the battlefield. These guys are vicious, especially their leader, and they'll kill anyone, anywhere, anytime. We can't match that."

Clay left the railing and moved next to Jason. "I agree that law enforcement needs to be involved, but they need our help. I know that we're not down range right now but I also understand that you and I have special training and skills suited to handle a unique situation like this. We need to help them capture or kill these psychopaths before more people end up like Josh and Tarek."

Clay put the straw back in his mouth and locked eyes with Jason. His perspective and reminder of the stakes helped drain the last bits of doubt clinging to Jason. He heard all he needed to refocus on the objective. Jason extended his hand to Clay.

"Justice for Josh and Tarek," Jason replied with resolve back in his voice.

Clay grabbed his hand and pulled Jason in for a quick chest bump. "That's the Jason Mulder I know."

"Can you do me a favor?" Jason asked.

"Sure. Shoot."

"Can you hang out here today while I run out for a few hours? I don't know if anyone else will come for me here, and I don't want them to be alone. You can bring your arsenal into my room. The smoke didn't get too bad in that part of the house."

"No problem. Is it okay for you to leave? Do the police outside need to talk to you?"

"I've already shared the entire story with two detectives, and my parents and Noah corroborated my account of what happened. I think they'll be good until I return."

"Where are you going?"

"I'm going to Whiteriver to talk to the WMAT PD. Be ready to go full-tactical within twenty-four hours because, by the time I return, we'll have a plan to take down the cartel."

Clay smiled. "I'll be ready."

CHAPTER 44

The speedometer in the old Ford truck dropped from 85 MPH back down to 70 MPH after Jason took his foot off the accelerator. He didn't want to add a ticket or even criminal speeding to his horrendous day. Halfway to Whiteriver, the phone chirped on the seat next to Jason. It was Shanna.

"Noah just called me. Is everyone all right?" she asked.

"Yeah. Everyone is okay. Nobody got injured, but everyone got a good scare."

"What happened? Noah said he had to help put out a fire with your mom and dad in your house. He sounded upset and asked if I was available for a therapy session today."

It surprised Jason to hear that Noah was upset. He seemed frazzled, but nothing out of the ordinary considering the circumstances. Jason had to remind himself that he'd been in hundreds of stressful situations and the fire was a traumatic event for most people, even if he could quickly process it and move on as if it had never happened.

"Can I stop by and tell you in person? I'm on my way to Whiteriver right now."

"You're coming to Whiteriver? Why?"

"Yeah, I'll be there in a little over an hour. I'm going to WMAT PD."

"Are you meeting with them about the cartel?"

"I am."

"Is the fire related to this meeting?"

"I'll stop over after my meeting and tell you everything."

"What time will you be here? I'm going to drive back down to Phoenix to see Tarek."

Jason checked his watch. It was almost 11:00 am. "I'll be there in two hours."

The middle-aged officer behind the counter stiffened when Jason entered the building. His eyebrows pinched and his face couldn't hide that he was concerned about the new visitor. Jason looked down at his shirt and pants. He was in such a rush to leave that he forgot to change and entered WMAT PD in tactical gear with his shoulder caked in dried blood. Jason understood the concerned look.

"I'd like to speak with Captain Selah."

The man behind the badge put both palms on the counter and leaned toward Jason.

"He's not available now. How can I help you?"

"My name is Jason Mulder, and I've been working with Lieutenant Luna and Captain Selah on an active case for your department. Is Lieutenant Luna available?"

The front desk officer eyed Jason for several seconds and left the counter. A minute later, he returned.

"He'll be with you in a few minutes."

Jason stood to the side and picked at a fresh scab on his elbow. He'd acquired several cuts and scratches during his scuffle with the cartel member that he didn't notice at the time.

Five minutes later, Luna arrived. "What happened to you?"

"The cartel came after my family at home and I had a confrontation with two of them."

"You're kidding, right?"

"I'm as serious as a heart attack. Two hitmen threw Molotov cocktails into our house and staked out the doors to shoot us as we came out. You can read the entire report once the Gila County Sheriff's Office finishes it."

Luna tilted his head and crossed his arms. "I'm looking forward to reading that report. Is it safe to assume the two guys look worse than you do?"

Jason nodded.

Luna continued to stare at Jason.

"Did you talk to Captain Selah about going after those thugs?" Jason asked.

"Yeah, he wants the cartel out of the forest and off the reservation, but he thinks the feds should go after them. We're so tight on resources now, especially with Sergeant Spencer still on leave."

Jason raked his short hair with his fingers and exhaled. "Can we get a few minutes with the captain?"

"He's really busy, so I don't—"

Jason put up his hand. "I know he's swamped, but we need to find the people that shot Tarek before they do it again," Jason interrupted.

"How is Tarek?"

"He's in serious condition with a long recovery ahead of him. Can you at least check with the captain to see if he has time to meet?"

Luna stared at Jason, exhaled loudly, and left the office. Ten minutes later, he reappeared.

"We've only got five minutes, so we need to make this quick. Follow me."

Jason hustled to catch up with Luna. They swiftly shut the door behind them after they entered Captain Selah's office. Jason took the chair in front of his desk while Luna stood.

"What can I do for you?" Captain Selah asked.

The captain remained seated behind his desk, covered with stacks of file folders and stapled pieces of paper. Jason noticed several rows of colorful ribbons on his uniform, highlighting a distinguished career in law enforcement.

"Thank you for seeing me. I'd highly recommend setting up a sting to take out the cartel tonight before they kill anyone else on the Fort Apache Reservation."

Captain Selah rocked back and forth in his chair as he considered the recommendation. Finally, he seemed to arrive at an answer and leaned over his desk toward Jason.

"I've already talked to lieutenant Luna about this. We don't have the resources to safely take down a drug cartel. Plus, that's the responsibility of the DEA or FBI."

"I understand, but the DEA thinks they've caught the entire cartel thanks to Sheriff Kellerman's campaign stump speeches, and the FBI passed the case to the DEA weeks ago. So it's WMAT PD, or the killing continues."

Selah was silent for several beats. "What do you propose?"

"We found their camp a little over twenty-four hours ago, so if we can coordinate a strike team tonight, we may catch them before they move again. It's only six to eight men, so we don't need a large group, but we need your best tactical team to go in and hit them hard."

Selah stood and shuffled to the window. He turned his attention from the oak tree outside his window to lieutenant Luna. "What do you think? Can we pull together a team to do this?"

Luna nodded slowly and then more emphatically with each passing second as he seemed to consider the operation. "Yeah. Yes, we can do it."

"Okay, set it up for first light tomorrow. I want a team of at least eight people on this, and the DEA on standby if it gets hot."

"Yes, sir."

Selah returned to his chair and opened a manila file. "Please close the door behind you."

Luna and Jason moved to the doorway but did not leave. Seconds later, Captain Selah looked up. "Is there a problem?"

Luna pointed toward Jason. "What about him?"

"And Clay. He's also Air Force Special Warfare and a big reason we've been able to find the cartel," Jason added.

"We'll find enough internal manpower, and the DEA will be on standby," Selah responded.

Jason didn't move or blink. He remained in the door and continued to stare at Captain Selah. It was like an old-fashioned grade school stare-down.

"Why are you still here?" Captain Selah asked.

"This mission needs all the manpower we can get, and Clay and I can help."

"Can we deputize them or something?" Luna asked.

"It's not that easy," Captain Selah replied.

"Can we do it as consultants or contractors? Clay does contract search and rescue work for Pima County. We could be your search and rescue contractors for this mission."

"We don't have money to hire contractors."

"We'll work for free and in a support role only."

Captain Selah pursed his lips for several beats then nodded. "Fine, you'll be search and rescue contractors, but in a support role only. Now get out of here and shut the door!"

Fifteen minutes later, Jason parked his truck in front of Shanna's house. She met him at the door and pulled him in for a hug.

"Do you want to come in?"

"Can we sit on your front porch?"

"Sure."

Jason and Shanna each chose a chair in the shade on the cozy concrete stoop. They talked about Tarek until Shanna's brother arrived in the driveway. He emerged from his brown sedan with a faded white hood from at least a decade of pounding from the Arizona sun.

"You've met my brother, Kai, before. He's home for the summer before he returns to Northern Arizona University for his senior year."

"Nice to meet you again," Jason said as he extended his hand. "What are you studying?"

"My degree will be in Criminology and Criminal Justice, but I'm also getting a certificate in Wildlife Ecology and Management. I want to work for Game and Fish." Kai smiled proudly.

"I'm jealous. That sounds like a fun career."

"You're jealous? Shanna said you're a badass in the Air Force and jump out of planes and helicopters."

"Shanna said that?"

Her face instantly flushed red. Shanna slapped Kai on the arm. "Time to go inside now."

Jason turned to Shanna. "You're pretty cute when you blush."

"Stop it," Shanna playfully demanded.

"Did you really say that?"

Shanna's mother saved her from further embarrassment when she pulled into the driveway behind Kai's car. She exited the vehicle slowly. Jason noted her droopy hospital scrubs on her short but sturdy frame. She slung a leather bag around her neck and shuffled like someone that had just finished a twelve-hour shift.

"Hi, Mama. This is my friend Jason."

Jason stood to show his respect. "Nice to meet you."

Shanna's mom smiled and continued toward the front door.

"How was your shift?"

The matriarch of the family stopped and glared at Shanna as though she had asked her to run a marathon. She turned, entered the house, and closed the door without answering.

"That went well," Jason quipped.

"She's just tired after working another long shift at the hospital."

Jason tilted his head and stared at Shanna.

"Okay, maybe she liked my ex and knows we won't get back together if I'm dating you."

"Were you serious with your ex?"

Shanna sighed. "We dated for a little over a year. I never saw a long-term future with him, but he wasn't a bad guy, so I let the relationship last longer than I should have. On the other hand, Momma wanted to pick out a wedding dress after a few months."

"Is he part of the White Mountain Apache Tribe?"

"Yes. He's the son of a doctor at Whiteriver Hospital. I think that had something to do with her desire for us to be together."

"He's the son of a doctor? He seemed pretty wasted that night in Pinetop-Lakeside."

"He's smart, but he puts more effort into picking the right ponies at the OTB. That was one of the many reasons I didn't see a future with him."

"I'm not a big gambler. I'd rather spend my money on outdoor gear, books, or something for my future off-grid home," Jason said with a smirk. When Shanna lifted her eyes to meet his, he playfully nudged his shoulder into hers.

"I know."

Shanna and Jason sat in silence for a few minutes until Jason checked his watch. He stood and helped Shanna to her feet.

"I have to get ready to go back out later tonight, so I have to head back to Payson now."

"What are you going to do?"

Jason managed a partial grin but didn't answer. Shanna heard the silence loud and clear.

"Please be careful."

Shanna completed the command with a soft kiss on Jason's lips. Jason smiled and pulled her closer to him. He looked into her eyes and gave her several quick kisses, then they walked toward Jason's truck.

The twenty paces to Jason's truck felt like a mile. He didn't want to go, but he still had to prepare for a return to the forest in a little over twelve hours. Jason opened the truck door and heard Shanna's phone ring before he entered. Her voice indicated it was a serious matter, and he studied her expression as Shanna listened to the caller. He hoped her face would give him a clue or at least some advance warning of the impending news, but he didn't have to guess. Shanna burst into tears, hung up, and collapsed onto the patchy grass. He knew the whole story at the sound of her first shriek.

Jason moved around the truck and knelt next to Shanna. He put his arm around her and felt her body heave with each guttural sob. Jason did not shed a single tear. He stared straight ahead across the street but didn't see the homes. Jason saw Tarek showing him the footprints near Cibecue Creek and then his smile after he got the job at Sunrise Ski Resort. Next, his mind flashed to the steely look of the cartel leader moments after he shot Sergeant Spencer. Rage detonated in his core and spread to his fingers and toes. Jason savored the feeling and planned to internalize it until he pummeled the smug face of the man responsible for so many deaths.

Shanna stopped crying, sniffed, and held Jason tight. He kissed her on the head and stood up.

"Internal bleeding?"

Shanna nodded.

"I have to go. I'll call you tomorrow after the mission is over."

Shanna looked up and moved her long hair to one side. "You're upset. You shouldn't drive right now."

"I'm okay, but I have to go."

Shanna embraced Jason for several minutes. She pulled away, and Jason watched her pass through the front door. He climbed into his truck and stared out the windshield before turning the ignition. Justice for Josh, Celeste, and now Tarek was hours away.

CHAPTER 45

Clay and Jason arrived at the predawn rendezvous point deep in the heart of the forest. Pine limbs scraped the side of Clay's truck like steak knives across a porcelain plate. He slammed his truck into park and shuddered.

"I hate that sound."

Jason didn't respond. He said little during the drive while he focused on the mission.

Clay parked behind a half dozen WMAT PD vehicles in a line along the fire road in the designated meeting spot. It rained earlier that night, and the thick, humid air felt more like Panama than Arizona. When Jason exited the truck, wet pine and mulch aromas dominated a forest full of scents and smells. Hints of the looming sunrise lightened the horizon as Jason and Clay geared up and strolled to the front of the caravan. A group of WMAT PD officers huddled around the hood of the lead vehicle. Lieutenant Luna used his flashlight to highlight points on the map.

Luna saw Clay and Jason approaching. "There they are. I'm filling in the team on the last known coordinates of the cartel."

He stepped to the side and waved to Jason. "Can you confirm our ingress route to the camp?"

Jason nodded and moved between two officers in black tactical gear to the vehicle's hood. He looked over the map for a few seconds and pointed with his gloved finger.

"The camp is halfway up the ridge, so they have one-hundred and eighty-degree visibility of the Cibecue Creek valley below. If we come from the north, cut across parallel to the camp, and then drop below the ledge the last two hundred yards, they won't see us. The terrain is steep, and the rocks are loose, so we all have to be careful of our footing."

"Are these guys DEA?" one officer asked.

"They're search and rescue consultants," Luna responded.

"Consultants?"

"They both have extensive mountaineering and search and rescue expertise that will be helpful on this mission. Plus, they're both in Special Warfare with the Air Force Reserve unit out of Tucson."

Another officer laughed. "I appreciate that weekend warriors want to help, but they're basically civilians. We can't have civilians tagging along on this mission."

Luna looked at Jason and Clay and then back to the officers surrounding the vehicle's hood.

"They're more than weekend warriors. These men are former full-time Air Force Special Warfare airmen with combat experience. They've seen more shit in a month in Afghanistan than some of us have seen in our entire careers. Plus, Jason lost his brother to the cartel and has found their camp twice now. It's two times, right, Jason?"

Jason held up three fingers.

"Okay, he's found them three times, while we've come up short every time we've tried. Plus, Captain Selah hired them as outside contractors for this mission, so we—"

Jason stepped back into the circle of men. His face radiated intensity.

"I'm not looking to step on any toes. Clay and I can get you to the camp and then wait back while you engage if that's what you prefer. If the shit hits the fan and a firefight breaks out, I promise you'll want us in the foxhole next to you. Our only goal is to ensure the cartel is removed from this forest by any means necessary. It's your call."

Jason backed out of the circle and stood next to Luna.

"Is everyone fine with these men coming as support to eradicate the cartel camp this morning?"

The concerned officer responded first. "If Selah is cool with it, so am I."

"Everyone else good?"

All heads bobbed up and down.

"Great. We'll head out in five."

Minutes later, Jason took point while nine men followed along the same path he had taken with Clay and Tarek forty-eight hours earlier. He stopped within two-hundred yards of the camp and motioned for Luna to join him in the front.

"This is where we need to fan out into the sectors we discussed. Clay and I have infrared sights on our weapons, so we'll lead the assault once everyone is in position."

"Captain said you two are support only," Luna protested.

"Fine. Who on your team has infrared sights or binocs?"

"Nobody."

"Do you want to ambush the camp blind, or would you like to know how many men are there and where they're stationed?"

Luna put his hands up. "Okay, I get it. Just don't get shot. My ass is on the line."

"I don't intend to."

Once Jason and Clay were in position, they slithered up to the level ledge area where they had found the cartel two days earlier. Jason remained in the prone position, brought his HK rifle and sight up to his eye, and scanned everything in front of him and to his right. Clay did the same for everything center and left.

Jason looked over at Clay and shook his head. Clay returned the same gesture. Did the cartel already move? Were they too late again?

The sun rose above the mountain peaks and splashed golden light across the camp. Jason rose to his knees and peered deep into the camp. Nothing.

He motioned for the rest of the WMAT PD to move up to their position. When they did, Jason and Clay stood and led them into the camp. They kept their rifles at the ready as they crossed through the camp and reached a sheer granite wall at the back of the ridge. Nobody was there.

"Clear!" Jason shouted.

Jason kicked piles of clothes and trash left behind in their hasty retreat. He took off his gloves and put his hand over a camping stove. It was faint, but Jason felt heat radiating from the steel grates that were likely red hot hours ago.

"We're too late again," Luna said.

"Yeah, but we're close. They haven't been gone long and left in a hurry. You think your team can look through all this crap for clues on their next destination?"

"Yeah, we'll check it out and bag any evidence."

Clay called Jason over. He held up a clear gallon-size bag full of stamp-like objects similar to the blotter paper Jason found in the fire tower.

"Were they working on the largest letter-writing campaign in state history?" Clay asked.

"Be careful not to open or puncture that. It's fentanyl."

"What? I thought fentanyl were pills."

"That's the most common type, but it also comes in liquid form for hospitals and places like that. We even had fentanyl in our kits over in Afghanistan. My guess is that pills were too hard to manufacture out here, so they went to plan B. Blotter paper that looks like stamps," Jason stated.

"I had no idea."

A WMAT PD officer approached Jason.

"Lieutenant Luna said I should show you this."

He handed Jason a pen from Whiteriver Indian Hospital and a crumpled-up visitor sticker with the name Daniel written on it.

"I can't believe one of them went to the hospital for treatment," Clay said.

"Me either. That's risky if you're in the country illegally and even more so if you're a cartel distributing drugs."

"That's not as uncommon in Whiteriver. Some residents don't have ID, and the hospital has to treat everyone. Maybe that's why they went to Whiteriver Indian Hospital instead of somewhere else," the WMAT PD officer shared.

Jason considered the possibility. The officer's explanation made perfect sense, but he couldn't shake the nagging feeling that he was missing something. He thought about what Tarek said about slowing down and letting the forest provide the answers.

"I need a minute," Jason said as he left the group.

He found an area away from the chaos of men rummaging through piles of trash. He exhaled and looked out over the Cibecue Creek canyon, still shaded from the horizontal rising sun.

"What secrets do you have for me?" Jason whispered to the wind in his face. He envisioned Tarek standing silently in the forest to gather new information.

Two minutes later, Jason walked back to the team sorting through all the cartel debris without an answer.

The hospital was a new lead, and Jason's gut told him it wasn't a coincidence. He kept racking his brain for the connection until he arrived next to Clay and Luna.

"Why would someone from the cartel visit Whiteriver Indian Hospital and risk being caught? Someone from a cartel won't go to the hospital for a cold, sore throat, or even a gunshot wound. It had to be for something important enough to risk detection."

"Maybe there were on a scouting mission. They may have been casing the place for the next big shipment of fentanyl to Whiteriver Hospital," Luna suggested.

"I administered fentanyl to a couple of amputees in Afghanistan. I know a little goes a long way. Would Whiteriver Indian Hospital receive enough fentanyl to interest a drug cartel?" Jason asked.

"Oh, yeah. They get a huge shipment of controlled substances three or four times a year. They're part of Indian Health Services, so IHS sends a truck with pallets of pharmaceuticals to one hospital in the region. Then they break it down and redistribute smaller shipments to hundreds of IHS hospitals in the West. It saves money, I guess. I know they request beefed-up patrols from us during these deliveries because of the high street value of the shipment."

"That has to be it!" Jason said. "When is the next shipment?"

"That's why patrol officer Massey couldn't be here. He's assigned to provide security to Whiteriver Hospital. The delivery is scheduled to arrive at nine this morning."

Jason checked his watch. "That's in less than ninety minutes!"

CHAPTER 46

Victor gazed out of the windshield without taking his eyes off the Whiteriver Hospital loading dock. Although he didn't show it, he was anxious about the heist he'd planned for weeks. It was a risky plan, but it had to succeed. Victor's future with La Palma, and perhaps his life, depended on it.

He leaned the driver's seat back a few inches for an unobstructed view of the hospital entrance and the road to the loading dock from his perch in the visitor parking lot. Carlos sat silently next to him, focusing on the highway leading to the hospital.

"I see a truck coming."

Victor nodded. His racing heart beat even faster. He'd planned every detail for weeks and tried to account for any potential problems. The thought of disappointing El Jaguar was strong motivation not to overlook any detail. Victor was already returning with half his crew headed to prison, and the La Palma boss didn't allow for three strikes.

A white GMC box truck with no logos or branding pulled in a few minutes after nine, just like Victor's local source said it would. The driver and passenger in the cab guided the delivery vehicle to the loading dock on the north end of the single-story hospital. This was ideal for Victor's crew. The dock faced miles of forest on the edge of town and was not visible from the main parking lot or the highway.

Victor pulled out of his parking spot and puttered toward the loading dock. He didn't want to get there too soon and alarm the drivers or hospital staff.

"Notify the rest of the team. We'll strike after they begin to unload."

The delivery driver in the passenger seat hopped out and waddled to the rear of the box truck. He stood on the loading platform and pressed a button to move himself up to the trailer door. The man in his early twenties cut the metal security tag, put it in his pocket, and pulled the door up. A minute later, he wheeled out a pallet loaded with brown cardboard boxes to the liftgate. Victor watched carefully for the white boxes with red and black ink. The vibrant colors notified the hospital staff, delivery drivers, and Victor's crew of its unique contents.

After watching the men unload the hospital supplies, four pallets full of white boxes with SUBLIMAZE (fentanyl citrate) stenciled on each side appeared on the liftgate.

"Go!" Victor ordered the other two trucks.

Seconds later, the delivery truck was surrounded by three pickup trucks and men armed with AK-74 rifles. The cartel members jumped out and motioned for the two delivery guys to raise their hands. Victor and Carlos kept their weapons trained on the delivery men while the rest of the La Palma Cartel moved the contents from the pallet to one of the pickup trucks. The transfer was completed in under four minutes.

"Check the truck for more boxes," Victor barked in Spanish.

"They have one more pallet," a man yelled from the darkness of the box truck.

"Hurry. Take it all!"

Victor ordered both delivery men into the back of the box truck, and he secured their arms and legs with zip ties. He applied duct tape over each of their mouths and leaned over to within inches of their ears.

"If you try to yell, I'll cut you to pieces," Victor hissed in broken English. He displayed his razor sharp four-inch blade to reinforce his threat.

Victor pulled the door down to secure the men in the back of the box truck when he heard yelling outside the vehicle.

"Policia!"

It was the last word Victor wanted to hear. He turned east and saw a WMAT PD cruiser moving toward them at high speed. Another WMAT PD SUV approached from the west.

"Carlos, take Miquel and do what we discussed. We'll hold them down out here," Victor shouted.

Carlos ran through the loading dock into the hospital while the remaining La Palma members took cover behind their trucks. Each WMAT PD vehicle parked diagonally to block access to the only exits. Doors swung open, and both officers aimed their weapons at the perpetrators.

"Drop your weapons!"

The demand was met with a deafening barrage of gunfire at the officers. The WMAT PD duo dove behind their vehicles to protect themselves from lead buzzing by like a swarm of killer bees. The firing stopped, and it was eerily quiet near the loading dock until the back door opened with a kick. Carlos appeared with a gun to the head of a middle-aged woman in hospital scrubs. She cried out in strangled yelps as he pushed the pistol harder into her cheek. Miquel followed with his weapon trained on a Whiteriver Hospital security guard. The white-haired security guard was stripped of his duty belt and limped ahead of Miquel with his hands held at shoulder height.

Victor rose from behind his truck.

"Back away, or we kill them," Victor yelled in English.

Neither WMAT PD officer moved.

"You have one minute to move your vehicle, or she gets a bullet in her head."

Victor nodded to Carlos, and he yanked on the woman's black hair until she screamed. The high-pitched cry reverberated throughout the loading dock area.

The WMAT PD officers kept their pistols trained on Carlos and Miquel. After a minute, Victor left the cover of the truck and walked across the asphalt loading dock.

"I warned you!"

Victor raised his Springfield 1911 Garrison 9MM pistol to her temple. Just before pulling the trigger, he swung his weapon to the security guard and shot him in the chest. The oversized man stiffened and fell face-first onto the pavement. A thud of flesh slamming against an immovable object followed the blast from the handgun. The sound was disturbing enough to turn the most hardened stomachs, but Victor didn't waste a nanosecond before executing his next move. While all eyes turned to the limp heap of the former security guard, Victor returned his weapon to the woman's head.

"Don't shoot. We'll move! We'll move!" the closest WMAT PD officer yelled.

Seconds later, the vehicle blocking the east exit reversed out of the way. Carlos forced the woman into the backseat of the nearest truck while Victor jumped into the second.

"Let's go!" Victor yelled into the radio.

He led the other two trucks out of the Whiteriver Indian Hospital parking lot and onto the highway. They turned south and drove through Whiteriver toward Gila County.

"Are you still going to Show Low to drop off the payment?" a voice asked Victor over the radio.

"No. It's not safe anymore. I'll make the deposit for our local contact later. We need to get this cargo to the meeting point with the buyer."

As soon as they left Whiteriver, they encountered a half dozen WMAT PD vehicles speeding toward town. Victor looked in his rearview mirror and hoped they'd keep racing to the hospital, but they didn't. The line of vehicles did a quick U-turn and began pursuing them. He'd have to kill more people before delivering his new inventory to the buyer.

CHAPTER 47

Clay stayed on the bumper of the rear WMAT PD vehicle as they pushed ninety miles an hour. Blocks into town, three pickup trucks blew past them in the opposite direction. The lead WMAT PD vehicle immediately did a U-turn and turned on his emergency lights. The following four vehicles did the same, but Luna's vehicle continued straight. Jason and Clay didn't have a police radio, so they weren't aware of the reason for the split up.

"What should we do?" Clay asked.

Jason looked at Luna's vehicle shrinking in their windshield and turned to catch a final glimpse of the three trucks.

"I think the cartel members are in those trucks. So, let's follow them."

"Why is Luna dropping out of the chase?"

"Not sure. Maybe he's going to check on Whiteriver Indian Hospital."

Clay completed the U-turn and slammed his size twelve boot on the gas pedal. The acceleration pushed Jason back in his seat, but he kept his eye on the WMAT PD vehicles pursuing the three trucks.

Jason pulled the phone out of his pocket and powered it up. He turned it off for the sting to avoid unwanted pings and dings or sending an inadvertent signal of his location. The phone vibrated with a new voicemail.

Noah's voice wafted from the phone's speaker. He sounded out of breath.

"You need to call Shanna right away. She called me a minute ago looking for you. She's tried to reach you several times, and it goes straight to voice mail. I don't know what it's about, but it seems super urgent—"

Before Jason could finish the message, he received a call. It was Shanna, so Jason clicked over to answer.

"I was just about to call you."

"Where are you?"

Jason could tell by Shanna's voice she was upset.

"I'm with Clay and the WMAT PD. Where are—"

"They have my mom. You have to help her."

"Who has your mom?"

"The cartel!"

Jason pulled the phone away from his ear and shook his head. He couldn't believe the words he was hearing.

"What?"

"A nurse that was working with my mom called me a few minutes ago. She said the cartel robbed a delivery truck at the Whiteriver hospital. When the police showed up, they went inside and kidnapped my mom and a security guard. They shot—"

Shanna started sobbing before she finished. Jason gave her a couple of seconds to respond but had to know the answer.

"Who got shot?"

"The security guard."

"And your mom?"

"They took her. Hurry! They left five minutes ago."

Jason's jaw clenched and his hands curled into fists. He wanted to catch the cartel with every fiber of his being.

"We're behind them now. As soon as we catch up with them, we'll get your mom and bring her back safely. I promise."

Jason knew it was a promise he couldn't honor, but he wanted to give Shanna hope.

"I may lose my signal soon, so I'll call you as soon as your mom is safe."

The crying stopped, and Shanna sniffed several times. "Call me as soon as you have her."

The pursuit vehicles slowed as the shoulder narrowed, and the number of sharp curves increased as the highway descended into the Salt River Valley. Guardrails were the only thing between their three-ton truck and the five-hundred-foot vertical drop to the valley below. Just when Jason thought it couldn't get any worse, Clay turned on his wipers as rain smacked the windshield.

Brake lights appeared on the vehicles ahead. It looked like they were underwater through the rain, and Jason hoped the cartel was giving up. Clay slowed to a few miles an hour when Jason saw the lead cartel vehicle turn off the highway onto an unpaved forest road. Jason figured they were heading toward familiar territory and knew that would make their capture more difficult.

"Dammit! I thought they were going to pull over," Jason shouted.

He craned his neck to forward get a better look at the cartel vehicles around the curve turning off the highway.

"What are they doing?" Clay asked.

"They're going back off-road. Probably heading somewhere they know that gives them a shot at getting away."

Clay's truck splashed through puddles as the low-speed chase entered the forest north of Cibecue Creek. They bounced on the unmaintained road for another twenty minutes when two vehicles appeared out of nowhere behind Clay.

"We have company," Clay said. His eyes alternated back and forth between the rearview mirror and the path ahead.

Jason turned around and saw two black Chevy Suburban SUVs join the pursuit. He recognized DEA special agent Holland in the front seat after the windshield wipers went back and forth several times.

"That's the DEA. We have a little more muscle now to take these guys down."

A minute later, the lead vehicles arrived at a T in the road and stopped. Jason held his breath, hoping the cartel was ready to turn themselves in. All the law enforcement trucks came to a halt behind the cartel vehicles at the intersection. The steady rain was the only sound in the cabin until Clay shouted and pointed.

"We have a runner."

A man jumped out of the second truck and ran left. After the man darted away, the cartel trucks turned right and continued on the unpaved road. All the WMAT PD vehicles followed the three trucks to the right.

"I think that's the leader," Jason said. He kept his eyes locked on the man darting in the rain as he verified his pistol was in his shoulder holster.

"Stick with the WMAT PD vehicles, but slow down at the T so I can jump out. I'm not letting him get away that easy," Jason said.

Clay reached the T intersection thirty seconds later, and Jason jumped out. The monsoon storm whipped up the wind, and the nearly horizontal rain soaked him to his boxer shorts in less than a minute, but Jason didn't slow down. He was determined to catch the man running from him.

The dirt road ended in a small parking area for two or three cars. A rough footpath led from the parking area down a steep embankment. Jason paused at the path's entrance as the trees swayed and branches bent. Pine trees rising five stories from the ground were called widow makers by local loggers due to their massive weight and girth. The potentially deadly trees bent and groaned under the force of the wind. The desire to catch up with the figure who passed through the area minutes earlier was strong, so Jason continued down the dangerous trail. His ears were keenly tuned to any snapping or cracking sounds that may give him a second or two warning of limbs or entire trees crashing toward him.

Jason rushed through the dense stand of trees and ended up on his butt. He slipped on hard, wet clay and slid across several feet of mud before taking a seat. He found his footing again and observed the water pooling on the path ahead.

"I better slow down or I'm going to break a leg," Jason whispered.

He shortened his gait and continued through an open, level portion of the path. Jason was relieved to be away from the trees until a flash of light filled the sky. A lightning bolt struck a tree on the ridge less than a hundred feet from where he stood. He felt it as much as he saw it. A roar of thunder followed a second later, indicating he was in the heart of the storm.

Jason left the clearing and entered another cluster of trees. Although taking cover under trees to avoid being struck by lightning was a terrible idea, Jason felt a sense of psychological comfort with tons of hardwood between him and three hundred million volts of electricity. He continued on the path until it opened up to the valley below. He didn't hear the swollen Cibecue Creek below over the rain before seeing it, but he stopped when it came into view. The once tranquil creek looked more like raging level four rapids. Jason scanned the area and realized he'd been there before. He was a hundred yards north of where he dove off the cliff with Clay and Tarek three days earlier.

Movement caught his eye, and that was when he saw the local leader of the La Palma cartel wading into the creek.

"Oh, no you don't," Jason said out loud. Jason didn't want Victor crossing the creek back into his home turf for the past couple of months. He could have weapons or even a vehicle stashed nearby, and Jason couldn't let him get to either.

Jason hopped down the path in controlled slides to reach the creek faster. Once he reached the creek bank, he took his eyes off Victor to observe the rust-colored water rushing violently through the canyon. The monsoon storm created flash flood conditions in the creek, and the current deluge would only worsen it.

When Jason turned back to find Victor, he didn't see him. He looked right and left until he spotted the cartel lieutenant downstream on the other side of the creek, clinging to a sheer cliff wall. The creek pushed him away from the level area across from his entry point, and now he was fighting the torrent of water pushing him like a giant hand. Victor edged slowly downstream while he passed from boulder to boulder. It would only be a matter of time before he reached the flat area where Jason pulled Tarek from the water. He was still too far to get a shot off with his pistol, so Jason had only one bad option remaining. He also had to cross the watery tempest daring him to enter.

CHAPTER 48

Five steps into the creek, water lapped over Jason's waist. After eight steps, it was up to his chest and he was moments away from being swept downstream. Jason suspected the water would be over his head after another step or two and he'd be at the mercy of the current. His target destination was a few feet upstream of Victor, so Jason had entered the creek twenty yards upstream to compensate for the current. It wasn't enough. Like the rescue mission in Cougar Canyon in Oregon, the torrent of water pushed him past his exit point. Jason used all his might and best technique to close the gap between himself and the cartel member. When he was a few feet from him, he got one foot on the creek bottom and pushed himself out of the raging water.

Jason landed on the bank five feet from the cartel leader. His eyes widened at the appearance of his pursuer and raised his pistol toward Jason. The barrel was inches from Jason's chest, so he didn't have time to remove his weapon. Jason quickly showed his hands.

"Don't shoot!" Jason said.

A half grin appeared on the cartel leader's lips and Jason prepared for the next move that could determine if he lived or died.

He had to redirect the end of the barrel six inches to his right or left before the cartel leader could pull the trigger. Not an easy feat, but the odds moved in Jason's favor if he could distract the shooter for a fraction of a second. During the hundreds of hours of weapons training in Krav Maga, Jason learned that acting afraid can cause a person with their finger on a trigger to relax. It takes the human brain a quarter of a second to react to unexpected movement and an average adult can strike at speeds of 22 feet per second. That's 5.5 feet in a quarter of second, which gave Jason five feet to spare.

"Please don't kill me. Let me go and I won't ever bother you again," Jason lied. His voice trembled with his palms out just above his waist. It wasn't hard to act afraid when a loaded weapon was pointed at your chest.

The cartel leader laughed.

"No, you won't Jason Mulder. I know who you are, and you've been after me for months," he replied in English.

Fury grew inside Jason as his name crossed the cartel leader's lips, but he remained focused on the mission. Get the cartel leader to drop his guard.

"You know my name, but I don't know yours. At least have the decency to let me know who killed my brother before you kill me."

"Very well. My name is Victor Romero and I will be the one that kills you and everyone else in your family."

Jason responded quickly. "Why? To sell more fentanyl?"

Victor's smile widened. Ego is a gift when it comes to self-defense. He wanted to tell his story, so when Jason saw Victor's mouth start to open and eyes move up to meet his, he seized the opportunity. Jason's left hand uncoiled faster than a rattlesnake strike, and he simultaneously leaned left as he cupped the barrel between his thumb and index finger. He pushed the barrel six inches to his right and eliminated the threat of being shot. Wide eyes and an open mouth signaled that Victor realized the countermove as Jason closed his fingers around the slide and bent Victor's wrist and pistol back ninety degrees. Jason followed quickly with his right hand over the pistol hammer and now had control over the weapon. He couldn't reach the trigger to fire, so he thrust the barrel into Victor's sternum.

Victor emitted a loud gasp and Jason was sure he'd drop the weapon, but he continued to hang on with his right hand while his left hand went to his chest. Jason pulled the weapon up and away with all his might. Victor lost his grip and Jason's upward momentum carried the wet pistol over his head, where it slipped through his fingers like a greased pig. It flew five feet into the air and splashed into the creek.

Victor straightened up and stared at Jason for what felt like an eternity. Jason ripped open his shirt to expose the SIG Sauer P226 in his shoulder holster.

Jason hoped he'd make a countermove, but instead. Victor turned and bounded into the creek. He couldn't shoot a fleeing man in the back, so he chased him into the water. Steps later, he caught the cartel leader by his shirt and yanked with all his strength. Jason held onto his collar as they fell back and drifted into the swift current in the center of the creek while Jason dodged massive tree limbs hurtling through the water at speeds that could inflict lethal damage. It wasn't how he had initially planned it, but Jason felt satisfied with his current position. He knew there was no way Victor, or almost any human without the title of Olympic swimmer, PJ, or Navy SEAL, had the extensive training in the pool he'd had. He would use this to his advantage and assist Victor in swallowing copious amounts of muddy creek water. The sensation of drowning took the fight out of everyone.

Victor Romero was not like anyone else. He wasn't a skilled swimmer but had no fear of drowning. Or death. He thrashed, pulled, and clawed at Jason's wrists to free himself.

After ninety seconds in the torrent, Jason heard a thunderous roar vibrate throughout his body. He hoped it wasn't what he initially thought but it confirmed his worst fear when he looked downstream. The brown mist ahead revealed that they were dangerously close to Cibecue Falls, and Jason had to get himself and his detainee out of the creek. He let one hand go from Victor to paddle himself back to the bank. Jason kicked hard to escape the grip of the raging current until he stood up in waist-deep water. Jason continued to hold Victor by the collar and noticed a chain with a key around his neck. He yanked the chain off Victor and punched him in the head with the key dangling in his fist. Jason examined the key for second before putting it in his pant pocket, but it was too late to react to the incoming strike. Victor stood tall and clocked Jason in the ear with a roundhouse punch. The force of the unseen blow caused Jason to lose his grip on Victor.

Both men found their footing and prepared for a fight, each man bobbing and weaving while looking for a weak spot until Victor stopped and belted out an earsplitting spartan yell.

"Te voy a matar."

Jason was familiar with the Spanish phrase. He didn't learn it from his mom, but he knew Victor yelled, "I'm going to kill you," from watching horror films in Spanish when he was ten or eleven years old. Celeste put parental controls on those types of movies in English but forgot to include Spanish, even after years of teaching her sons the language of her home country.

"¡Vámonos!" Jason replied with a sinister smirk. The Spanish expression for "bring it" caused Victor's eyes to widen.

"You know Spanish," the cartel leader noted.

"I can say you'll rot in prison for the rest of your life in German too if you'd like. That's if you leave here alive."

Victor smiled. "Those deaths are nothing compared to what is coming. A hundred kilos of meth laced with fentanyl is on its way to a buyer right now. In a week, your morgues will overflow with bodies."

Jason blinked several times as he tried to wrap his mind around the tragedy that could unfold in towns across the Southwest. Another wave of acid detonated in his stomach at the thought of more families planning funerals.

"Time to shut up. You're going to spend the rest of your life in prison."

Victor mustered a weak laugh. "Over my dead body."

"Be careful what you wish for," Jason replied. He snuck in a quick jab that grazed Victor's cheek. He was tired of talking and was ready to administer the justice Josh and Tarek deserved.

Jason wiggled his feet in the river rock to get a secure stance. He was ready to neutralize the cartel lieutenant when Victor reached into his cargo pocket and removed a knife. Jason stumbled back a step after Victor pushed the button to reveal a four-inch steel blade.

Victor held the knife pointed toward Jason's torso, barely exposed above the water. Jason sensed Victor was skilled with a blade as he cautiously inched toward him.

Jason removed his Sig Sauer and pointed it at Victor.

"Drop the knife or your dead!" Jason barked.

Victor loosened his grip and angled his hand to let the knife drop into the water. Jason kept his finger on the trigger as the knife disappeared into the murky liquid and saw Victor's eyes move past him and widen. Jason turned to see a tree trunk twice as thick as a telephone pole racing toward him. He didn't have time to move, and it collided with Jason's back and drove him underwater. Stars filled Jason's eyes before they closed as he sank further below the surface. Seconds later, he wiggled his fingers in the rocky creek bottom and waited for the log to clear when he felt pressure around his neck. At first, Jason thought the massive log was still above him but realized Victor had both hands on the back of his neck and was holding him underwater with all his might. Jason lost his weapon when the log struck him from behind so he couldn't shoot Victor to release his grip. He tried to push off the bottom by doing a massive push-up off the creek floor, but he couldn't get his head above the water. He tried grabbing Victor's legs, but Victor stood arched over him and he couldn't reach them. After a sixty-second struggle, Jason's lungs burned, and he still couldn't escape Victor's clutch. Panic ensued, and Jason believed he'd die in the muddy creek in under a minute. Memories of his family, Gaby, and his old teammates in the Air Force flashed through his mind. His mind switched from friends and family to visions of past training of buddy breathing in the pool at Lackland Air Force Base. He felt the same burning in his lungs then and thought he would die, but he didn't. He lasted another sixty seconds. Next, Tarek appeared in the tunnel Jason saw closing rapidly in his mind. He recalled Tarek in the truck telling him that we must first die to live. The proverb confused Jason when Tarek first told him, but now it was clear. Jason knew what he had to do.

A minute and a half after Jason first slipped under the surface, he stopped fighting and let his body relax. Victor continued to pin Jason to the creek bottom. After Jason was limp under the water for another thirty seconds, Victor let go and backed away. He stared at the rusty water, as if waiting for final confirmation of Jason's demise.

Victor exhaled and let his shoulders relax when Jason burst from the water and drove his left fist into Victor's throat. Victor grabbed his throat with both hands, and Jason followed with a right hook into his face. All four fingers slammed into his jaw below the ear. A textbook knockout punch. Victor went limp and fell backward into the water. Jason tried to snag his leg, but the current had already claimed its property. The cartel leader floated face down toward Cibecue Falls, so Jason moved out of the creek and up the bank to get a better look. Victor did not appear conscious when he reached the edge, hung suspended for several seconds, and disappeared over the falls.

Jason stared at the mist dancing over the falls for a full minute. He couldn't imagine how an unconscious man could survive the forty-foot plunge with that volume of water pounding him like a million fists.

Almost on cue, the rain slowed and stopped. Now Josh Mulder could finally rest in peace, but the storm wasn't over.

Jason had to save Shanna's mom before she joined the long list of lives taken by the cartel.

CHAPTER 49

After the black spots in Jason's vision disappeared, and his breathing returned to normal, he retrieved the key from his pocket. It didn't look like a car or house key, but something smaller, like a safe or post office box. He jammed the key back into his front pocket and stumbled up the muddy bank. Soon, he reached the small parking lot and relished being back on level ground. He jogged on the muddy path until he reached a slew of stopped vehicles near the T junction. The doors of the rear vehicles were open, but nobody was taking cover behind them. He heard yelling as he approached the black Suburbans belonging to the DEA. Ten more steps and his heart sank.

One of the cartel members stood with his back to a gigantic pine tree that must have fallen onto the forest road during the storm. He had Shanna's mom, Judy, in a headlock with his left arm and his pistol in his right hand pressed against her temple. Another cartel member stood to Judy's right with his gun trained on her.

Several members of WMAT PD and the DEA had their weapons aimed at the cartel members from behind the cover of the two front WMAT PD vehicles.

The guy holding Judy yelled. Jason couldn't make out everything but understood his last command.

"¡Váyanse de aquí o la vamos a matar!"

He yelled for them to leave or they'd kill her.

"Drop your weapons and let her go," an agent shouted back.

Jason continued toward the confrontation and listened to the verbal pissing match when he passed Clay's truck halfway to the front. Jason assumed it would be empty but spotted Clay sitting at the wheel and jumped inside.

"What's going on?"

"They took the guys in the first two trucks into custody within a few seconds, but these two jokers grabbed the lady and are trying to negotiate their way out of here. The police aren't having any of that," Clay responded.

"How come you aren't out there?"

"I was up there until a guy in a DEA jacket got in my face. He told me to back off and stay in my vehicle. So, I moseyed back to my truck and have been watching from here ever since."

"That's Judy, Shanna's mom, up there. We need to do something fast before they kill her."

Clay stiffened and pulled the straw out of his mouth. "You serious?"

"Yeah, Shanna called me just before I jumped out. I was over there last night. That's her mom."

The cabin grew quiet as the two Air Force Special Warfare operators turned to observe the standoff. Jason could see the fear on Judy's face and noticed the stains from tears across her cheeks. Despite her disdain for him, his heart ached for the unbearable dread she must be feeling. His gut told him to act quickly.

Jason scanned the forest to his left and then to his right.

"I have a plan."

Clay returned the straw to its rightful place. "I'm all ears."

"Do you still have all the kit in your truck?"

"Always."

They exited the truck, and Clay removed two HK416 Carbine rifles and four loaded twenty-round magazines. He handed one to Jason. Jason popped in a magazine, pulled back the charging handle to load a round in the chamber, and then brought the rifle up to his face to peer through the sight.

"We need to fan out from here and sneak through the woods. I'll go right to get a shot on the guy holding Shanna's mom and you go left and get a beat on the other guy. You'll set up at eight o'clock, and I'll set up at four so we don't hit each other in any crossfire."

A shrill cry from Judy caused both of them to turn in her direction. The man with a gun to her head grew more animated with his threats to shoot her.

"Both sides are getting antsy, so we don't have much time," Jason barked. "We need to set up and be ready to take the shot in five minutes. I'll give the sign to shoot, so we do it simultaneously."

"What's the sign?"

Jason smiled. "You'll know, so be ready."

Clay smiled back. "Let's do this."

Jason dashed from Clay's truck into the forest twenty yards before he stopped. He took a knee to assess the situation and turned left toward the standoff. Jason and Clay had to approach in complete silence to not alert the cartel members or the police. The element of surprise was essential for Jason's plan to work.

Three minutes later, Jason was even with the officers and agents in the standoff. He found a natural hump in the ground nearby and dropped into a prone position. Jason felt the cold, rain-soaked ground under his elbows, stomach, and legs but forgot about any discomfort when his eye lowered to the sight. He located the target and raised his head to verify he was looking at the right guy. Jason confirmed that the cartel member holding Judy was in the proverbial crosshairs of his sight. He also noticed a problem. From his angle, Judy shielded most of the kidnapper's body. Only three or four inches of his head was exposed. Jason wished he had planned for Clay to take this shot. Jason was no slouch as a marksman, but a moving target as wide as a soda can from fifty yards was a challenge for anyone. If Jason missed to the right, he'd shoot and kill Judy. If he missed to the left, the cartel member would have time to pull the trigger and kill Judy before anybody else got a shot off. He had one option. Hit the bullseye, or Judy dies.

After five minutes, Jason used his thumb to turn the selector from safe to fire and focused on his breathing. With each passing second, the two cartel members grew more desperate and agitated. Jason wanted a few more minutes to get completely set but knew he didn't have it.

The red dot in the sight moved from the cartel member's head and then over to Judy's head and then back across the forest as he tried to slow his breathing. He could hear his old Air Force Range Master in his head.

Don't pull the trigger. Squeeze your finger and let it surprise you.

This calmed Jason, and when he was at that point where his lungs were between exhaling carbon dioxide and inhaling oxygen, the red dot froze an inch above the kidnapper's ear and three inches above Judy's skull.

Jason squeezed.

He saw a burst of red explode like liquid fireworks through his sight. Both Judy and the cartel member collapsed to the ground. A half beat later, he heard a second shot and saw the other cartel member take a step back and fall awkwardly.

Jason froze in place. He wasn't sure if he shot the man holding Judy hostage or if he was a few inches off and killed Shanna's mom.

Several DEA agents and WMAT PD officers pointed their weapons into the forest while the others moved closer to the downed cartel sicarios. Jason and Clay laid their weapons down and stood with their hands up.

"Is she okay?" Jason yelled.

Special agent Holland looked over and recognized Jason.

"Those two are okay. Let's make sure these guys are down."

Jason jogged toward the lifeless cartel members. He was twenty yards away when a WMAT PD officer reached Judy. He bent down and put his fingers on her neck. Jason stopped.

Did I hit Judy too?

Jason took two more steps when he saw the officer reach down and help Judy stand up. She shook uncontrollably and was likely in shock. Jason exhaled and continued toward the bodies.

"They're both deceased," a DEA agent proclaimed after checking for pulses.

Jason arrived next to Judy.

"Are you okay? Are you hurt anywhere?" Jason asked.

Judy glared at Jason. He could see the fear and hurt in her eyes. Jason wondered if she would cuss him out, and then she lunged toward him. She put both arms around him and laid her head on his chest. Her body shook as she broke down and sobbed.

A minute later, Judy looked up at Jason. "Thank you. Thank you for saving me."

Jason smiled back. It was the most heartfelt expression of gratitude he'd ever felt.

He wanted to bask in the aftermath of the safe recovery of Shanna's mom and the successful apprehension of the cartel but he had a new mission on his plate. Stop the buyer of the fentanyl-laced meth from killing hundreds of people.

Chapter 50

A WMAT PD officer put a blanket around Ms. Dosala and led her back to his vehicle.

"Come with me," Special Agent Holland said to Jason and Clay.

They followed him to the back of the caravan until they reached a Suburban parked behind Clay's truck.

Holland leaned against the front grill and put his palms on the hood.

"I need both of you to help escort the frightened lady back to the White Mountain Apache Tribe Police Department for me."

Jason looked at Clay and then back to Holland.

"Are we done here? Jason asked.

"For you two, yes, you're done here. We're going to head out soon to apprehend the buyer."

"You found the buyer for all the fentanyl in the back of these trucks? How?"

Holland pushed away from the vehicle. "During the standoff, one of my bilingual agents stayed in the Suburban with the four detainees. He gave them all one chance for a deal with the DA. No names, no ratting out anyone. Just the time and place of the exchange with sixty seconds to respond. Those men have heard about the gang retaliations at the state prisons, so the guy with the nasty scar on his neck caved in under twenty seconds. We'll see if we can get him a nice cell with a view."

"When and where is the meeting with the buyer?"

"Behind the lumberyard in Globe at noon."

Jason looked at his watch. "That's in less than an hour, and it takes at least an hour to get there."

"I know. Time to stop talking and start moving."

Jason turned to Clay. "Can you help take Shanna's mom back?"

Clay looked like he was going to protest but stopped. "Yeah, I'll help."

"You both need to take her," Holland barked. He pointed his index finger at Jason, and the agitation in his voice grew more pronounced with each syllable.

"I'm not stopping until this is over. Go ahead, Clay."

Clay left to help transport Shanna's mom and Jason pulled out the key on Victor's chain. "I have another clue that more people are involved."

"Where'd you get that?"

"Off the neck of the cartel leader just before he floated over Cibecue Falls. I'm sure it leads to more people that are involved. I'll tell you more on the way."

Special Agent Holland looked at his watch, whistled, raised his hand high, and moved his index finger in a circular motion. "Let's go."

"Are you taking all the detainees with you?" Jason asked.

"We have to. These are our only vehicles."

Jason looked up and down the line of parked vehicles. "We should take one of the cartel trucks. The white pickup the leader jumped out of is best just in case the buyers know the vehicle."

Holland stared at Jason for several seconds. "Fine. Hop in. The vehicle with the detainees can head to Phoenix while we take down the buyers. I'll call for backup on the road."

Holland started the white pickup truck loaded with cases of liquid fentanyl and fishtailed along the soggy dirt road. Neither Jason nor Holland spoke until they were back on the paved road and halfway to Globe.

"So, what's up with the key?" Holland asked.

Jason had thought about his answer to the inevitable question about the key. He didn't have concrete answers but had a couple of plausible theories. His primary theory involved another member of law enforcement. Jason wasn't sure he should reveal his prime suspect yet.

"It looks like a post box key, similar to the one your team found."

Holland nodded. "So, what does it mean?"

Jason wasn't sure if Holland had already pieced everything together and was testing him or if he was still formulating his hypothesis. He was learning how to better work with law enforcement and chose not to play all his cards just yet.

"I think it means they had local help. This key probably leads to a box to exchange money and transfer information. If we find out who was expecting this key, we identify the traitor."

"What makes you think that key was for someone else?"

Jason looked out the window. The desert scrub brush passed by at a high speed. Jason leaned over and saw Holland driving eighty-six miles an hour. He looked at his watch and noticed they had to cover twenty miles in the next fifteen minutes.

"The key was around the leader's neck, like a reminder for a future exchange."

Holland pursed his lips and nodded. "Makes sense. Who do you think it was for?"

This was the question Jason was hesitant to answer. He suspected Detective Caldwell from the Navajo County Sheriff's Office was stonewalling him from the beginning. He was always a few minutes late after Jason called in their location, and he provided the tip to the DEA when half the cartel was caught. Jason couldn't be sure it was Caldwell, so he chose not to reveal his suspect.

"That's the one-hundred-million-dollar question. We may never find out now."

"What exactly happened to the cartel leader back there?"

Jason cleared his throat and looked out the window again. "We had a disagreement, and he lost."

"Disagreement over what?"

"Who got to live."

Holland jerked his attention toward Jason and did a double take. He turned his eyes back to the road ahead and didn't ask any more questions. They'd entered the outskirts of the mining town of Globe, Arizona, and he needed to get to the lumber yard in minutes to beat the buyer.

"There it is!" Jason shouted.

Holland turned the wheel and cut across two lanes of traffic. The locals responded with honks and middle finger salutes. They shot past a handful of customers in the parking lot and drove behind an eggshell white structure that housed racks of lumber. The narrow parking area was between a barren rocky hill and a large windowless retail building that obscured the views of any curious onlookers. Jason understood why they chose this place.

They parked a few feet away from the building, and Holland called the driver of the Suburban. "Park in the customer lot and monitor the alley to the back. If you see any vehicles drive past you toward us, burn two minutes and then get back here."

"Roger."

It was three minutes past noon, and Jason wondered if the buyer would show. Perhaps somebody from the cartel warned them and they were halfway back to Texas now. He didn't have to wait long because a box truck pulled into view. It inched toward Jason and Holland in the pickup truck loaded with stolen fentanyl and stopped. Jason couldn't see inside but knew the delivery vehicle couldn't hold over three men inside the cabin. Both vehicles faced each other, motionless behind the lumberyard as if they were sizing each other up for a game of chicken.

"What now?" Jason asked.

"We wait," Holland whispered. He had his weapon in his right hand and his left hand on the door handle, ready to pounce. His eyes never left the glare on the windshield of the box truck.

The box truck flicked its headlights on and off twice a minute later. Holland mimicked the move, and the box truck doors opened. Two men in their twenties exited the driver's side and waved for Holland to pull his vehicle toward them. Jason could see that both men had sidearms tucked into their waistbands. Holland put the truck in drive and drove slowly toward the men. A slightly older man dropped from the passenger side of the box truck and put on a Texas-sized cowboy hat. He looked around cautiously and walked to the front of the box truck.

"That's him," Holland whispered. "Come on, where are those guys?"

Jason saw the black Suburban come around the building and creep behind the box truck. He wasn't sure if Special Agent Holland saw it from his vantage point in the driver's seat.

"The other team is behind the box truck."

Without warning, Holland put the truck in park, opened the door, and wedged himself in the open door and body of the truck with his Glock .40 caliber pistol aimed at the buyers.

"Federal agents. Put your hands up!"

All three men from the box truck looked at each other and ran toward the vehicle's cab. They didn't make it.

Four agents in tactical gear with DEA emblazoned on their backs arrived, two on each side of the box truck. They pointed their M6A2 carbine rifles at the buyers and ordered them to put their hands up and get on their knees. They complied, and the DEA agents quickly cuffed the buyers.

Jason slid across the seat and pulled the truck forward. Special Agent Holland was with the tactical team sharing congratulations for another safe and successful bust. Three agents took the buyers back to the suburban while Holland joined another DEA agent at the back of the box truck. They pushed up the rolling door and saw two pallets in the back. This wasn't even their only stop.

"This is a huge bust, sir." The DEA special agent fist bumped Holland, closed the door, and jumped back down to the pavement.

Jason watched the door slam shut. "You should test those boxes already in the truck for a lethal dose of fentanyl."

Holland tilted his head and raised his eyebrows. "Why? What else do you know?"

"The leader said something about our morgues overflowing with people killed by over one-hundred kilos of meth laced with fentanyl. I pray that's it in the back of the truck."

Holland stared at Jason and turned to his men. "Take those guys to Division in Phoenix and have the investigative team come out for the contraband. Make sure they test the brown boxes in the box truck for fentanyl."

The other agent returned to his vehicle, and Jason walked back toward the truck with Holland.

"What a wild and crazy day," Jason muttered as he entered the truck.

"We haven't even had lunch yet. It's only half over."

Jason sunk into his seat and turned to Holland. "So it can only get better, right?"

CHAPTER 51

Holland turned the ignition in the cartel truck, but before they could pull away, a black and white marked police vehicle pulled behind the lumberyard. Jason assumed it was the local police but couldn't believe his eyes when he saw the Navajo County Sheriff logo on the side. The police cruiser parked between the two vehicles, and a man in uniform exited.

Jason's jaw nearly hit the dashboard when he saw Sheriff Kellerman unfurl himself onto the pavement. His gut howled with suspicion.

Why is the sheriff here?

Holland and Jason exited the truck. Sheriff Kellerman looked like he saw a ghost when he saw Jason and the DEA special agent approach. He looked right and left and attempted to get back into his vehicle when Jason yelled out to him.

"Hey, Sheriff. What are you doing here?"

Kellerman shut his cruiser door, looked at Holland, and cleared his throat. "I heard about the shootings at Whiteriver Health Center and thought you guys may need some backup." His voice did not exude the same confidence Jason had seen in person and in all the TV ads.

"You came all this way into Gila County to see if we need backup?"

"This ain't Phoenix or Tucson. That's what we do in these rural counties."

Jason took a few steps toward Sheriff Kellerman and his cruiser. He was now ten feet from the NCSO vehicle.

"Too bad you didn't get here a few minutes sooner. The DEA team was amazing. They already caught the entire cartel and their buyer."

Sheriff Kellerman looked around and swallowed hard. "Where are they?"

"On the way to the DEA Division office in Phoenix for processing and further questioning."

Kellerman nodded. "Excellent work, guys. I don't think you need my help here, so I'd best be heading back now."

"How did you get here from Show Low so fast? Were you already in the area?"

"Lights and sirens, my friend."

"You must have driven Mach two after the call from Whiteriver Hospital. I'm impressed."

Sheriff Kellerman put both hands on his hips. "I don't like where you're going with this, son. What exactly are you trying to say?"

Jason looked over to Special Agent Holland and then back to Sheriff Kellerman. "I think it's suspicious that you're so far out of your jurisdiction to provide backup that was never requested. Why are you really here?"

"I told you. I came here to provide backup. As a former DEA agent, I want to support the good guys whenever possible. Pretty standard procedure in law enforcement, but you know nothing about that. Stick with the combat medic thing because you're barking up the wrong tree."

Jason observed Sheriff Kellerman unsnap his holster and then wipe his brow with a handkerchief. He was sweating more than Jason and Holland and they'd been active in the sun longer than Kellerman.

"So, you aren't here to collect your cut from the cartel?"

Sheriff Kellerman removed his pistol and pointed it at Jason. "You've gone too far now. I've always suspected you had some vendetta against me, but your outrageous lies prove you have some agenda. You've interfered with our investigation from the beginning, and now you're slandering a public official. You'll have to explain yourself to a judge."

Jason looked over to Holland and saw he had his right hand near his holster. His face screamed confusion as he listened to Jason and the sheriff exchange accusations.

"Can you explain why you have a carry-on suitcase in your front seat? Planning a trip sometime soon?"

Special Agent Holland and Kellerman's eyes both shot to the front seat of the cruiser, where a gray carry-on suitcase with a retractable handle was visible in the passenger seat.

"It's none of your damn business, but I'm going to a fundraiser right after work and need a change of clothes."

Kellerman pointed at Jason's dried blood just above his right temple with his non-weapon hand. "I see you have a pretty nice knot on your head. You should get that looked at. You're talking crazy right now."

"Victor Romero didn't think it was so crazy when he told us you'd be coming to get your cut from the big buyer that's also in custody," Jason said. He saw Holland's head snap in his direction out of the corner of his right eye.

If Sheriff Kellerman was playing poker, he'd just lost this hand. After hearing the cartel leader's name, the sheriff's body language screamed concern, and panic set in. He raised his weapon until the barrel pointed between Jason's eyes.

"Time for you to shut up and go to jail."

Jason hoped Holland had also caught the sheriff's obvious tell. He turned to the DEA special agent, "I think you should arrest the sheriff for his involvement with the cartel."

"Don't tell me who to arrest," Holland barked.

Jason's heart sank. He couldn't believe Holland had missed all the signs.

As Jason stared down the barrel of a gun, a wave of clarity washed over him. He had one last option to expose the sheriff and had to go for broke. If he didn't, a crooked cop would arrest him. Jason figured once the sheriff got him inside his vehicle, he'd get shot during the drive to the Navajo County Jail for supposedly trying to escape along a stretch of desolate high desert.

"Victor's talking," Jason shouted.

The sheriff lowered his pistol several inches and tilted his head.

"That's right. He told us you'd be expecting a key. A key that opens a postal box with enough money to fill that travel bag in your car so you can take a vacation somewhere.... like Canada."

"That's not true. Nobody in that cartel is a rat."

Jason shook his head. "It's true. He gave us the key and I have it in my front pocket."

The sheriff swallowed hard. Jason noticed that the hand holding the pistol was shaking.

"I want to see it. Show me nice and slow, or you'll be eating nine millimeters of lead for lunch."

Jason reached into his front pocket and removed the chain with a key dangling on the end. He held it high to ensure Special Agent Holland could also see it from twenty feet away.

All the blood seemed to leave Sheriff Kellerman's face. His once rosy cheeks turned pale white.

"Now, do you want to change your story?" Jason asked.

Before the sheriff could respond, Holland raised his pistol and aimed it toward Jason.

"Shut up! I can't let you slander a former DEA agent. Put your hands behind your head, interlock your fingers, turn around, and kneel."

If Holland hadn't sounded so pissed, Jason would've assumed he was joking. He couldn't believe that a professional member of law enforcement, like DEA Special Agent Holland, couldn't see that Sheriff Kellerman was an accomplice to the cartel.

Holland took a step toward Jason. "Do it now!"

The color returned to Sheriff Kellerman's face followed by a grin. "Thank you. It's nice to know the DEA can smell through thick bullshit like that."

"Cuff him. If he moves, I'll shoot him," Holland said. He never took his eyes off Jason.

"My pleasure," Sheriff Kellerman replied. He reholstered his pistol and removed his cuffs from his service belt. He approached Jason waiting on his knees from behind and snatched the key from Jason's hand. When the sheriff pulled Jason's arms down behind his back, Holland turned his weapon on Sheriff Kellerman.

"You're under arrest, Sheriff! You came here to collect your cut, and now you're going to prison."

Jason felt the sheriff loosen his grip on his wrist.

"What are you talking about, Special Agent Holland? Has this kid got you in on this, too?"

The sheriff let go of Jason's wrist, so Jason pulled his hands down from behind his head and turned ninety degrees on his knee to see both Kellerman and Holland.

"I've seen you on the news at several fundraisers this year. You always have your service uniform on. You didn't bring your suitcase to change clothes."

Holland took his aim slightly off Sheriff Kellerman as he talked. Kellerman noticed, and Jason saw his right hand move toward his holster. Jason pivoted another ninety degrees until he was facing the sheriff. When the sheriff removed his pistol and aimed to fire, Jason rose and raised his left arm simultaneously. His forearm collided with Kellerman's shooting arm above the wrist and a split second later Jason heard the report from Kellerman's pistol. The nine-millimeter slug whizzed three feet over Special Agent Holland's head. Although Jason's ears were throbbing after the blast, he didn't hesitate. He slid his left hand over Kellerman's wrist and right hand over his shooting shoulder. Now Jason had control of the sheriff and he delivered three successive up knees into his groin and abdomen like an angry mule. Kellerman gasped and bent in half. Jason saw movement from the corner of his eye and a beat later heard the distinct tone of hardened metal hitting pavement. Kellerman had a size advantage, but Jason trumped it with extensive combat self-defense training and controlled rage. He executed an arm drag and easily spun the lawman thirty years his senior a half turn. Instead of applying the rear choke hold with relentless pressure on the carotid artery until Kellerman passed out, Jason chose to inflict pain. He pulled the sheriff's shooting arm behind his back and thrust it up in a quick jerk.

Pop.

A blood-curdling scream immediately followed the sound of snapping ligaments. The sheriff's arm dangled inside his long sleeve service uniform like a small child playing in an adult coat. Jason let go and the sheriff fell to the ground writhing in pain.

"That was for Josh."

Holland lowered his weapon and jogged to the crooked cop. "I guess I'd better call an ambulance."

"Nah, I can fix this."

The sheriff lay on his side, mumbling incoherently, so Jason straddled his oblique and pulled on his dangling arm.

"This is going to hurt," Jason said. He secured his arm, jerked again, and reset the shoulder. The sheriff yelped and clasped his shoulder as he rocked back and forth in pain.

"That was for Tarek."

Chapter 52

Two black SUVs belonging to the DEA arrived behind the lumberyard. Special Agent Holland walked the traitor and the cartel's local source to the vehicle and transferred him to another agent. Holland returned to Jason, leaning against the cartel truck.

"Now that was wild and crazy," Holland said.

Jason laughed and let his body relax for the first time in hours.

"I'm going to be filling out reports until Christmas because of all this, but it's worth it. I want to thank you for all your help."

"I had to ensure justice was served to the people who murdered my brother. Plus, I've developed a special hatred for drug dealers."

Holland leaned up against the truck next to Jason.

"When did you figure out the sheriff was working with the cartel?" Holland asked.

"To be honest, I'd suspected someone from NCSO early on, but I thought it was Detective Caldwell. He seemed to always be a step too slow or fast with the cartel. I didn't suspect it was the sheriff until he stepped out of his cruiser. His reaction when I said the cartel leader's name and showed the key confirmed it was him."

Holland nodded.

"How about you? When did you figure out the sheriff was working with the cartel?"

"I also had my suspicions, but showing up sixty miles out of his jurisdiction with a suitcase raised them even further. Similar to you, his reaction to the key when you pulled it out was the clincher for me."

Jason stepped away from the truck and tossed his hands in the air. "Okay, so why did you pull your weapon on me?"

Holland looked down at the ground and then laughed. "Sorry, but that was the only way I could think of at the time. He had his pistol pointed at your head and the only way to get him to put it away, was for him to think I was on his side."

"So, you knew it was the sheriff after I said Victor's name and showed him the key?"

"Yep."

"Wow, that was acting worthy of Hollywood. I thought for a minute you were really on his side."

"Nope. All an act."

Jason slapped Holland on the back. "You deserve an Oscar for that performance."

"You didn't do so bad yourself, Sherlock. Now go home, sit back, and relax this weekend."

"I'll be in Tucson this weekend for an Air Force Reserve drill. I'll be rappelling out of helicopters for two days, so not exactly relaxing, but I love it just the same."

Holland extended his hand, and the two shook. "I'm taking the sheriff to Phoenix. The second vehicle will take you back to Whiteriver to rendezvous with your buddy."

Holland got into the front passenger seat and rolled down his window. "You said something earlier that caught my attention. I happen to work for an agency that likes to put dirtbag drug dealers in prison. Would you ever consider a career in the DEA?"

Jason shook his head. "Thank you, but this was enough excitement for me. I'll stick with being a PJ once a month for now."

"Fair enough, but if you change your mind, call me."

Special Agent Holland pushed his business card through the window, and Jason took it.

Jason strode to the other DEA vehicle and climbed inside. He stared at the business card several times during the journey back to Whiteriver.

When Jason arrived, he found Clay leaning against his truck in the WMAT PD parking lot. He jumped out of the SUV and marched toward Clay.

"I'm so glad to see you in one piece," Clay said. He put out his hand to shake, but Jason kept moving until his friend and wingman was in a bear hug.

"Thank you for all you've done. You risked your life, gear, and truck to help me. I appreciate all of it."

Clay took a couple of steps back and removed the plastic straw.

"No problem, buddy. It's what we do in Air Force Special Warfare. You PJs do it for other people all the time."

Jason heard a whistle as he was about to climb into Clay's truck. He turned to locate the source and saw Lieutenant Luna standing next to Captain Selah outside the front entrance to the White Mountain Apache Tribe Police Department. They waved him over.

"Thank you both for all your support," Jason said when he reached the two men.

Both men nodded, and Captain Selah stepped forward. "I have some updates from all the agencies on the case that may interest you. Do you want to go inside?"

"No, right here is fine," Jason said. He felt his muscles tense again at the thought of the cartel.

"I spoke with Detective Caldwell at NCSO. He apologized for the way he treated you and said he was being manipulated by the sheriff. Kellerman convinced him you were some half-baked nut case driven by grief and revenge. He also shared they found the business in Show Low with the key. It belonged to White Mountain Post and Shipping, and deputies found it stuffed with over two hundred thousand Canadian dollars."

Jason nodded. "I thought it may be something like that. Did you ever find the cartel leader that went over Cibecue Falls? Victor Romero?" Jason asked. It was a question that weighed heavily on his mind since Victor disappeared into the mist.

"Not yet. A team has searched the area for a couple of hours, but nothing has turned up. During that time, we got more information on him from a detainee. Victor Romero is a lieutenant with the La Palma cartel in El Salvador. He has a reputation as a ruthless killer according to his people. We'll keep looking for his body, and eventually, he'll turn up."

Jason hoped that was true.

"You probably want the update you've been waiting to hear, don't you?" Captain Selah asked.

"Yes, sir," Jason whispered.

"Shanna is with her mom at Whiteriver Indian Hospital. Judy seems to be okay, but they are holding her for observation. You should head over there now."

Ten minutes later, Jason entered the hospital room. He saw cords and tubes attached to Judy, but she slept peacefully in her bed.

Shanna sat in a chair next to Judy, and when she saw Jason, she jumped up and ran to him. They held each other tight at the end of the bed as if they'd spin off into space if either one let go. No words were exchanged, but the communication was intense. He sensed Shanna's appreciation and growing trust in him. She was no longer holding back.

Jason felt something he hadn't experienced in over seven years. He finally understood it was okay to let go of Gaby. He realized he couldn't completely let go before because nobody else was worthy. Until now.

CHAPTER 53

Two weeks later, Jason joined Shanna at her home in Whiteriver for dinner. Jason's eyes widened, and his mouth watered as he scanned the spread on the table. He practically drooled like a dog at the sight of the quinoa salad, chili-marinated avocado, and cured salmon overflowing on the plate in front of him. Shanna handed another plate of food to Jason.

"What's this?"

"Apache fries. They're smashed and fried potatoes topped with aioli. It's an appetizer," Shanna replied.

"Wow, I don't know where to begin," Jason remarked.

Judy returned from the kitchen and sat down at the table with Shanna and Jason. Together, they enjoyed their dinner with little conversation.

"Jason, do you want more of anything?" Judy asked. Jason could still see the bruises and remnants of the trauma from two weeks earlier, but cherished the thin smile on her face.

"No, thank you. I'm stuffed."

"Be sure to save room for dessert."

Judy returned a minute later with a plate full of pastries.

"You have to try these. They have a few wild oxalis petals harvested nearby and are all topped with piñon-infused whipped cream."

Jason plucked a pastry from the passing platter and put it on his plate. He was still uncomfortable with the five-star hospitality Judy provided the last two times he was over.

After dinner, Jason and Shanna moved to the concrete patio outside the front door. They left the light off and watched the stars shimmer in the inky black sky. Jason leaned over and kissed Shanna. After kissing for several minutes, Jason moved from her mouth to her neck when the front door opened. He jumped away from Shanna and looked up to see it was Judy. Jason remembered her threatening scowl the last time she caught Jason kissing her daughter and prepared for her rebuke.

"Oh, sorry. I'll leave you two alone," Judy said. She quickly shut the door.

After Judy's reaction, Jason and Shanna laughed like pre-teens kissing under the school bleachers.

"I think your mom likes me now," Jason said.

"You think? I feel that she likes you more than me."

They kissed again.

"All kidding aside, my mom is very grateful for what you did. It was very brave."

"Anybody else in my position would have done the same thing."

"That's not true," Shanna stated.

"I know Tarek would have. He'll always be a hero to me."

The mood changed from cheerful to somber in an instant. Tarek had been buried a week earlier, and Jason couldn't stop thinking about his senseless death.

"Me too."

Shanna leaned over and put her head on Jason's chest. He wrapped his arm around her, and they sat outside, enjoying each other's presence until it was time for Jason to leave.

Jason and Shanna returned to Show Low to celebrate their one-month dating anniversary. They repeated their first date activities with burgers and cornhole. Shanna and Jason also returned to the bar and grill in Pinetop.

They selected a booth inside this time because of the warm and humid weather July brought to the High Country in Arizona.

The server brought them nachos and beer while they discussed their day.

"Your new house is looking great. I love the location by the river. Now that they poured the foundation, when will you get the walls up?"

Jason inhaled deeply and started to speak but stopped.

Shanna tilted her head. "Is everything okay?"

Jason reached across the table and pulled Shanna's hand inside his. "I'm excited about my new off-grid house, but it was supposed to be Josh's house too. Sometimes the house reminds me of how much I miss him." Jason squeezed Shanna's hand. "I wish he could have met you. He would've liked you."

The door chimed, indicating a new patron had entered the establishment, and Jason looked over Shanna's shoulder again.

"Are you looking for someone?" Shanna asked.

"No. Why?"

"You keep looking over my shoulder while we're talking."

"Sorry. I keep thinking that Victor Romero will walk through that door. It still bothers me that they never found his body after he figured out who I am and where I live."

It was Shanna's turn to squeeze Jason's hand. "He's gone, so you don't have to worry about him anymore. You saw his body go over the falls, right?"

Jason nodded.

"It will take some time, but you have to let go of him. He's still haunting you from the grave, and you can't give him that power."

The door chimed again. Jason dropped Shanna's hand, and his eyes widened.

"What's wrong?" she asked.

"Somebody just walked in, and I don't think you're going to like it."

Shanna turned around and saw her ex-boyfriend meandering toward them. Her body stiffened and both Shanna and Jason grew more interested in the drinks in front of them.

The ex strutted past their booth, stopped, and returned to their table.

"Well, look who's here. Shanna and her bully boyfriend."

Neither Shanna nor Jason looked up to acknowledge him.

"We never had that talk we were supposed to have. I have a lot to tell you. We should have it right now."

"Right here?" Shanna asked.

"No, let's go outside."

Shanna looked at Jason, and he raised his eyebrows but didn't move a muscle. She looked back at her plate, and Jason could tell she was thinking about her next move.

"Come on," the ex chirped.

Shanna stood up, folded her napkin, and placed it on the table. She looked into Jason's eyes again, and he returned a blank stare. The ex grabbed her wrist and jerked her toward the door.

"Let's go."

Shanna's arms shot up as if propelled by a catapult. She grabbed her ex with both hands above the elbows and thrust her knee into his balls.

His gasp filled the room, causing people at nearby tables to put down their drinks and look at the commotion. The ex bent over and leaned against the wall.

"Don't you ever touch me again!" Shanna roared.

A minute later, the ex regained his balance but remained hunched over. He looked at Jason and then back at Shanna before limping away.

Shanna stood tall next to the table as he slunk out the door.

Jason remained silent when Shanna returned to the booth. She looked down at the nearly empty plate of nachos.

"You going to take this last one?"

Jason shook his head. She snagged the last nacho chip and chewed it intently.

Jason waited until she was finished. "I thought you hated violence."

"I do, but unfortunately that's the only language he speaks. I think he heard me this time."

Jason's lips curled up. "Now you sound like me."

Shanna didn't respond.

Jason put his hands in front of his face like a boxer avoiding a jab. "I didn't know you had moves like that."

A wry grin formed on Shanna's face. "There's a lot more to learn about me if you want to get to know me better."

"I'd like that."

Epilogue

Jason parked in his usual spot at the north end of the cemetery lot. He slid out of his truck and ambled underneath the metal arch of the fenced property. Eighty-four paces later, he arrived at his destination. Jason realized he could reach Josh's grave blindfolded by now.

He stared at the dash between the two dates on Josh's marker. Jason accepted that a simple straight one-inch line on a gravestone encompassed the entire lifetime of the person buried below. For Josh, the number after the dash should have been decades later. Jason couldn't do anything about that now, but he could alter the story for his dash on the mark of his future eternal resting place.

Jason twisted, sat, and leaned back against the smooth granite. The familiar position and the coolness penetrating his back were a welcome reprieve from the unrelenting afternoon sun.

Jason found several pea-size pebbles nearby. He collected them in one hand and tossed them lightly with the other.

"Josh, what am I going to do now?"

The sound of the light breeze tickling Jason's ears and a crow perched high atop a ponderosa pine were the only responses. The outrage against the cartel for killing Josh and Tarek was replaced by frustration. Why did the cartel come to Arizona in the first place? Why were they willing to kill to protect their way of life?

The reason was the source of his frustration. The cartel came to Arizona to serve America's highly lucrative and unquenchable appetite for drugs.

"Josh, I've been thinking something different must be done with all these drugs. What we're doing today doesn't seem to be working."

Another pebble landed past Jason's feet.

"Maybe I could make a difference if I joined the DEA."

Jason dropped the last of the pebbles. He watched the shadows extend across the well-manicured lawn and inhaled the aroma of the freshly cut grass. He closed his eyes and sat in silence.

Several minutes later, Jason rose and turned to the headstone. He pulled out the compass and plant identification guide Josh had with him the last day he was alive. He tapped the top of the monument with the glossy guide like he always did since the day they buried Josh. A tombstone fist bump of sorts.

Jason pulled Special Agent Holland's business card out of his pocket. He ran his finger over the embossed round logo of an eagle. United States Department of Justice was printed at the top of the sphere, with Drug Enforcement Administration below it. The thought of putting drug dealers like the La Palma cartel away before they killed innocent Americans grew more appealing with each passing second. He removed his phone from his pocket, found Holland's number, and tapped on the virtual keyboard.

Special Agent Holland, this is Jason Mulder. Call me. I've made a decision.

Jason stared at the text message for several seconds and hit send. He strolled back to his truck with a smile. He was ready to add more adventure and a new purpose to the dash in his life.

***

Thank you for reading Cartel Hunter! I appreciate every reader and hope we can stay in touch.

I have a FREE eBook for those that want to read more about Jason Mulder, including his first kill as a PJ while leading a team behind enemy lines on the Georgia-Russia border to save a downed F-22 Raptor pilot. Visit **RobertGoluba.com/FREE** to download *Raptor Down: A Jason Mulder Thriller Mission*.

If you're ready to jump into Book 2, Reverse Pursuit, in the Jason Mulder Thriller Series, visit this link: **geni.us/Revpur**

Reverse Pursuit: A Thriller
Facing years in prison, Jason Mulder fights back... as a fugitive.

A drug sting in a double-wide trailer in Northern Arizona leads to the arrest of DEA Special Agent Jason Mulder.

When the court finds him guilty and sentences him to federal prison, he knows his only hope of vindication lies in escaping and uncovering the truth. He disappears into the unforgiving Arizona wilderness, and a relentless manhunt ensues.

In a thrilling race against time, he must evade determined US Marshals and battle ruthless criminals eager to eliminate Jason and those closest to him.

As he gets closer to identifying the men that framed him, the stakes reach a crossroads with his freedom and life on the line.

The hunted becomes the hunter.

Will Jason save his family and clear his name in time, or will he mourn the death of loved ones while locked up behind bars forever?

Reverse Pursuit is Book 2 in the Jason Mulder Thriller Series

Robert Goluba is an author of thrillers and suspense novels. He was born and raised in Central Illinois, where he attended college, served in the Army National Guard, and met his wife. At age thirty, after a self-diagnosed allergy to snow, he moved to sunny Arizona where he now lives with his wonderful wife, two kids, and canine companion. He published his first book in 2016.

The Jason Mulder Thriller Series is his current project.

Visit **RobertGoluba.com** to learn more.

Made in United States
Orlando, FL
29 May 2024